The
Fugitive's
Trail

J.C. FIELDS

Paperback-Press
an imprint of A & S Publishing
A & S Holmes, Inc.

ISBN: 0692395954
ISBN-13: 978-0692395950

DEDICATION

This book is dedicated to my mother.
You gave me your love of books and reading.
Because of that gift, my life has been so much richer.

ACKNOWLEDGMENTS

Completing a debut novel for any writer is an exhilarating event, it is also a bit scary. Without the help of the following individuals, this book would still be a file residing on the hard-drive of my computer.

First and foremost, I want to thank my editor, Scott Alexander Jones, who sanded the rough edges off the manuscript. His patience, comments, encouragements, and suggestions have accelerated my growth as a writer.

To Norma Eaton, many thanks for the fine tuning. Your suggestions smoothed everything out.

To Sharon Kizziah-Holmes of Paperback-Press, thank you for believing in the project and helping this writer realize a dream held for many years.

To Stan Williams, your work on the cover has been amazing. Thank you for your talent and your enduring friendship.

To my daughter-in-law Miranda, thank you for encouraging me to keep writing and for being my first fan.

Finally, and above all else, I give thanks each day for my wife Connie. She is my best friend, my partner in this journey called life, and the person I most love being with. Thank you for enduring my early mornings, late nights, and disappearing into my office on weekends to write.

PART 1

After descending from the thirty-fourth floor, the elevator doors opened revealing an expansive deserted lobby. Glass and steel comprised the front wall from floor to the top of the atrium four stories above. Crystal chandeliers hung from the ceiling, adding a note of elegance to the otherwise industrial look of the lobby. A firm hand on the man's back pushed him out of the elevator toward the building's entrance.

Two security guards escorted the man. Both were big and muscular, biceps stretching the material of their dark gray suits. One was slightly taller and on the right of the man. The other guard was shorter, to his left and slightly in front. The only other occupant of the lobby, besides the three men walking toward the front door, was at the security desk. He was a tall young black man dressed in a dark blue blazer, white shirt, and tie. He nodded at the guards as they escorted the guest toward the front door.

The man being escorted could see through the front glass a black Suburban waiting at the curb—the same vehicle he had been pushed into earlier in the morning. As the guard in front reached to open one of the building's front doors, he was turned slightly toward the guest, exposing his weapon.

While the guard's attention was trained on opening the door, the guest's left hand extracted the Glock from the belt holster on the man's right hip. At the same time he was reaching for the gun, his right leg lifted. With as much force as he could, he kicked at the leg of the taller guard behind him. His shoe slammed into the kneecap of the man's left leg, which bent in the wrong direction and the guard collapsed screaming in pain.

His left hand, which now held the Glock, rose and the trigger was pulled twice. The shorter guard was forced back against the adjacent glass door and collapsed. The now unescorted man rushed through the door in front of him, turned to his right, and ran.

Before the guard at the front desk could get out of his chair, the entire incident was over. The man had disappeared into the crowd on the street.

The lobby guard hurried over to the two men on the floor, saw a pool of blood spreading under the shorter guard. The taller guard was writhing on the floor, trying to straighten his now ruined left leg. Hurrying back to his desk, he picked up a phone and dialed 911.

***

The driver of the black Suburban sat stunned as he watched the man rush out of the building, turn right, and disappear into the midday crowd. He slammed the Suburban into park, opened the door, and rushed into the building. As soon as he was through the front doors, he stopped.

His first sight was the carnage of the dead man slumped against the glass and the shattered leg of the other. At the same time, his cell phone rang. Glancing at the caller ID, he sighed. The pending conversation would not be pleasant.

***

Staring out the window of his thirty-fourth floor office,

Abel Plymel realized he had made a hasty decision, a decision made in anger. He needed the man alive.

Turning back to his desk, Plymel picked up his cordless phone and dialed the cell phone of one of his security guards. It went unanswered, totally unacceptable. He paid them to answer their phones twenty-four seven.

He dialed the cell phone of the second guard, no answer. Finally he called his driver, who answered on the fourth ring. His eyes grew wide as he listened then suddenly threw the handset at his office door.

CHAPTER 2

Kansas City, MO

Standing in the front room of the now empty house, it seemed alien to him. Not the place where he'd raised his son. Looking around the room, he smiled, opened the front door, and stepped out. He twisted the knob to make sure it was locked, closed it, and walked to his new car parked in the driveway, a Ford Mustang. Sitting in the driver's seat, he stared at the house for several minutes before making a call on his cell phone. It was answered on the second ring. He said, "Sandra, this is Sean Kruger."

"Sean, I was just about to call you. Did the cleaning service do a nice job?"

"Yes, they did. They left about ten minutes ago. Thank you for recommending them. Please let the Carsons know I'm out of the house a day early."

"They'll be thrilled. Have I told you how much they love the house?"

"Several times, Sandra."

"And the neighborhood, their little girl is already planning sleepovers—"

"Sorry, Sandra, I don't have a lot of time. I just wanted

to tell you my keys are on the breakfast bar in the kitchen."

Sandra was quiet for a second and then said, "I'll give the Carsons a call and let them know."

"Thank you for all your help these past few months. I wish I could talk longer, but I'm late for an appointment."

"You're more than welcome. Why don't you call me after you settle into your new condo. We can have dinner." She paused for half a second. "My treat."

Hesitating for a few seconds, he finally said, "I'll do that." Although he knew he never would. He ended the call and smiled. Sandra O'Dell was a nice person and a very good real estate agent. But, if he had not cut her off, she would still be chattering about sleepovers. As for the dinner, the thought of listening to her for several hours made him shiver.

He sat in the car for a few seconds, then opened the door and stood up to look at the house one last time. It had been his home for seventeen years. A lot of good memories were here: his parents moving in to help raise his then one-year-old son, the joy of watching them interact with their grandson on a daily basis, watching a little boy turn into a bright and talented young man. There were also sad memories.

Finally, after staring at the house for several minutes, he sat back down in the car, started the engine, backed out of the driveway, and accelerated the Mustang toward his new home. It was the first day of a new chapter in his life.

The condo was a newly renovated two-bedroom unit on the west side of the Kansas City Plaza. The extra bedroom would serve as his office and a place for his son Brian to sleep when home from college. One of the reasons he had chosen this particular unit was the open living space. The living, kitchen, and dining area were all one room separated only by a breakfast bar in the kitchen. But the main reason he liked the place was the balcony. It had a clear view of the Plaza, which was spectacular at night.

Fifteen minutes later, the Mustang was parked in his designated parking slot. It was approaching dusk and the shadows from adjacent buildings were growing long. He sat quietly in the car and thought about the hectic and emotional four months since his mother's death. The doctors had told Kruger it was a heart attack, but he disagreed. He had a Ph.D. in psychology and knew the mind was far more complicated than most people imagined. His father and mother had been married for sixty years, marrying right after high school. Something died inside his mother when his father passed away two years ago. She would put on a happy face and say nothing was wrong. But Kruger could tell she was hurting. Finally, after Brian moved away for college, she quietly passed away one night in her sleep.

Even as a non-practicing Catholic, Kruger believed in a hereafter. He was comforted with the concept of his mother and father together again. But occasionally doubt crept into his faith. As one of the FBI's premiere profilers, he had seen the darkest recesses of the human psyche. And sometimes he wondered how a benevolent God would allow such terrors to occur. But that was for religious philosophers to debate, not him.

As he opened the car door, he heard a woman scream, "Let go of me, you bastard."

His first reaction was to draw his service pistol, a Glock 19, and run in the direction of the voice. As he rounded the northwest corner of the building, he saw two muscular, tattooed young men: one white and the other black. The black guy was holding a woman by the arms as the white guy dug through her purse. Kruger was fifteen yards away when he stopped. Taking a Weaver stance, he yelled, "FBI, on the ground *now.*"

The black guy was startled and released the woman, who quickly ran toward Kruger. The white guy turned around, stared at Kruger, and said, "Shiiiittttt, you ain't no FBI. Show me a badge, mutafukr."

Kruger yelled again, "*On the ground now!*"

The black guy looked at Kruger and then at his partner. He appeared to be choosing whether to get on the ground or run. The white guy threw the purse on the ground. Reached behind his back and pulled out a snub-nosed revolver. As the guy raised the revolver in his direction, Kruger didn't hesitate and fired the Glock twice. Both shots hit their target. The white guy dropped the revolver and grabbed his chest. Two circles of red appeared high on his chest and shoulder. He dropped to his knees and then fell back. The black guy bolted in the opposite direction as fast as he could. Kruger quickly moved to the fallen gun and kicked it aside, still pointing his Glock at the man on the ground.

He looked back at the woman, saw she was okay, and reached for his cell phone. He punched in 911 as he trained the Glock on the prone assailant. He said to the operator, "My name is Sean Kruger; I'm a special agent with the FBI. I have shots fired and a man down. I need an ambulance and a squad car." He was asked for the address, which he gave and ended the call.

The white kid stared up at him with wide eyes. The blood loss was moderate. Kruger did not offer assistance and kept the Glock pointed at the man. Within five minutes, a patrol car arrived and one of the two officers told Kruger to drop his weapon and stand aside. Kruger complied, laying the Glock on the ground. He put his hands above his head and backed up ten steps. One patrolman checked the wounded man, and the other officer cuffed Kruger and led him to their squad car.

Within ten minutes, five patrol cars and two ambulances occupied the parking lot of Kruger's new condo. He watched from the back seat of the patrol car as the wounded man was placed on a gurney and loaded into one of the ambulances. As it sped away, a Kansas City police sergeant opened the squad car's back door and leaned in.

"You want to tell me how you got involved."

Kruger stared at the police officer and said, "The lady was in trouble, I helped her out."

"You live around here?"

"Yes, second floor, apartment A."

The sergeant continued to stare at Kruger. "Lady lives on the second floor also and she's never seen you before."

"Because I just moved in today, *sergeant.*" Kruger spat out the police officer's title with as much sarcasm as he could muster. "Are you going to take these cuffs off?"

"Not yet, just cool your heels." The sergeant shut the door and walked away.

Sitting back in the seat with his hands cuffed behind him was difficult and uncomfortable, but he managed. Dusk had turned to night and the area was bathed in the artificial glow of street lamps, police car headlights and the rotating blues and reds of their emergency light bars. Finally after another fifteen minutes elapsed, a man in a suit opened the door.

"You Kruger?"

Nodding, "Yes, who are you?"

"Detective McAdams. Get out."

Swinging his legs out of the squad car, Kruger leaned forward and stood. McAdams reached around and unlocked the cuffs. "Sorry about the cuffs, Agent Kruger. Your story checks out."

Kruger rubbed his wrists, trying to get the feeling back. He said, "May I talk to the victim?"

The detective shrugged and nodded his head in her direction. "Suit yourself, you're free to go."

As he was walking toward the woman, she rushed to him, hugged him, and said, "Thank you. I'm not sure what would have happened if you hadn't come along."

Surprised by her embrace, he limply returned the hug and said, "Glad you weren't hurt. My name's Sean Kruger."

The woman backed away, smiled, and said, "I'm Stephanie. I really don't know how to thank you, Sean. I've never been in a situation like this."

"Well, to be honest with you, it's a first for me too."

Stephanie smiled and said, "One of the officers asked me if you lived around here. I've never seen you before. Do you?"

Nodding, Kruger said, "I bought 2A and just moved in

today."

She stared at him for a few seconds and said, "I moved into 2B a week ago, but I've been out of town on business. I had just gotten home from the airport when those two grabbed me. Hope this isn't a common occurrence around here."

Shaking his head, he said, "This can happen anywhere. It's safe—at least that's what I was told."

She smiled. "Good, I like the area. And with a good-looking FBI agent living next door, I feel even more secure."

Kruger returned the smile. It had been a long time since he had enjoyed a conversation with a woman. The conversation felt out of place in this situation, but he didn't care. He immediately liked her. She was a petite woman in her late thirties or early forties, several years younger than he was. She was strikingly beautiful, with naturally curly brown hair she wore touching her shoulders. Her pale blue eyes sparkled in the streetlights of the parking lot, and her smile was infectious. Realizing he was staring, he said, "I'm glad you feel safer." He chuckled. "Hell of a way to meet your new neighbor."

She brushed the hair off her forehead, tucked her newly returned purse under her arm, looked up at him and smiled. She said, "It will be a great story to tell our grandchildren." She walked over to the police sergeant, thanked him, and headed toward the building's rear entrance door.

Kruger watched as she opened the door, walked through it, and disappeared into the building. Not really sure how to take her last comment, he decided it was going to be fun trying to find out.

***

Stephanie Harris climbed the one flight of stairs to her condo. She was intrigued by this man who had just prevented something very unpleasant from happening. The ability to assess individuals quickly had allowed her to rise to the level

9

of senior vice president of sales at a large greeting card corporation. Her assessment of Sean Kruger was very positive. Maybe it was an infatuation with the white knight coming to her rescue, or a high school–type crush, she didn't know. Her experience tonight should have left her shaking and concerned about the safety of her new residence. But it didn't. Knowing he was next door gave her comfort. The decision was made; she wanted to get to know this tall, good-looking FBI agent.

She unlocked her front door, walked to her bedroom and threw her purse on the bed. Exhausted from her business trip and the parking lot incident, she changed into jeans and a baggy sweatshirt. After checking her messages on the phone, she had an idea. Since he wasn't wearing a ring on his left hand, she assumed he wasn't married. But she wanted to find out for sure. She grabbed her apartment keys and walked to his front door.

***

Kruger was unlocking his door when Stephanie walked up to him and said, "Hi, I didn't properly introduce myself when we met in the parking lot earlier. Too many distractions, I guess."

He smiled and said, "You could say that."

She offered her hand and said, "Stephanie Harris, Mr. Kruger."

Shaking her hand, he said, "My dad was Mr. Kruger. I'm Sean. It's nice to meet you, Stephanie Harris."

"I really appreciated what you did in the parking lot. Do you think that young man will be okay?"

He nodded. "Probably. One of the patrol officers told me before I came up, both the white guy and his partner were well known to the local cops. In fact, they already had the black guy in custody. Both were out on parole. I imagine this little incident will change that status."

"Good. But, I would really like to thank you properly.

10

Can I buy you dinner tomorrow night at a place of your choosing?"

He shook his head. "No, I'm afraid that won't work."

"Oh… I'm sorry, I mean…" She paused for a few moments, looking disappointed, "I didn't realize you were married."

Kruger laughed. "No, I'm not married, that's not what I meant. I'm a little old-fashioned. I'd love to have dinner with you tomorrow night. But you can't pay for it. I will. Since you've lived here a week longer than I have, you get to pick the restaurant."

Smiling, she said. "Houston's. It's my favorite place. Knock on my door at seven."

CHAPTER 3

New York City

NYPD Police Detective Preston Alvarez was approaching his mid-forties and had over twenty years in the department. During those twenty years, his blue-gray eyes had seen a lot. This morning he saw barely controlled chaos as he pulled up to the crime scene. At least ten patrol cars sat parked around the office building. Their light bars were rotating and reflecting off the building's glass façade.

An EMT vehicle was just pulling away from the scene, its light flashing and siren screaming. He pulled in behind a patrol car and put his unmarked detective car in park. Pushing his rimless glasses up to the bridge of his nose, he stepped out and stared up at the building, forty stories of glass reflecting the midmorning sun. He ducked under the crime-scene tape, gave his badge number to a patrolman with a clipboard, and walked through the unblocked side of the glass front entrance.

A crime scene tech was taking pictures of a body on the floor to his right, just inside the front entrance. A patrolman stood next to him, watching. Alvarez said, "Any witnesses?"

The patrolman nodded and pointed to a black man dressed in a dark blue blazer standing next to the large reception desk. The desk was situated in front of a bank of elevators. The witness was talking to another patrol officer with three stripes on his sleeve. Alvarez walked over to the two men, showed his badge, and said, "I'm Detective Alvarez. What's the story here, Sergeant?"

The sergeant turned to Alvarez and said, "This is David Leonard. He mans the security booth for the building. He was here when the incident occurred." The sergeant turned to Leonard. "Tell him what you just told me."

Leonard stared at the sergeant and then at Alvarez, his eyes wide. "Man, the guy moved like lightning. One second he's walking between these two big guys and the next, the big guys are on the ground and he's running out of the building."

"Whoa, slow down," said Alvarez. "Who did what to whom?"

"Well, see, the two big guys, they work for P&G Global on the thirty-fourth floor. They brought this guy in thirty minutes before all this happened. That's when, see, they pushed him out of the elevator and walked toward the front door. The shorter guy—I don't know his name, but I see him and the taller guy all the time with Mr. Plymel. See, the smaller guy was in front; the taller guy behind. Anyway, see, the guy in the middle is looking scared, man, real scared. Just as they're going out the front door, the guy in the middle does this karate thing, and man, just like that"—Leonard snapped his fingers—"the guy kicks the guy in back in the knee. He grabs the gun off the hip of the guy in front and shoots him. He did all of that in one fluid motion, man—one fluid motion. Man, he was fast." He paused and shook his head. "I never seen anything like it. It looked more like a movie stunt, but it was real. He then pushed the front door open and ran that way." Leonard pointed to the right side of the building.

Alvarez said, "So they brought him in thirty minutes before all this started. Is that what you're telling me?"

Leonard nodded. "Yeah, man, thirty minutes. I checked my computer log. I'm supposed to keep track of who comes and goes."

Alvarez wrote in a small notebook and said, "Do you know why he was brought here?"

Leonard shook his head. "Nah, I don't ask questions man, I just watch the lobby."

Alvarez nodded. "Okay, Mr. Leonard, don't go anywhere. I'm going to the thirty-fourth floor and see what they say." He pointed at the sergeant and said, "Would you come with me?"

The scene on the thirty-fourth floor was the same as the lobby: police officers talking to various individuals, and crime-scene investigators taking pictures. As soon as Alvarez walked out of the elevator, a man several inches shorter and in a very expensive suit walked up to him.

"Are you in charge of this investigation?" the man asked.

Alvarez stared at the man. "Who are you?"

The shorter man snorted. "I'm Abel Plymel, CEO of P&G Global. Have you caught the man responsible for this mess?"

Alvarez shook his head. "Not at the moment. We're trying to find out what happened."

Plymel's face reddened. "Isn't it obvious? A man stormed in here and started threatening my employees. My security guards subdued him and escorted him out of the building. Now one of them is dead and the other severely injured. What are you doing about it?"

Alvarez frowned. "He stormed in here?"

"That's what I just said. Are you deaf?"

Ignoring the last comment, Alvarez turned to the sergeant standing next to him. "Go back down and see if you can find any more witnesses. I'll stay here and try to straighten out the conflicting stories."

The sergeant nodded and headed back to the elevator.

Plymel continued to glare at Alvarez.

Alvarez said, "When you say 'stormed in,' what do you

mean? We have a witness that said he was escorted by two men into the building."

Plymel turned and looked at a taller man standing a few feet away and then looked back at Alvarez. Alvarez watched as the taller man turned, walked to a hallway, and quickly vanished out of sight. Plymel said, "Just that. The elevator opened and this crazed man steps out and starts threatening our associates. He was very belligerent and knocked a vase of flowers off the receptionist's desk. Then he started yelling. When we confronted him, he threatened everyone with bodily harm."

Alvarez nodded and wrote in his notebook. "Who saw the man?"

"I and several staff members tried to reason with him. He wouldn't settle down. That's when our two security guards forced him back into the elevator."

Nodding again, Alvarez said, "Okay, I'll need to talk to each of the individuals who were involved. Is there an office I can use?"

***

Several hours later, Alvarez stepped off the elevator. He looked around and saw David Leonard and walked over to him. "Mr. Leonard, tell me again, what time did you see the suspect escorted into the elevator?"

Leonard looked down at his desk and was silent for a few moments, then said, "I didn't see him enter the building. I must of missed him."

Alvarez frowned, stared at the black man, flipped a few pages on his notebook, and said, "Two hours ago, you told me you saw the suspect escorted into the building by two men. The same men he later killed and wounded."

"I must of misspoken. I didn't see that."

Alvarez leaned over so he could whisper. "Are you fucking with me, Mr. Leonard?"

The man looked away, shook his head, and said, "No, I

didn't see him come in the building. Honest, I didn't."

Alvarez straightened up, shook his head, and walked out through the front door of the building.

An older man, who had been standing several feet from the lobby reception booth, watched as the detective walked out of the building. He took a cell phone from the inside breast pocket of his suit coat and dialed a number. It was answered on the second ring. He said, "Yes, this is Alton Crigler. Would you tell the director I need to speak to him." He paused and listened, then said, "I understand. Tell him it is of the utmost urgency." Another pause. "Yes, he has my number. Thank you."

CHAPTER 4

Kansas City, MO

At exactly six fifty-eight the next evening, Kruger knocked on Stephanie's front door. She opened it and greeted him with the infectious smile he couldn't stop thinking about. She said, "I made reservations for us at seven-thirty. I know the front-end manager. He has a table in a back corner reserved for us. It's quieter back there, so we can talk and get to know each other."

"Sounds like a plan."

She wore black jeans tucked into tall medium-heel black leather boots. Her gray cashmere sweater complemented her figure and was accented by a necklace made with pipe bone, plated silver beads and Turquoise inlays. As she passed, Kruger caught a whiff of jasmine. She was simple and sexy.

Dating was not a common activity for Kruger, so he was quiet for a few moments, afraid he would say something stupid. Finally as they walked down the hall toward the stairs, he said, "You look nice tonight. I like the necklace."

Smiling, she looked up at him and said, "Thank you. It's one of my favorites. I found it on a trip to Phoenix last year. The person I bought it from claimed it was made on a nearby reservation. But if you look hard enough, you can see 'Made in Taiwan' on several of the beads." She chuckled. "It doesn't matter, I still like it."

He smiled and said, "Do you want me to drive?"

She shook her head. "No, let's walk, just in case we drink too much wine."

"Then, I'd better leave my gun in the apartment."

She looked at him with concern. "Aren't you supposed to carry it all the time?"

He nodded as he stepped through his now-opened door. Ten seconds later, he was closing the door and twisting the handle to make sure it was locked. "Yes, but I don't carry it if I'm planning on drinking. It's a personal decision I made a long time ago. I normally don't drink much when I'm on a case, only beer."

"I don't like guns, but I'm glad you had one last night."

They were both quiet as they went down the stairs to the ground level exit. Once on the sidewalk and walking to the restaurant, the conversation turned to small talk. At dinner, the conversation centered on cities they had both visited and the good restaurants they had tried in each city. After the dishes were cleared, Stephanie said, "So now that we've avoided talking about ourselves for the past hour, I want to know why a handsome man with a great personality isn't married."

Kruger shrugged and said, "I was once, a long time ago. I met her in college and we dated off and on while I worked on my doctorate. We got along great, until we got married. After the wedding, I taught abnormal psychology at a liberal arts college on the East Coast. I hated it. A friend suggested I apply to the FBI because they were looking for individuals with advanced degrees. It sounded more glamorous than grading Psych 101 papers, so I applied. She disapproved of the idea but didn't say anything."

Stephanie smiled and said, "Should I call you Dr. Kruger?"

"You'd better not." He returned the smile. "As a new

agent, we had to move around a lot. She resented disrupting her life every six months and let me know it. Then she got pregnant with our son Brian and things got worse. We settled in Kansas City and she absolutely hated it. One day when Brian was about ten months old, I came home from a two-day trip to St. Louis and found him alone in the apartment. He was in his playpen, soiled and crying his lungs out. I never did find out how long he'd been alone, but I suspect it was at least twenty-four hours, maybe more. She had packed her clothes, a few personal items, and walked out of our lives."

Kruger paused, took a sip of wine, and then stared at the liquid as he swirled it in the glass. Stephanie remained quiet, so he continued, "Anyway, a lawyer friend of mine filed an injunction prohibiting her from being with Brian unless my parents or I were present." He smiled and looked at her. "There was really no need. She didn't try to contact him until he was almost five. Apparently she didn't want to be in his life, except when it was convenient for her. Brian's a good kid, he doesn't dwell on it much. She's just someone who calls him on Christmas and sometimes his birthday."

Stephanie said softly, "How did all this make you feel?"

Kruger shrugged. "You can let it eat you up or you can move on. I moved on. I bought a house and my parents moved in with us. They took on the role of helping raise Brian while I traveled and saved the world."

He paused and frowned. After staring at his glass of wine for several moments, he said, "They're both gone now and Brian's in college. During those years I didn't put a lot of effort into establishing a relationship with anyone. I just concentrated on Brian and my job."

Stephanie remained quiet. Then she took a sip of her wine. "I'm sorry, I didn't mean to drag up painful memories."

Kruger straightened in his chair and smiled. "You didn't. It's just the way it is. Now that Brian's in college, maybe I'll find the right woman and put some effort into a relationship." He paused as he took a sip of wine. "Now that I've bared my soul, what about you? Why aren't you married?"

She smiled and said, "My story's not quite so heroic. My younger sister and I grew up thinking our parents didn't know each other. They're both doctors and we never saw them together, except on holidays." She laughed, took another sip of wine, and continued, "It got so bad that when I turned ten and my sister was eight, we started calling our nanny Mom. That didn't go over very well. But it did wake them up and a lot changed. I'm not complaining. They were good parents, but they were better doctors. I guess I followed in their footsteps with my devotion to my career. After I got my MBA, I joined the company I'm with now. I worked my tail off to climb the corporate ladder. It's amazing how many men are intimidated by successful women. I just haven't met a guy who can handle it yet. I tried at first and then gave up, deciding if it happened, great. If it didn't, well that would be fine too."

Kruger took a sip of wine and looked over the glass at her. "What if you find a guy that can handle it?"

She smiled. "He'd have to put up with my traveling."

"I can if you can put up with my traveling."

They both laughed and she said with a smile, "What are you proposing? We get married tonight?"

"Nothing that drastic." He paused, looked at her, and said, "I've never met anyone like you. In my line of work, the individuals I deal with are different in each case. They're local police or sheriffs' departments, and sometimes they resent…" He stopped, chuckled, and said, "No, that's not correct; they always resent the FBI showing up. So, I just don't talk about myself. Talking to you is different. I know it sounds corny, but the minute I met you, I felt I could tell you anything. I like that feeling."

She was quiet for several moments. "I know, I've been thinking the same thing. I've never asked anyone out for a date before, but I didn't even hesitate with you. What's going on, Sean, you're the psychologist?"

He shook his head. "I don't know. Maybe we're just two

people who finally stumbled onto their soul mates."

"Sounds like New Age mumbo jumbo to me." She displayed the smile he was falling in love with. "I thought you were the one with the Ph.D.?"

"You haven't read my dissertation, have you? It's titled *Acquiring a Soul Mate Using Metrics of Tea Leaves and Mumbo Jumbo.*"

They both laughed and went quiet.

Finally she said, "You may be right. I always thought when I met the right person, there would be fireworks. I'm wondering if meeting the right person is more like putting on a favorite sweater. It's comfortable and keeps you warm."

As the restaurant started to close, they were still sitting at their table talking. Kruger apologized to the waiter for staying so long and left him a substantial tip. As they walked back to their condos, Kruger walked with his hands in his pockets. Stephanie hugged his left arm and put her head on his shoulder. "So what's next, Sean?"

He shrugged. "Not sure. This is new territory for me." He looked back over his shoulder at the restaurant and continued, "Have you ever had an evening you didn't want to end?"

She hugged his arm tighter and looked up at him. "No, not until tonight."

He nodded. "Me either."

They walked in silence until they got within a block of their condos. Finally, Stephanie said, "Tomorrow's Saturday. Do you have any plans?"

"No, other than getting the condo straightened up from the move. Why?"

"This is going to sound strange, but would you do something domestic with me?"

He looked at her and smiled. "What did you have in mind?"

"I was planning on looking for a new sofa and love seat. We could do it together. I'd like your input. Plus we could have lunch somewhere, on me this time. We could make a day of it."

He put his arm around her. "Sounds like fun."

***

Sunday evening, Kruger finally managed to find a little time to start unpacking and arranging his condo. Around eight, his cell phone chirped. He glanced at the caller ID, shook his head, and answered, "Kruger."

"Sean, it's Alan."

"What's happened, Alan? You never call on Sunday." Alan Seltzer was an assistant deputy director with the FBI and Kruger's immediate supervisor. They had known each other since their academy days. In his current position, Kruger reported to Seltzer.

"I need you in New York City sometime tomorrow."

"Again, what's happened?"

"I got a call from the SAC in the New York City office this afternoon. They have a situation that doesn't smell right. Apparently someone jumped a couple of security guards in the lobby of an office building on Wall Street. One of the guards was killed and the other crippled. Now the NYPD has called in the bureau because the security guards worked for a company co-owned by a former deputy attorney general."

"Okay, he's pulling in favors; I get that. What's this have to do with me?"

"Well, apparently the two guards were ex-special forces, guys with a lot of experience and training. The guy they were escorting out of the building took them both down in less than five seconds according to witnesses."

"Alan, this sounds like a local problem. Why do I need to get involved?"

"Because the director of our fine agency is an old college friend of the former deputy attorney general, that's why."

"Oh goodie," he said sardonically. "Who is he?"

"Alton Crigler."

Kruger remained silent long enough for Seltzer to say,

"Are you still there?"

"Yeah, I should hang up. He and I don't see eye to eye on anything. It doesn't make any sense he would ask for me. Besides, he's an asshole."

"I agree he's an asshole. But the fact of the matter is the director's involved, and now so are you, whether you like it or not."

"Great, just great." He paused. "All right."

"Good, when you have your itinerary, call me. I'll have someone pick you up at the airport."

CHAPTER 5

New York City

"From what we've been told, the guy suddenly appeared in the offices of P&G Global and started threatening everyone. No one saw him enter the building or get on the elevator. Did I mention there's a guard in the building's lobby at all times?" Brad Metzger paused and took a sip of water. As the Special Agent in Charge of the New York City FBI office, he was the one who had called Alan Seltzer. Metzger was a tall athletic man, with coal black hair, which he kept short and perfectly styled. His brown eyes, movie star looks, and a passion for expensive Brooks Brothers suits rounded out a look the FBI embraced. Today he looked frazzled. His suit coat was off and the sleeves of his wrinkled shirt were rolled up to his elbows.

He continued, "As the guy was being escorted out of the building, he took two guards down. Martial arts kick to the knee of the guard on the right, stole the gun of the guard on the left, and shot him point blank. One dead, the other needs complete knee reconstruction. We interviewed the EMTs; they said the knee was at a forty-five degree angle the wrong way."

Kruger grimaced. "Ouch." He cocked his head to the left. "So how was he being threatening?"

"Good question, but the answers are confusing. Some witnesses said he was waving a gun, others said he was yelling, others said he was waving a knife. There are no corroborating stories."

Kruger chuckled. "Figures."

Metzger continued, "We were told the man had worked for a company purchased by P&G Global. They're a private equity company, specializing in buying companies, making changes and then selling them for a profit."

Kruger said, "Yeah, those changes usually include letting everyone go and shipping their jobs overseas."

Metzger nodded. "Apparently that occurred in this situation, a disgruntled ex-employee."

"So who is the guy? You ID him?"

"Yes, but we can't find any trace of him."

Kruger smiled, "Not that hard to do in New York."

"No, I mean we can't find any records of him. No driver's license, no birth certificate, no credit cards, no social security number—poof, nothing. He's a ghost."

Kruger frowned. "Then how did you ID him?"

Metzger handed a file to Kruger. "Here's his personnel file from the company P&G Global bought. Everything in that file does not exist in the real world. The guy worked there for ten years as a computer geek. He debugged software. We contacted the original owner of the company. He and the suspect met in college. He told me the guy helped start the company and was brilliant, best hacker he'd ever seen. When we called the bursar's office at their college—"

"Let me guess," Kruger interrupted. "No record he was ever there."

Metzger nodded. "They went digital five years ago. Everything is computerized."

Kruger stared at Metzger. "I was joking."

"I'm not. There's no record of him. Someone is erasing all the public records of his existence. We think he's established a new identity somewhere, but we have no idea of where."

Kruger stared out the window of the conference room. "That could make finding him problematic. Have you found any friends or relatives?"

Preston Alvarez sat across from Kruger at the conference table; he was now the lead NYPD detective on the case and an old friend of Kruger's. He said, "Nope— seems our suspect was a loner."

Kruger looked at Alvarez. "You've been quiet this morning. What do you think?"

"I think the whole story's bullshit."

Metzger smiled. "Preston feels P&G Global is being less than truthful."

"Less than truthful? They're lying their collective asses off and covering something up," said Alvarez. "I was the first NYPD detective on the scene. I asked the guard at the front desk what happened. He told me those two guards brought the guy in a half-hour before the incident. Two hours later, he tells me he was mistaken." He rolled his eyes toward the ceiling. "Give me a break."

Kruger said, "What about security cameras in the lobby? They would have recorded the guards bringing the guy in."

"They don't." Metzger shook his head. "There's a fifteen-second gap about thirty minutes before the incident. It's hard to detect, but our tech guys found it. There's also no record of him entering the building alone."

Alvarez said, "Like I said, the story's bullshit."

Kruger nodded. "Okay, their story's bullshit. How do we prove it?"

Alvarez slid two file folders across the table to Kruger, tapped them with his index finger, and said, "These are NYPD files on the two guards. They're both ex-military and left the service under less than ideal circumstances. Their first encounter with the NYPD was right after discharge about ten years ago. Both have numerous priors: aggravated assault, extortion, assault with a deadly weapon, etc. Each time, the charges were dropped after the victims refused to testify."

Kruger frowned. "Why?"

Alvarez shrugged. "Same old story, money, threats, who knows."

"The bullshit gets deeper."

Alvarez nodded.

Metzger said, "Five years ago, P&G Global bought a company specializing in security for business executives working overseas. These two worked for that company. They returned to the states a year ago and have been Abel Plymel's personal security ever since."

Kruger said, "Does the guy who took them out have a police record?"

Alvarez shook his head. "Not that I could find, but then we can't find anything on him."

Kruger turned to Metzger. "What about military records, did you find any?"

Metzger shook his head.

Kruger was silent and sipped his now-cold coffee. Finally he said, "What is Alton Crigler's role at P&G Global?"

"He's the managing partner," said Metzger. "Plymel's the president and CEO, from what the SEC told me. On paper they're equal partners, but Plymel holds a little higher status within the company. He does the deals and Crigler handles the politicians in Washington. There's a board of directors made up of their largest investors. Both men report to them."

"Why did he want me involved?" Kruger said, almost to himself.

Metzger shook his head. "Don't know, maybe you should ask him."

***

With his hand extended, Alton Crigler stepped out from behind the massive oak desk. "Thank you for heading the investigation Agent Kruger." The office was ornate, professionally decorated, and smelled of old leather and

Lemon Pledge. At six foot two, Crigler was slender and dressed in a dark gray pinstripe Armani suit. A crisp white-on-white shirt accented with a maroon tie completed his wardrobe. He was in his mid-sixties and still had a full head of coal-black hair, although streaks of gray were visible at his temples. During his early career, he had held various positions in the Justice Department, following his graduation from Yale Law School. After being the deputy attorney general for ten years and getting passed over numerous times for the top spot, he left public service to become a principal in P&G Global.

Kruger shook the extended hand. "Right now I'm just a consultant."

Crigler gestured to a leather wingback chair in front of his desk. He returned to his seat. "That's disappointing. I was led to believe you would be the agent in charge."

As Kruger sat down in the leather chair, Crigler picked up his desk phone and punched in a number. "Doris, I need to speak to Phil. Yes, that will be fine." He replaced the handset. "This will only take a second." The phone buzzed. He picked it up and said, "Yes. Thank you, I'll hold." He turned his chair around toward the floor-to-ceiling window behind his desk. After a few moments of silence, he continued, "Phil, thanks for taking my call. I understand Agent Kruger is only a consultant on this investigation." He paused as he listened to the response. "Yes, he's sitting in front of my desk." Silence again. "Splendid, I'll let you tell him." Crigler turned his chair back around, stood, and reached over his desk with the phone handset in his hand. "The director would like to speak to you."

Kruger smiled, knowing that Crigler had just called in a favor. He stood and took the offered handset. "This is Agent Kruger."

"Director Wagner here, Agent Kruger. I know you were just called in as a consultant. But, I believe it would be in the best interest of the bureau for you to lead this investigation."

"Special Agent Metzger is a very capable investigator.

I'm not sure he needs my assistance."

There was silence on the other end of the call for a few moments. Finally, the director said, "I do not believe this is a debate, agent. You are in charge. Is that clear?"

"Yes sir, but this is not my area of expertise, Agent Metzger..."

"Agent Kruger, this is not a request—it's an order."

"Yes sir."

"Give the phone back to Alton. I will explain the mix-up."

Kruger smiled again and handed the phone back to Crigler. As he sat back down in the leather chair, his curiosity about the just-witnessed power play grew. He watched as Crigler finished his conversation with FBI Director Phillip Wagner and returned the handset to its cradle.

"Now that we have that settled," said Crigler, "when will you catch this person?"

Kruger almost laughed, but he kept his face neutral. "Why do you want me on this case so bad? This isn't what I normally do."

"Come now, Agent Kruger, you're much too modest. Your reputation is stellar. You've tracked down some of the most dangerous criminals this country has ever seen."

This time Kruger laughed. "Don't believe all the urban legends coming out of the bureau."

"Seriously, your reputation for never giving up is why you're perfect for this case. My company needs to have this man caught and brought to trial." He leaned forward in his chair, put his elbows on the desk and stared at Kruger. With a sober voice, he said, "P&G Global's position in the financial community is based on appearances. This little incident threatens our prestige in the world of Wall Street. I'm sure you can understand our position here. Can't you Agent Kruger?"

Kruger was silent for a few moments. He suddenly realized there was more going on than someone attacking two security guards. "I'm going to need access to the security camera tapes and any witnesses who saw this man."

"By all means, you have full access."

Kruger stared at Crigler, paused briefly, and said, "How much money is missing?"

Crigler stiffened and his eyes narrowed, but he recovered quickly. "There is no money missing. Why do you ask?"

"The man is a computer genius. He might have gained access to some of your bank accounts and illegally transferred funds."

"I can assure you, none of the company's funds are missing."

Kruger smiled, stayed silent for a few moments, and realized how the question was answered. None of the company's money was missing. He wondered how much personal money had been taken. But he kept that question to himself. He stood. "I'll schedule appointments with your associates and start the interviews this afternoon. Do you have a conference room I can use?"

Crigler nodded.

CHAPTER 6

New York City

As the elevator descended to the first floor, Detective Alvarez stared at the floor indicator lights and said, "Well, that was a cluster fuck."

Kruger nodded. "You're right, their story is bullshit. Everyone's version was too rehearsed and too much alike for my taste. There wasn't one degree of deviation in any of their stories."

The elevator door opened and they both walked toward the front door in silence. Once they were on the street outside the building, Kruger turned to Alvarez and said, "I want to talk to the driver. By himself, without the firm's lawyer sitting at the end of the conference table staring at him. He acted like he wanted to say something, but wasn't sure if he could."

Alvarez nodded. "I'll find him. Where do you want to do it?"

"Let's keep it friendly, say a corner bar close to his residence."

"Got it. I'll call you when it's arranged."

***

The call came at 7:30 p.m. The driver would be at McGuire's Bar and Grill in an hour. Arriving thirty minutes early, Kruger found a secluded table in a back corner. When he asked for a Boulevard Pale Ale, he was mildly surprised when he was told the bar served the Kansas City brewed beer. At 8:35 p.m., the driver, Ron Lekas, entered the pub followed by Alvarez. Lekas hesitated when he saw Kruger. He looked back at Alvarez, who pointed toward a chair at Kruger's table.

After the waitress took his drink order, Lekas said, "Didn't know you'd be here."

Kruger said, "Thank you for coming."

Lekas looked at Alvarez. "I wouldn't have come if I knew the Feds would be here."

Alvarez said, "Shut up and listen to him."

Lekas was five foot seven, dark haired, and a descendant of immigrants from the Mediterranean. He wore his leather jacket over a light-blue silk shirt and black dress slacks. Running his left hand through his black hair and smoothing it back, he said, "I need to go. You guys are going to get me fired."

Kruger smiled and said in a low voice, "That's not my intent, Ron. No one is going to tell them you spoke to us. I felt like you wanted to tell us something when we interviewed you this afternoon. But, you didn't feel comfortable talking in front of the firm's lawyer. Am I right?"

The waitress sat a draft down in front of Lekas; he grabbed it and took a long pull of the amber liquid. He shook his head. "Ahhh—man. I need this job. They threatened to fire me if I didn't tell you what they wanted me to."

"Who threatened you, Ron?" Kruger had leaned forward.

Lekas took another long drink. "Mr. Plymel."

Kruger looked at Alvarez, who smiled. He returned his attention to Lekas. "What did you see, Ron?"

Lekas took another long pull on his beer, but remained silent.

Alvarez said, "We find you lied to us in that room this afternoon, you could be in big trouble. You could lose your job anyway. I looked at your jacket this afternoon, Ron. You've got a felony bust for distributing. You ever carry a weapon on the job Ron?"

Lekas jerked up straight and shouted, "No—hell no. Those other guys did, but I never have."

Kruger leaned across the table again. "What's going on, Ron? Tell us."

Silence was Kruger's answer. Finally, Ron Lekas looked between Alvarez and Kruger and said, "They brought him to the meeting. He didn't just break into the office like they claim. We picked him up at his apartment earlier that morning. From what I heard, he broke into Mr. Plymel's apartment, messed with his computer, and stole some money. Not sure how much, but Mr. Plymel went crazy."

"Why did he go crazy?" asked Alvarez.

Lekas shrugged. "Don't know. Franklin, the guy that was killed, said it wasn't the company's money. It was Mr. Plymel's personal money."

Kruger sat up straight. "What's your position with the company, Ron?"

"I'm one of two personal drivers for Mr. Plymel."

"Two. Why two?"

"We're on call—twelve on, twelve off. I was on call the night Mr. Plymel first ran into the guy you're looking for."

Kruger's eyebrows went up. "What do you mean, first ran into?"

"I had just escorted a couple of Mr. Plymel's lady friends to his apartment. I was getting ready to go back to the car when the doorbell rang and Mr. Plymel answered it. The guy you're looking for delivered some pizzas. Mr. Plymel recognized him, gave him a hard time, and then handed him a two-cent tip."

"How'd he recognize a pizza delivery guy?" said Alvarez.

"He used to work for a company Mr. Plymel bought. He was let go. At least that's what Mr. Plymel told his guests. I left right after that. I didn't hear any more of the conversation."

"Where did you pick him up at?"

"Right outside his apartment. Franklin escorted him to the Suburban. I was the driver. They called when they were done with the meeting. I had the Suburban parked at the curb waiting for them. I saw Franklin push him out of the elevator toward the front door. Just as they got to the door, the guy shot Franklin and messed up Harvey's knee."

"What was the plan when they got him back into the Suburban?"

Lekas shrugged. He hesitated for a few moments then said, "Not sure. I wasn't told."

"You can guess, Ron. What was the plan?"

The driver remained silent.

"Were your orders to kill him and get rid of the body?"

Lekas shrugged. "I wasn't told."

Kruger sat back in his chair. "So, he might have been defending himself, is that possible?"

Lekas nodded. "Yeah, I'd say so."

Alvarez said, "Has anything like this happened before with Plymel?"

Shrugging, Lekas said, "Not that I've seen, but I'm usually the day driver. I've heard stories. You know, from the other driver. He talks about picking up investors and women." Lekas stared at his now-empty beer. "These rich guys get all the pussy."

Kruger stared at Lekas. This opened up the investigation into something entirely different. They needed to find the fugitive and talk to him.

Alvarez's cell phone chirped. He stood, walked toward the back of the bar, and answered it. Kruger looked at Lekas and said, "Thank you for talking to us. We'll remember your cooperation."

Lekas put his head in his hands and said, "Ahh, jeez

man. Don't get me involved."

"We'll try not to."

Alvarez hurried back to the table and said, "One of our guys found a cabbie who says he recognized the guy. You wanta meet him?"

Kruger stood and threw a twenty-dollar bill on the table. "Have another beer or two on us." Then he walked out of the bar, following Alvarez.

***

Two uniformed cops were talking to the taxi driver when Kruger and Alvarez arrived at the cab company. Having just finished his day shift, he was not pleased about the delay in going home. He was a short man, five foot seven or less, with a full black beard, dark complexion, and dark brown eyes. He was sitting at a table in the break room, drinking a bottle of water and smelled of curry and sweat. Alvarez spoke to the officers; they nodded and stood back a few steps. Kruger showed him a picture. "Tell me about this man."

The cab driver looked at the picture and in broken English said, "I dropped him off at Newark International. He gave me a hundred-dollar bill, told me he would give me another one if I got him there by one o'clock. I did. He gave me another hundred. He ran into the airport. I drove off. End of story. Can I go home now?"

Kruger looked at Alvarez, who said, "I'm on it. I'll have someone get the security tapes."

Returning his attention to the cab driver, Kruger said, "Where did you pick him up?"

"Library at Thirty-Fourth and Madison."

"What did he say to you during the ride?"

Shaking his head, the cab driver said, "Nothing. He only spoke about the money."

"Did he have any luggage?"

"No. Just backpack."

Kruger smiled and said, "Thank you, sir. I appreciate

your cooperation." He walked away toward where Alvarez was talking on his cell phone and waited for him to finish. After the call ended, Kruger said, "What?"

Alvarez shook his head. "It's New Jersey, for gawd sake. We have to get a freaking warrant."

Kruger smiled. "Let me handle it."

***

Charlie Craft was a twenty-seven-year-old, pencil-thin forensic technician with the FBI. Years of slouching over a computer screen had given him a slightly stooped posture. He wore black square glasses, his only fashion statement. Clothes were a necessity, but not a priority. He owned a half-dozen khaki Dockers, which made it easy to decide which pair to wear with one of a dozen black or navy polo shirts. A pair of black Converse tennis shoes complemented the Dockers on a daily basis. Meeting Charlie on the street would be a non-event and quickly forgotten. But he was an expert forensic technician and wizard with digital media, including computers. Sean Kruger liked him; therefore, Charlie had prospered within the FBI.

The next day, Charlie took an early-morning flight from Washington DC to Newark Liberty International, where Kruger and Detective Alvarez met him. As he walked up to Kruger, Charlie handed him an envelope. "I believe this is what you wanted, Sean."

Kruger smiled, looked at the federal search warrant, and said, "Perfect. Charlie Craft, meet NYPD Detective Preston Alvarez. He's our local contact on this little endeavor."

Craft and Alvarez shook hands and they all started walking toward the airport security office. Charlie said, "What are we looking for, Sean? You were a little cryptic when you called."

"We're looking for a fugitive. We need you to search the security tapes. Hopefully, you can determine which flight he took. Once we know where he went, we can start the

36

manhunt in earnest."

"Huh…" He paused, blinked a couple of times and said, "That's going to take a while."

***

Harvey Ramirez was still in the recovery room after his second operation to repair his badly injured knee when Kruger and Alvarez arrived at the hospital. While Alvarez checked in with the two uniforms guarding the man, Kruger asked a nurse at the nurse's station if he could speak to the attending surgeon. Ten minutes later, the doctor was shaking Kruger's hand.

"How bad was the injury, Doctor?"

Doctor Kendra Rivera, was as tall as Kruger, slender, dark brown hair pulled back in a tight ponytail, rimless glasses sitting in front of hazel eyes on a slightly up-turned nose. She was attractive, but her demeanor distracted from her appearance. "In my judgment, it's permanent. He'll likely have a stiff leg the rest of his life. Why do you care Agent Kruger?"

Kruger smiled slightly. "I really don't, but I need to talk to him. How long before that's possible."

She stared at him for a few moments. "Not today, maybe not tomorrow."

"I really don't have that kind of time, Doctor. Can you give him something to wake him up?"

She frowned. "Absolutely not."

"The man has information I need…"

"Not at the expense of his well-being, Agent."

Kruger leaned in closer to the Doctor, who did not give up any space. "Doctor, there is a fugitive out there who has already killed one man and severely injured your patient. My concern is for the public well-being. I need Ramirez awake."

She glared at him for a long time. Finally her face relaxed. "Very well, follow me."

Kruger and Alvarez stood next to the bed containing the

groggy Harvey Ramirez. Doctor Rivera stood on the other side, arms crossed over her chest. Ramirez was larger than Kruger realized. He was at least six foot six and weighed close to two seventy five, all muscle. The wounded man was blinking his eyes and struggling to gain consciousness. Kruger looked at the doctor, who nodded. Kruger said, "Harvey, tell me about the man who did this to you."

Ramirez focused on Kruger and shook his head.

"Harvey, I'm an agent with the FBI, I'm trying to find this guy. Can you help me?"

In a voice barely above a whisper, Ramirez said, "Not a chance. Go away."

Kruger looked at Alvarez, "See what you can get out of him. I'm going to check with Charlie." He walked out of the room and was followed by the doctor.

As Kruger walked down the hall the doctor caught up and said, "I tried to warn you, it will probably be a few days before he's cognizant enough to really answer your questions."

Kruger stopped and looked at her. "I had to try. In a few more days, the fugitive will be long gone and my chances of finding him will be nil."

She nodded. "You don't sound like you're from this part of the country."

Kruger shook his head. "I'm based out of Kansas City."

"Do you spend much time in New York City?"

He shook his head.

She smiled, turned to walk back to Ramirez's room and said, "Shame."

***

Kruger's cell phone vibrated as he got a cup of coffee in the hospital cafeteria. He said, "Kruger."

"Sean, it's Charlie. You're not going to like what I've found."

"What?"

"You need to see this. How quickly can you get back here?"

"One hour."

When Kruger was back at the airport, minus Alvarez, he sat next to Charlie at a security monitor. Charlie pointed to a figure entering the airport. "Here's the cab you told me about. See the license? It matches." Kruger nodded and Charlie continued, "We see him enter the airport on this camera." He pecked at a keyboard and another camera angle popped up. "Here we see him stop once he's inside. He watches as the cab drives away. He looks around, finds what he's looking for, and walks into a trinkets-and-trash store. At first, I didn't see him come out. But after a closer look, I found him." He pointed to a man with a ball cap, a dark windbreaker, and sunglasses. The man's head was down as he walked. Charlie said, "Ten minutes after our suspect goes in, this guy comes out of the shop."

Kruger said, "Same guy?"

Charlie nodded. "Same backpack. That's how I identified him. Now, watch as he takes the escalator down to baggage claim and transportation." More typing on the keyboard and the view changed again. "Here he's coming down the escalator. He doesn't pause and look around after he gets off, like most people. He goes straight outside to the taxi queue." He typed on the keyboard again and pointed to the screen. "There he is, getting into a cab. He didn't take another flight, he left the airport."

Kruger stared at the video monitor and was silent for a few moments. Finally he said, "Damn. We may have lost him."

Charlie nodded. "That's a strong possibility."

"Why would you pay two hundred dollars to a taxi driver to get you to the airport if you weren't late for a flight?"

"Maybe hundreds were all he had."

Kruger shook his head. "No, there's something else."

"The cabbie remembered him because of it."

"Charlie, that's why I like working with you. Exactly, he wanted the cabbie to remember him. See if you can identify this new taxi. If you can, we'll go talk to the cab company."

Charlie handed Kruger a piece of paper. "Already did. Let's go."

***

The cab company had records of where the taxi Charlie identified had dropped off the passenger. The Westminster Hotel in Livingston, New Jersey, a twenty-minute ride from Newark Liberty International Airport.

At the hotel, Kruger identified himself as an agent with the FBI and asked for the manager. She was a short, overweight lady in her late-fifties with unnaturally black hair. She looked at the picture and name Kruger gave her. She went to one of the computers at the front desk and typed. "No, no one by that name ever registered. We still have the security disk for that day. You're more than welcome to review it."

Fifteen minutes later, Charlie found what they needed. "There he is, Sean, getting out of the cab. Once again, he watches the cab drive away and starts walking west. He never even came in the door."

"We've lost him, haven't we?"

Charlie looked up at Kruger. "I'm afraid so. There no telling where he went."

"Okay, it's time to go back to basics. The NYPD searched his apartment, but you haven't. Let's get over there and see if you can find something they missed."

CHAPTER 7

Springfield, MO

JR Diminski handed Senior Vice President Brian Quest a three-page report. It had been a week since Diminski convinced Quest he needed a security audit of his banking systems. Quest gave it a quick glance, expecting to find a clean report. He stopped halfway down the second page and returned to the first page. This time, he read more carefully. He read the memo two more times. He laid it down on this desk, took his glasses off, and shut his eyes. Squeezing the bridge of his nose with his right thumb and forefinger, he said, "How hard was it to find?"

"Not very. I'm surprised you haven't had a lot of complaints from your customers."

Quest's eyes were weary and it looked like he hadn't slept in a couple of days. "My team can't find it. We knew we had a problem, but knowing and correcting are two different issues. Can you fix it?"

"How much has the bank lost so far?"

"About a hundred thou..." He caught himself. "The amount is not for publication. The bank has covered all the losses, not one customer has lost a penny."

Diminski nodded. "FDIC. Do they know about the security breach?"

"No, it would raise our rates. Can you fix it?"

He nodded. "Yes, I can."

Quest stared at the report, then at his computer screen. "Draw up a contract. I'll take it to the president for his signature. Can you start tonight after the bank closes?"

Diminski reached into his computer bag, withdrew a prepared contract spelling out his obligations to the bank and the bank's obligation to him. Standing, he handed the contract to Quest. "I'll be here at six."

Three days later, a smiling Brian Quest handed Diminski a check. "I've been authorize by the board to offer you a long-term retainer."

Diminski raised his eyebrows. "Why?"

"The holding company that owns the bank wants to be able to request your services and receive immediate attention."

"Are there other banks with similar problems, Brian?"

Chuckling, Quest nodded. "The same company designed the systems for most of the banks within our network, JR." He smiled, his eyes looked rested. "They want you to do a complete audit of our online security structure."

Diminski smiled. "Sounds like something I would enjoy. Tell them I accept."

After all the paperwork was signed, Quest said, "I've been meaning to ask you, what does JR stand for? Are you a junior?

Hesitating for just a moment. "It stands for J and R. My parents never told me why they named me that way; they died when I was young."

His parents had died when he was young, but the name had really come from a gravestone he had found in a large cemetery in the northern part of town. The child had died within a month of its birth, but the birthdate was the same as his: same year, same day. The child's name was John Robert Diminski. After several days of manipulating databases in

New York and Missouri, Diminski had a new identity. There was now a credit history, New York driver's license, Social Security card, and birth certificate for a person called JR Diminski. His former identity had been permanently erased; no public records remained, except behind a very secure firewall at the Pentagon. A firewall even he couldn't get past.

Since arriving in Springfield, his residence had been a hotel on the south side of town. The contract with the banking group was going to increase his workload, creating a need for more space and something more permanent. It was time to find an apartment.

After several phone calls, he stood in a two-bedroom unit four blocks from his hotel. The building manager stood behind him and said, "How about this one?"

Diminski said, "I need at least twenty megabits-per-second internet speed."

The manager, a bald, short man with a round belly hanging over his belt, sighed. "We offer free cable, but you can get whatever service you want, you just have to pay extra."

Diminski nodded. "How much?"

"The internet service?"

"No, the apartment."

"Oh, seven-fifty a month, with a two-hundred-dollar, nonrefundable security deposit."

Diminski smiled. His apartment rent in New York City was three times that amount and only had one bedroom. "I'll take it."

"I have to run a background check. Once I know you're not a pervert, you can move in."

Diminski turned around, removed his wallet from his left front pants' pocket and extracted twenty one-hundred-dollar bills. "There's two-thousand dollars, my first two months' rent, security deposit, and a little extra for you, if you let me move in today."

The man stared at the money and moistened his lips with his tongue. He looked up at Diminski and then back at the money. Finally, he said, "Follow me to the office; I need you to sign a lease agreement."

The first real test of his new identity came next: applying for a Missouri driver's license. An independent contractor operated the Missouri Department of Revenue offices, usually staffing them with low-wage clerks. Diminski picked a day when he knew the office would be busy and the staff would be trying to push as many people through the system as possible. After standing in line for forty minutes, he was motioned forward by a young, stocky woman with spiked purple hair. As he approached her desk, she stared at him with a blank expression.

After handing his paperwork to her, she glanced at it and started typing on her keyboard. She frowned at the computer screen, turned to him, and said, "I have to have a name. The computer won't take initials."

He smiled and said, "My name is JR."

She stared at him without emotion. "But the system has to have a name. It's not allowing J period, R period."

"That's not my name; it's simply JR, no periods, just the letters."

She once again stared at the computer, then back at him. Finally she shrugged and typed in the letters without the periods. "Huh, it took it." As she continued typing, she said, "Weird. Who'd name their kid JR?"

Barely able to keep from laughing, Diminski said, "My parents."

She stopped typing, stared at him with her blank expression, and shrugged again.

Fifteen minutes later, he walked out of the office with a brand-new driver's license issued by the state of Missouri. His confidence in his new identity was growing stronger every day.

It had been three weeks since the incident in New York City. Diminski's old identity had been erased. His new identity had passed government scrutiny, and he had a contract with a bank holding company for the next six months. With the signing of the lease for his apartment, a feeling of stability was returning to his life. If no one found him in the next few weeks, he felt he had a good chance of permanently disappearing. This thought made him smile.

CHAPTER 8

New York City

Alton Crigler opened the door to Abel Plymel's office and noticed he was on the phone. Plymel sat in his desk chair, his back to the door, facing the window. Crigler shut the door quietly, walked to the leather sofa against the wall, and sat down. He unbuttoned his dark-gray Brooks Brothers suit coat, crossed his legs, and cleared his throat loud enough for Plymel to hear.

Plymel looked over his shoulder and saw Alton sitting. He nodded ever so slightly and said into the phone, "I have to go. Something just came up."

He turned around, faced Crigler, and placed the phone back in its cradle. "How long have you been sitting there?"

"Just walked in. The FBI has assigned one of their top agents to this incident. I tried to stop it, but I have little control over the internal politics of the FBI."

"Bullshit. You're still tight with the director."

Crigler shook his head. "Not anymore. He won't even take my calls."

"Then what do you want me to do?"

"I personally don't care what you do. But the board is

unhappy with this." He hesitated for a second. "Embarrassment in the front lobby. They are concerned because we do not need any negative publicity right now. The current administration is looking for reasons to put their thumb down on private equity companies, and this incident will only help fuel their obsession."

"You're the goddamn liaison with Congress. Talk to your contacts. Take them to lunch and spread more money around. Every single one of them has a PAC you can pour money into." He paused and sat back in his chair. "Hell, our activities increase the goddamn GNP."

Crigler chuckled. "You're talking like a true Wall Street insider. You have no idea of how Main Street views our industry. Do you?" Crigler shook his head. "It takes enormous amounts of cash from this company and our fellow private equity brethren to keep Congress, the Justice Department, and the SEC out of our little sandbox. So like I said, get this episode behind you. Get it resolved before the FBI finds out exactly what happened."

Plymel's face grew red. He jumped out of his chair and leaned across the desk. Pointing a finger at Crigler, he said, "Keep those moronic senators and the FBI off my back. That's why you're here enjoying the twilight of your career. You're the one who's supposed to take care of problems like this. I will not be lectured to by a semi-literate Senate Finance Committee chairman from Tennessee ever again..."

Crigler raised his left hand with the palm toward Plymel. "Spare me your platitudes. Say a mantra and shut up, Abel. Your temper will cause you to have a heart attack or a stroke, probably both."

Plymel's jaw clinched tight. He took a deep breath. His temper was flaring more lately and not dissipating as fast as it had in the past. Secretly, he was worried. His blood pressure was high, and he wasn't sleeping well. Not that he had ever slept more than five or six hours a night. But now it was down to three hours or less. The presence of a headache reached his awareness. He walked to an armoire on the opposite wall from Crigler. He opened the doors, revealing a fully stocked bar. Grabbing a glass, he poured two fingers of twelve-year-old Glenfiddich. He turned to Crigler. "Want one?"

Crigler shook his head with disgust. He glanced at his watch. "For god sakes Abel, it's only eleven o'clock in the morning. No I don't want one. Get a grip, man. You're on the edge. The board is already asking questions about your stability, and quite frankly so am I. You haven't produced a high-profit takeover in twelve months. In fact, they think we've been out-bid on several recent deals. Deals we should have won. Instead, we're looking at them from the sidelines."

Plymel shrugged. "Tell them not to worry. We'll make it up on the one I'm going to close in a few days."

Crigler stood and headed toward the door. Before he opened it to leave, he turned back toward Plymel. "I'm just the messenger. The board's lost confidence in you. They said for me to tell you to get this mess straightened up or resign. In my opinion, it's going to be hard for you to regain their trust." He turned back to the door, opened it, hesitated, and looked back at Plymel. "It took a lot of arm-twisting to keep them from asking for your resignation this morning. I'm done sticking my neck out for you. The next messenger won't be so congenial." With that comment, Crigler walked out of the room, closing the door behind him.

Plymel stared at the door and started to tremble. He closed his eyes and took several deep breaths. He poured another scotch. Staring at it for a few seconds, he downed it in one gulp.

***

When Kruger and Charlie arrived at the fugitive's apartment, Alvarez was already there. He said, "Not sure what you're trying to find. All our people found was a lot of DNA."

Kruger smiled. "Nothing against your team. Charlie just

wanted to get a feel for the guy. If he finds anything, you will be the first to know."

Ten minutes into his search, Charlie said to Alvarez, "Is this how you found the apartment?"

Nodding, Alvarez said, "Guy lived like a monk, if you ask me."

Charlie had just finished looking through a desk in one of the two bedrooms. He now stood in the living room looking around. Kruger was sitting on a worn sofa, he frowned, stood and said, "Did you find something?"

"No, I didn't. That's what's wrong with this apartment." He turned to Kruger. "Remember Paul Bishop's house in St. Louis?"

Kruger nodded and looked around. "Yeah I do. You're right, this place is similar. There's nothing personal here."

Alvarez looked at Kruger and then Charlie. "Who's Paul Bishop?"

Kruger said, "It was the first time I meet Charlie. Paul Bishop killed himself and left a suicide note confessing to four unsolved murders. The guy lived in a house for twenty years and it looked like this."

Alvarez nodded. "The landlord said he moved in a couple of months ago. It's a furnished apartment. Apparently, all of this was here when he moved in."

"Is it possible he was planning his disappearing act for awhile? Maybe that's why you couldn't find any records of him." Kruger stopped. "By the way, how did you find out where he lived?"

Alvarez was quiet. He shook his head. "The receptionist at P&G Global gave it to one of the first responders." He looked at Kruger. "Before they got their stories straight."

Kruger smiled. "How did they know his address? I thought he just appeared out of the elevator."

"Fucker's keep lying to us, don't they?"

Kruger nodded. "Yes they do. I bet no one knew she'd given it to one of your officers."

Charlie interrupted, "Where's the laptop you found?"

Alvarez said, "Lab."

"What did you find on it?"

"Damn thing would make a great door stop. The hard drive's been crashed. Our computer guys think it was sabotaged."

Charlie nodded. "If this guy's as good as we've heard, he might have had a booby trap on it. I'd like to see it, if possible."

"Soon as we're done here, we can go to the lab."

"I'm uncomfortable with the timeline." Charlie pointed to the bedroom and continued, "His clothes and luggage are still in the closet. We know the cabbie dropped him off at Newark at twelve fifty-five p.m. So he had to get in the cab somewhere around noon, with only a backpack. If he came back to the apartment and cleaned it out, what did he do with his personal effects? Why didn't he take clothes? Nothing fits."

Kruger said, "How long was it before your team searched this apartment?"

Alvarez pulled out a notebook, flipped a few pages, read for a few moments, and said, "We got the call at nine-thirty a.m. I showed up at ten-oh-three. Let's see—here it is. We had someone here by three-thirty p.m., why?"

Kruger was silent for a few moments. He looked at Alvarez. "He didn't come back here. The cabbie said he picked him up outside the library at Thirty-Fourth and Madison. That's on the other side of town, closer to P&G Global than here."

Charlie grinned. "What's at a library?"

Kruger looked at him, thought for few moments, and said, "Books?"

"Yes, but they also have public computers." Charlie's smiled widened. "He didn't have to come back here to erase his computer. He did it remotely. Bet he had backup off site and was more interested in getting it than the computer. Computers can be replaced—the data and programs, not so much."

Alvarez frowned. "Where would he keep back up?"

Kruger snapped his fingers. "A safe deposit box. A bank."

Alvarez took his cell phone out and made a call. When the call was answered, he said, "How many banks are within a half-mile of the library at Thirty-Fourth and Madison?" He paused for a few moments listening and said, "That many? Really? I would never have guessed. Well, start calling them and find out if our fugitive had an account or lockbox. We'll be back there in about an hour." He ended the call. "They might have a location for us by the time we get back. Damn, I didn't realize how many banks are in this city."

***

Charlie was looking at the computer back at the precinct house, while Kruger and Alvarez discussed the timeline. A young detective handed Alvarez a piece of paper. Alvarez thanked the man. "He has an account at Bank of America. There's a safe deposit box in his name at a location eleven blocks from the library at Thirty-Fourth and Madison."

Kruger said, "We'll need a search warrant for the lockbox." Alvarez nodded and left the room.

Charlie said, "This guy is good. There's nothing on this hard drive. It's completely wiped clean." And more to himself than Kruger, he said, "How the heck did he do that without leaving residual data…"

Alvarez came back into the room. "We'll have the search warrant as soon as we can get it signed by a judge, probably thirty minutes."

***

With the proper paperwork in hand, the bank's branch manager opened the lockbox and left. Using latex gloves, Kruger opened the now empty box. He handed it to another detective, who started dusting it for prints.

Alvarez walked up to Kruger. "Just got his balance. He has over twelve-hundred dollars in a checking account."

Kruger was silent. Finally he said, "The guy comes in, empties his lockbox, and doesn't withdraw twelve hundred bucks. What's wrong with that statement, Preston?"

Alvarez shook his head. "Didn't need the money?"

Kruger nodded. "Yeah, he didn't need the money. He had cash in the lockbox. Plymel's driver said our fugitive stole money from Plymel. This guy's been planning to disappear for a long time. If he's paying cash, we're screwed. He won't leave a money trail we can follow."

Charlie sighed. "The only way we're going to find him is if he makes a mistake or we get lucky."

Kruger nodded. "This guy is smart, real smart. I doubt he's going to makes any mistakes. I have a feeling we aren't going to get lucky anytime soon."

CHAPTER 9

New York City

Crigler returned to his office and immediately went to the coffee service in the corner. He poured a cup and absent-mindedly added a packet of Equal to the strong black liquid. The view out his floor-to-ceiling window included Midtown, Central Park and the upper East Side; he saw none of it as he stood sipping his coffee and staring into the distance. Plymel downing a scotch at eleven in the morning played into his plan. He had seen this type of conduct during his years at the Justice Department in Washington. Perfectly stable men, when confronted with a crisis they couldn't resolve, resorted to self-destructive behavior. Plymel was now heading down that slippery path.

Plymel was skimming funds from the company—of that, he was sure. He also suspected the incident in the lobby involved those funds. But, the board would not act on suspicions. He needed proof the man was diverting funds into personal accounts. How to get this proof was the current dilemma. After several minutes of staring out the window, he smiled.

Turning back to his desk, he opened the top left-hand

drawer and retrieved his personal cell phone. After finding
the number he needed, he pressed the call icon. It was
answered on the fourth ring.

"You are either in trouble or need a favor Alton, which
is it?" The voice was gruff, without a hint of humor. If Crigler
had not known the man for over thirty years, he would have
ended the call.

"I have a job for you, Adam. Are you interested?"

"Not sure yet. How much does it pay?"

"Going rate."

"Don't be insulted if I hang up."

"I need you to find out something about someone."

Adam Weber chuckled on the other end of the call.
"That has to be the vaguest job description I've ever heard.
Meet me at O'Hara's Pub in an hour. You're buying lunch."

***

O'Hara's Pub was crowded, as usual. It was a popular
hangout for Wall Street workers. Executives didn't go there
very often because lunch was inexpensive for New York City
standards. Plus, it was hard to conduct business in the loud
atmosphere. But it was a good place to meet for discussions
concerning illicit matters. Not that all discussions at O'Hara's
were illicit. But a fair portion did lean that direction. Adam
Weber was sitting at the bar nursing a Guinness when Crigler
arrived.

Weber was a large man in his late-fifties. His thinning
brown hair was kept short, not quite a buzz cut. With a face
to match his gravelly voice, Weber was a master at
intimidation. His line of work demanded good physical
strength and agility, so he worked out regularly. An ex-U.S.
Marshal, he now owned a private company specializing in
finding and recovering white-collar embezzlers and the funds
they had liberated. Crigler had used Weber several times over
the years, both for legitimate reasons and for a few
illegitimate endeavors. Weber preferred the illegitimate ones;

they paid better.

Crigler joined Weber at the bar. "Why do you like this place? It's loud and crowded."

Weber raised his beer to his lips and before taking a swig said, "Exactly. No one will hear what you have to say. Let's go to our table. There's one in the back reserved for us. We can talk there."

The waiter was an older man who appeared to have been present when the restaurant opened back in the late forties. But he was efficient, took their order, and kept the crowd away. After the waiter left with their order, Weber said in his gruff voice, "Okay, what's the job?"

Crigler took a sip of his Guinness and sat back in his chair. "What's your specialty, Adam? What do you do best?"

Weber frowned. "I'm not here to play games. What's the job?"

Crigler didn't deviate from his question. "What you do best is find individuals who have stolen money from a company and return both to the proper authorities. It's your calling, and you do it better than anyone I have ever seen."

"Yeah, yeah. What's the job?"

"It seems my partner Abel Plymel had some funds stolen recently. Funds he may have stolen himself. The FBI is trying to find the man who stole the money. But he has vanished into thin air. I need to know how much was stolen and where it is located."

"What about the guy who stole it?"

Crigler shrugged. "Don't care. He's inconsequential, just find the money. Once you find it, I can take the information to the board and Plymel is history."

"I need a starting place. Who took the money?"

Crigler handed Weber a security camera photo of the two guards and the suspect as they exited the elevator.

Weber looked at the picture then back at Crigler. "What's his name?"

Crigler told him and added, "The security guard on his left was killed during his escape, and the other one had his knee shattered. The man disappeared into the crowd and hasn't been seen since. The FBI has a seasoned agent looking for him—even he can't find him."

"Impressive," Weber said, taking a long pull on the Guinness. "Sounds like the guy had some military training. I'll start looking there." He paused and stared at Crigler. "By the way, my fee just went up."

Smiling, Crigler said, "I'll give you a hundred to start, plus expenses."

Weber laughed as he stared at the photo. "Five hundred up front, and another after I find him."

It was Crigler's turn to laugh. "Obviously you see the challenge of finding this man, don't you? All right—I'll give you five hundred thousand up front. Then you'll get another five when you bring me a picture of his corpse and the location of the money. "

Placing the photo in the inside pocket of his sport jacket, Weber raised his Guinness. "Plus expenses."

Crigler nodded.

***

It was a dingy hole-in-the-wall bar not far from Fort Bragg. Adam Weber was waiting for an old friend who still called the army home. It was five minutes before six in the evening, and his friend was due at the top of the hour. At exactly six, a man in his late forties, dressed in desert BDUs, walked into the bar. His gray hair was cut in a style reminiscent of the early sixties: a flattop. With a barrel chest and a narrow waist, his physique resembled a Y. To round out the cliché, he had an unlit cigar in the corner of his mouth and sergeant major stripes. He smiled when he saw Weber and headed to the table at the back of the pub.

"I'll be damned. If it ain't Major Adam Weber. Visitin' from New York City. How ya doin', sir?"

They shook hands. "Good. But I'm not a major anymore. I work for a living."

They both enjoyed the laugh. Before sitting down at the table, the sergeant gestured toward the bar by pretending to lift a mug to his lips. He watched as the bartender poured a beer and handed it to a waitress. He started pulling one of the chairs out from the table, but before he could sit down, a middle-aged woman set a tall mug in front of him. She smiled, kissed him on the cheek, and left.

"I take it this is not your first time in this particular establishment," Weber said in his gravelly voice.

"Yeah, the ladies in this town just love me. What's going on, sir?"

"Well, I need some help, sergeant major. I need to find someone who was in the military at one time."

"Where'd he do his training?"

"Not sure." Weber pulled a picture out of his sport coat pocket and handed it to the sergeant. He continued, "This is the only picture I have of him. He's a ghost." Weber told his friend a name, which the sergeant wrote on the back of the picture. Weber then said, "I've checked DMV. No such person, no records in the IRS—he doesn't exist. But, he's a computer guy and has the moves of someone trained by the military."

"Huh." The sergeant looked at the picture, then at Crigler. "How so?"

"See the gorilla in front of him?"

The sergeant nodded. "Yeah, looks like hired muscle. What about him?"

"Our friend here grabbed the big guy's gun, shot him, then crippled the man behind him with one kick to the knee—and from eye witness accounts, all in one move."

Nodding again, the sergeant said, "Huh." He continued to stare at the picture. "Sounds like someone I might have trained. You said he's a computer guy."

"Some kind of computer expert. He's been erasing all of the public records of his real name. That's why I can't find any traces of him. My bet is, there's probably a military file on this guy somewhere." Weber pushed an envelope across the table, which the sergeant palmed and quickly slid into one of the side pockets on his pants.

"You want me to find out if he was in the military?"

Weber nodded.

"When was he in? Do you know?"

Weber shook his head. "No, but I would guess at least within the past fifteen years."

The sergeant continued to stare at the picture. He looked up at Weber. "Give me a few days. I have a few ideas how to find him. But, it will take some time."

Weber nodded. "I'm aware of your ability. That's why I like doing business with you, sergeant major."

CHAPTER 10

New York City

Two weeks after the fugitive walked out of sight at the Westminster Hotel, Kruger called his boss, Alan Seltzer. When the call was answered, Kruger said, "We lost him." There was silence on the other end. Then Seltzer said, "The director isn't going to accept that, Sean."

"Then the director can take over the case." Kruger paused, waiting for Seltzer to respond. After several moments of silence, Kruger said, "The guy disappeared into thin air, Alan. We can't find a money trail. My guess is, he's planned this disappearing act for a long time and so far hasn't made a mistake. You can put more agents on it if you want to, but they'll get the same results."

"Have you told Alton Crigler yet?"

"No. I thought I'd deliver that tidbit of news on my way to the airport."

"Okay, I'll let the director know. Don't be surprised if you get a call. He's had an unusual degree of interest in this case. I have to give him a daily update."

Kruger's frowned. "Why?"

"Crigler and the director went to college together, so be

careful of what you say. It will get back to the director."

"I'm going to tell him the truth. If the director doesn't like it, too bad, he can take me off the case."

"Just be careful what you say, Sean."

***

Kruger was shown into Alton Crigler's office immediately. The tall man smiled, walked around the desk, and shook hands. He said, "I take it the fugitive is in custody."

Kruger shook his head. "No. But I wanted to give you an update."

Crigler frowned, his broad smile gone. He sat on the corner of his desk. "Tell me."

"We lost his trail in New Jersey. He was last seen by a security camera at a hotel in Livingston. The videotape shows him getting out of a cab and watching it drive away. Once it was out of sight, he walked out of the camera's field of view and disappeared."

Crigler was silent. He stood, walked back to his chair, and sat down, "Have you given up?"

"No." Kruger paused and stared at Crigler. "There's a possibility the man was defending himself."

Feigning surprise, Crigler shook his head. "Not from what I was told."

"It's one of the theories we're investigating. I'm not convinced everyone on your staff was truthful with me. Maybe I should interview all of them again."

"That's unacceptable."

"Why?"

"They've told you all they know. You don't need to bother them again."

Kruger shrugged. "That may be your opinion, but I'm not going to waste any additional resources on this case until I have better cooperation and people start telling me the truth."

"I've always suspected you were lazy, Agent Kruger, and a bit of a prima donna."

Kruger stared at the man. Inside he wanted to reach out and strangle him, but he kept his expression neutral. Remembering Seltzer's warnings, he paused before saying anything. Finally he said, "You're entitled to your opinion, Mr. Crigler, but the fact remains, the fugitive disappeared. He's out there; I just can't find him right now."

"Maybe I should call the director and have you replaced."

Kruger reached over the desk, lifted the handset of Crigler's desk phone. He offered it to him. "Go ahead."

His bluff called, Crigler stood up. He walked around the desk, took the handset from Kruger, and placed it back in its cradle."

"You're not easily intimidated, are you?"

Kruger shrugged.

Crigler walked over to the coffee service table and poured himself a cup. He lifted the cup to Kruger. "Do you want coffee?"

Kruger shook his head. "No, thank you."

"I like you, agent, but you have an independent streak I find irritating. You're not a team player. Sometimes that can be dangerous in an organization like the FBI—career-wise, that is."

Kruger remained quiet and stared at Crigler.

"The director and I were fraternity brothers in college. I can help your career or I can hurt your career." He paused, took a sip of his coffee, and walked back to his desk. "Find this man, Agent Kruger."

The implied threat lingered in the room like fog on a crisp fall morning. Kruger smiled. "I'll find him. But, it may not be on your timeline. It could happen tomorrow, a year from now, or maybe never. In the meantime, I have other pressing matters that need attention. Call the director if you feel the need." He stood, walked to the office door, and opened it. Just before leaving, he turned. "If I find proof anyone here at P&G Global lied to me—and I mean anyone—my next visit will not be as cordial." He walked out and closed the door before Crigler could respond.

***

Kruger opened the door to his condo and went straight to his bedroom. The constant traveling and lack of a home life were starting to catch up with him. He threw his overnight bag onto the bed with the intentions of unpacking and taking the contents to the laundry room. As he headed to the bathroom, he heard a knock on his front door. He glanced at the digital clock on his nightstand: 10:12 p.m. Who would be knocking this late?

He opened the door and found Stephanie standing there with two open bottles of Boulevard Pale Ale. "I heard you come home and thought you might be thirsty."

Kruger smiled. He grabbed her and drew her into a bear hug. "Damn it's good to see you." Her hair smelled of coconut and papayas, with a hint of vanilla.

"I'd hug back, but the beer might spill."

He released her. Took one of the beers and they kissed. The kiss lasted for almost a minute. Afterwards, they stood in the living room holding each other. Finally, Stephanie said, "This is nice."

They laughed. He took her hand and led her out to his balcony overlooking the Plaza. A small bistro table and four chairs had been purchased before he had left for New York City. Stephanie chose a chair facing the Plaza, and Kruger scooted one of the chairs closer to her. He sat down, propped his feet up on an adjacent chair, and placed the beer on the table. "I could get used to this real easy."

She smiled and took a sip of beer. "Thank you for the phone calls. You'll never know how much I enjoyed them."

Kruger looked at her. He shrugged. "You're welcome, but there's no need to thank me. I wanted to talk to you."

"I know. I wanted to talk to you too. It's just that in the

past when I was seeing someone, the calls weren't...uh, enjoyable. They would whine and complain about me being out of town. Our calls are different." She paused for a brief moment and gave him a slight smile. "I look forward to them."

He smiled but didn't say anything. They sat in the cool night air and stared at the lights on the Plaza. The silence lasted for several minutes as they held hands. Finally, Kruger said, "I may be losing my touch. I lost a fugitive and can't find him."

She looked at him. He was staring off into the distance, deep in thought. "You're not going to catch everybody, Sean."

"I have up till now." He frowned after he said it.

"Maybe you really don't want to find him."

"That's the problem, I desperately need to find him. Two very powerful men are lying to me about this case. I need to know why. I think the fugitive can answer that question."

She squeezed his hand tighter. "Why are they lying to you, Sean?"

"I think the guy was brought there against his will and threatened."

"What do you mean, threatened?"

Shaking his head, "I'm not sure, he may have stolen some money. They were going to take him somewhere, probably to kill him, when he attacked the two guards."

"He was defending himself."

Kruger nodded. "I think he was. But it bugs me. I can't find a trail to follow. The man just vanished. We have absolutely no idea where he might be. Charlie found an article in a Jacksonville, Florida, newspaper about someone with this guy's name walking into the ocean. He supposedly left a suicide note."

"Maybe he's dead, that's why you can't find him."

Kruger shook his head. "I'm not buying it. The guy did a thorough job of erasing his identity. No birth certificate, no

driver's license, no credit cards, no social security number—
nothing. The man goes to all that trouble and commits
suicide." He shook his head. "No. He did it to throw us off
the trail. He's still out there somewhere, I can feel it."

"You never know. People get depressed and do stupid
things."

Kruger shook his head. "No, the story was planted. We
had an agent in Florida check out the hotel. No such person
was ever registered. There would be all kinds of police reports
on a suspected suicide. The local police never received a
report of a suicide." Kruger shook his head again. "He's still
out there."

They were silent again.

A minute later, Kruger said, "I didn't eat. Are you
hungry?"

She nodded. "Even though it's Friday night, it's too late.
Most of the restaurants are closed."

"We could order pizza?"

She nodded. "As long as it has veggies."

"I'll order it. Want another beer?"

She shook her head. "No, I've got a bottle of Merlot at
my place. I'll go get it."

It was after midnight when they finished the pizza. The
conversation had turned from work to more personal topics.
Suddenly, Kruger stopped talking and was quiet.

Stephanie looked at him for several moments. He was
staring out over the Plaza. "What's the matter?"

"Not sure I want to do this anymore."

Her eyes widened and her hand covered her mouth.
"You don't want to see me anymore?"

"No. No, no, no, that's not what I meant. I was talking
about the job."

She relaxed, but didn't respond. She just kept looking at
him.

"I'm tired of fighting the bureaucracy and the good ole
boy network. Plus I'm starting to resent the traveling."

She nodded. "I can relate to those feelings. Planes are

not comfortable anymore."

"There's that, but…" He hesitated for a second. "It's more than the uncomfortable plane rides; it's resentment. I'm not even sure what I resent. But if I know I have to travel the next Monday, I start dreading it on Saturday."

She watched him and nodded slightly. "Yes, I feel that way sometimes. It depends on the trip and what I have to do."

Shaking his head, he said, "It's every trip for me. There was a time, not too many years ago, I relished being on the road working a case. Now…" He stared at the lights of the Plaza and just shook his head.

Grinning, Stephanie said, "What's different? A certain neighbor?"

Kruger grinned and turned to look at her. "Yes, I suppose that's part of it. I do enjoy our time together. But there's more. I've been trying to figure it out." He shook his head. "Haven't been able to diagnosis myself yet. If it gets to the point these feelings affect my work, I'll have to retire."

"What would you do?"

He shrugged. "Not sure. Teach. Go back to school. Be a Walmart greeter. Hell, I don't know."

She chuckled. "You'd look funny standing there saying, 'Welcome to Walmart,' wouldn't you?"

He didn't say anything; he just stared at the Plaza.

"Something happened, didn't it, Sean?" She reached for his hand and squeezed it lightly. In a soft voice she whispered, "Tell me."

"The director called just before I got on the plane. He normally doesn't get involved with the day-to-day workings of a case. But he's got his nose out of joint on this one. One of his old college buddies is a part owner of P&G Global. He's accusing me of not working the case hard enough."

"Are you?"

Kruger was quiet.

"Follow your instincts. Prove the man was defending himself."

Kruger turned and looked at her. He smiled and nodded. "I knew there was a reason I was falling in love with you." She smiled back and squeezed his hand harder.

***

Kruger awoke the next morning with Stephanie curled up next to him. The warmth of her bare back against his, comforting. He looked at the digital clock on his nightstand and smiled; he hadn't slept this late in a long time. He pushed the covers aside and sat on the edge of the bed and yawned. Stephanie rolled over and put her hand on his back. "That was a pleasant way to welcome you home."

Kruger lay back down and embraced her. "I could definitely get used to this."

An hour later, they sat at the breakfast bar drinking coffee—Stephanie in one of Kruger's gray long-sleeved OU Sooner t-shirts with the sleeves pushed up past her elbows. He could still smell the coconut and papaya with the hint of vanilla from her hair. She got up to get more coffee. "How long before you have to leave again?"

"Probably not for awhile. I'm behind on paperwork. I normally just work out of the local bureau office when that happens. A friend of mine from the academy is the special agent in charge here in Kansas City. What about you?"

"The shareholder meeting starts two weeks from Monday. I have to prepare for it, so I'm in town."

"Good." He looked at the clock on the microwave. "It's almost noon. I need to make a phone call. Afterwards we could do whatever you want."

Smiling, she started walking back to the bedroom. "I'll go clean up and then be back. Let's say, an hour."

Kruger took a quick shower and made the phone call. Charlie Craft answered on the third ring. "What's up, Sean?"

"Charlie, I've been thinking. How much trouble would it be to get all the new business applications from the various secretaries of states around the country?"

Silence was his answer. Finally Charlie said, "Don't know. We would have to send an official request to each state attorney general, I guess. Depending on the detail and length of time you want, the data could be massive. Why?"

"Our fugitive is a computer expert, right?"

"Yeah."

"He's going to need to work, wherever he might be."

"Okay, I'm starting to see where you're going with this. See where new computer companies have incorporated."

"Exactly."

"That will be a lot of data and lots of variables. Maybe he didn't start his own company. Maybe he hasn't started yet, and so on and so forth. What then?"

"Then we're in the same situation we are in now. No idea of how to find him."

"Are we still officially on this case, Sean?"

"Well, not officially. But it bugs me we can't find a trail. If you'll get the information, I'll dig through it in my spare time."

***

A week later, Kruger and Stephanie were enjoying lunch together on the Plaza, when his cell phone vibrated. He glanced at the caller ID and quickly accepted the call.

Charlie Craft said, "I don't have good news, Sean. We've received information on over five thousand computer-related companies registering as corporations, LLCs, or S-Corps, just in the past two months alone. I used that timeframe since we don't know if he might have started the process before he disappeared or after."

Kruger was silent for several moments, he stared at Stephanie.

She said, "What is it, Sean?"

He shook his head, held up one finger, and said into the phone, "Okay, how can we narrow it down?"

"I don't know if we can, we would run the risk of

eliminating the correct one. Heck, we don't even know if he will be on this list."

"Okay, at least it's a start." Kruger sighed. "Send the information to me. It could take months, but I'll start sifting through it."

PART 2

Five Months Later
Springfield, MO

It was a Friday, JR Diminski had just finished signing a contract to improve internal and online security for S&W Technologies, Inc. It was a high-tech company that designed and manufactured microchips for everyday household consumer goods. Diminski's task was to make sure no one stole their chip designs by hacking into their servers. The job included a complete computer security audit. Today he was on a plant tour, becoming familiar with their systems.

He saw her at a design table next to a high-end Macintosh. He stopped listening to his tour guide and basically stared at her. She was of Asian descent, petite, long black hair pulled back in a tight ponytail, and the most piercing dark eyes he'd ever seen. She looked up from her design table, smiled, and extended her hand for him to shake. "Hi, I'm Mia. Yes, I'm single, and yes, I'll have dinner with you tonight. I should be done around six. Pick me up in front of the office."

He stood there holding her hand, not knowing if he was shaking it or not. He remembered to breathe and suddenly felt like a dorky teenager at his first boy-girl party. After several awkward moments, he said, "Okay. Six sounds good. I'll see you then. Uh, I'm JR."

"Yes, I know. One of my friends works in the IT department at First National Bank. She was extremely impressed with you. I want to know if she was right to be impressed." She smiled and returned to her work. "Don't be late. I like Italian." The rest of the tour, of which he remembered nothing, was a blur.

They had dinner at an Italian restaurant she suggested in the downtown area. She liked it because the food was authentic Italian and it featured an extensive wine list. She smiled when they sat down. "What kind of wine do you like?"

Diminski said, "Well, the only kind I've ever had was in college and it cost two bucks. I really didn't care for it."

She laughed. "Allow me, nothing beats a good Merlot."

Diminski could hear a slight accent, which he found intriguing. As the waiter poured their wine, he said, "Nice accent. Where's it from?"

Mia smiled. "I was raised in Austin, Texas, by my grandparents. I'm a graduate of the University of Texas at Austin and a huge Dallas Cowboys' fan."

He chuckled. "You don't look like a Texan." He hesitated and then said, "You're too... petite."

She laughed. "I've been told that before." She paused for a few seconds, took a sip of her wine, and continued. "My father came to the United States from China to study engineering at Berkley. My mom was there, supposedly, studying sociology. But, I think she was more interested in experiencing the culture than studying about it. They met, she fell in love, and I came along nine months later. Just about the time he graduated."

She took another sip of Merlot and sighed. "According to my grandparents, after his graduation he disappeared. They believed he returned to China. He didn't even tell my mother. She couldn't handle being a single parent, too much of a burden, I guess. So she and I left California and went to

Texas to live with her parents. After a few years, she grew restless. One day, she left a note telling my grandparents she was going back to California to join a commune. To my knowledge, they never saw her again. I continued to live with them. Pappy taught me how to be a Texan and Granny taught me how to think. I love them a lot. Wish they were still here."

She grew silent, staring into the glass of wine. Diminski noticed she had said *love*, not *loved*. "Do you ever see your mom?"

"No," she said with a hint of bitterness. "I tried several times to reach her when I was in high school. I wrote letters telling her what was going on and asking her to come and see me. But I never heard back. My grandparents never did understand what happened. They always believed, up until the day they each passed away, she would come back. They never said anything to me about her leaving, but I can imagine how much it hurt. After I graduated from college, I went to California to see if I could talk to her. The commune was still functioning, but I was told by several of the members she wasn't receiving visitors. I gave up after that." She looked up at JR. "I've never tried again."

She looked back at her glass of wine. He could see tears welling up in her eyes. But suddenly she blinked a few times and was out of the funk. She smiled and returned her attention to him. "Okay, you've heard my sad tale. Tell me about yourself."

Diminski wasn't prepared, so he stayed as close to the truth as possible. That way it would be easier to remember what was said. "Not much to tell, really. I don't remember too much about my parents. They were killed by a drunk driver one night coming home from the movies. I was six at the time. Both sets of grandparents were gone, so I was placed in a foster home. They were good to me, and I stayed there until I was out of high school. I joined the army to be all I could be. I had a knack with computers. So after they taught me to be a soldier, I received intensive training on computers. After the army, I went to college and graduated with a degree in computer science. I've been doing that ever since. I moved here about six months ago, and now I'm having dinner with you."

Everything he told her was true. He just chose not to elaborate about the foster parents. They had been wonderful people and raised him like their own son. But, like her grandparents, they too had died some years ago.

Through their conversation, Diminski learned Mia was thirty one, six years younger than him. She was barely five feet tall, and he guessed her weight at a bit over a hundred pounds. Her smile was magnetic and her personality was anything but small.

"We have something in common," Mia said. "We were both raised by someone besides our parents—interesting."

He shrugged, "Not much we could do about it. Sometimes life happens."

"Yeah, I guess. But it would be nice to at least meet my father. I sometimes wonder where he is and what he's doing. I don't even know if he's still alive."

"Do you know his name?"

She nodded. "His name is Chun Mao Ling. There must be at least thirty million Mao Lings in China. I'm not sure it would be worth the effort to find him." She shrugged. "He hasn't tried to find me."

Feeling he was getting into another sad part of her life, he took a sip of wine. "I'm curious, why is an attractive, intelligent woman like you still single?"

She gave him a mischievous grin. "Haven't met the right guy yet. And you?"

"Oh, I've met them. They just didn't know they were the right girls."

She laughed. "Well said. Let's hope the next one you meet knows she's the right one." He was really starting to enjoy her smile and laugh.

She raised her wine glass. He lightly touched his to it and heard a crystal clink. "And when you meet your right guy, he knows it as well."

A serious look crossed her face. She leaned forward and said, "Okay, mystery guy, what does the JR stand for?"

He shrugged. "It stands for JR."

"Are you a junior, named after your dad?"

He shook his head. "Nope. That's how it is on my birth certificate: JR. No first or middle name, just JR." He felt he needed to steer the conversation away from this. He took another sip of wine suddenly remembering something. "Uh…" He hesitated and said nervously, "Uh, would you be interested in helping me pick out some furniture tomorrow?"

Mia smiled. She reached for his hand and squeezed it. "I'd love to. What's the occasion?"

"Well, I've signed a lease on a one-floor apartment downtown. My current furniture consists of a mattress, a desk, and a broken-down sofa I bought at a garage sale. I've got to furnish two bedrooms, an office, a living room, a dining area, and a kitchen." He shrugged. "I've got zero decorating sense and could really use some help."

She laughed. "Oh my god, I'd love to. Do you have veto power?"

He shook his head. "Nope. It would be totally up to you."

He would remember the look of joy on her face forever.

Five months since the incident: he had a new identity, a new career, a more permanent place to live, and someone special in his life. Maybe it was time to start seriously thinking about putting his past behind him and protecting this new life.

***

It was a Thursday evening; Diminski was killing time at a downtown pub waiting for Mia to join him. She had a deadline and was working late. The local news was on one of the overhead TVs in the bar area. He wasn't really listening, just waiting for the upcoming sports report. The talking head on the screen was introducing a feature story about the increase in home break-ins around the metro area. After the story was over, the guy next to him started a rant. He was a distinguished-looking gentleman in his late fifties, salt-and-pepper hair, half-rim glasses, which sat low on his nose, and a solid white mustache and goatee. He bore a striking resemblance to the actor Morgan Freeman. His khaki chinos, white polo shirt, and navy-blue blazer gave him a professional look. The man said, "If more citizens were trained and prepared with firearms, that kind of crap wouldn't happen."

Diminski was politically neutral and didn't care if someone was liberal or conservative. But he was intrigued with the man's comment. "What do you mean?"

The gentleman looked over his glasses, smiled, and said, "I mean just what I said. Train the public to use firearms and these idiots wouldn't be entering homes. They'd be afraid of getting their asses shot."

Diminski thought back to his own military training. He was good with a rifle and pistol, having won all of the marksmanship tournaments he had ever entered. "Yeah, I see what you mean. What kind of training are you referring to?"

The gentleman smiled and offered his hand. "My name's Joseph. I do that kind of training myself."

Diminski shook it. "Nice to meet you. I'm JR. You're talking about handguns, right? I didn't know you could own one in this state."

He nodded. "In Missouri you can and most of the surrounding states. You must not be from around here."

"I am now, I moved here almost a year ago." His thoughts went to Mia. Could this be a way to protect them if he was found? "I had a little training in the military. But, like you said, rifles aren't real practical, unless you're under siege by a horde of gangbangers."

Joseph chuckled, nodded, and said, "I operate a security company. I also own a small gun shop and do CCW training for those who want to qualify."

"What's CCW?"

"Concealed carry of a weapon permit, allows the common citizen to carry a concealed handgun. A lot of states allow it; it's just not publicized very much. Politicians love to vote for these types of bills. It keeps the NRA off their back. It's unfortunate there's so much negative discussion right now about guns in this country. With the right enforcement of current laws, we could keep guns out of the hands of the bad guys and train the good guys to defend themselves."

Now Diminski was intrigued. He needed to get a security system for the condo. As the number of computers in his office increased, so did his risk. He said, "Looks like I just found someone to help with two problems. I need a security system for my home office, and I would like to get a concealed carry permit."

Joseph reached into the inside pocket of his blazer, pulled out a business card and handed it to JR. "What type of business are you in?"

"Computer security. I do both corporate and financial."

Now Joseph smiled. "I've got a problem myself. Let's talk trade."

***

Over the next several months, Joseph and JR became good friends. Joseph's company installed a high-tech security system in JR's condo, and JR designed a secure website for Joseph, allowing his company to increase its e-commerce presence on the internet. Plus they set up an agreement that Diminski's company would be the subcontractor for any computer security Joseph needed for a client. JR completed his CCW qualifications, secured the permit through the Sheriff's Department, and purchased a Glock 19. The significance of this event told him a background check into his new identity revealed no problems. His hope for the future improved.

***

One night, while JR waited for Mia to complete another long night, Joseph was talking and suddenly said, "JR, where did you go through boot camp?"

Without thinking, he said, "Fort Benning. Why?"

"You were on the pistol team in the spring of ninety-seven, weren't you?"

JR paused before answering. He couldn't determine if his answer would reveal too much. "Yeah. I was."

"I knew it. I never forget how someone shoots. I can't remember names, but I do remember how a person handles a pistol. After working with you on your CCW, I thought your style looked familiar. I just couldn't place where."

JR's heart skipped a few beats. He stared at Joseph. "I don't remember you. Did we meet?"

"No. I don't think so. I was watching one of the competitions and remember several really good marksmen on the squad that year. You were one of them. Why didn't you say anything while we worked on your permit?"

"It's been awhile. Besides, it was no big deal. I was shooting because it kept me out of doing real duty."

Joseph nodded. "You're good enough to be an instructor."

"I'm too busy with Mia and work. But, thank you for the compliment." The last thing he needed was to draw attention to his abilities with a handgun. New York was less than a year ago and not forgotten by some very dangerous people.

Joseph smiled and sipped his beer. "Too bad. I need more instructors."

JR took a deep breath. He was starting to feel like he could maybe trust Joseph. But not quite yet.

CHAPTER 12

Kansas City

It was close to midnight when Kruger shut the lid to his laptop and rubbed his weary eyes. Too many nights of staring at letters of incorporation and business filings. Too many dead-ends and still no leads on where his fugitive had traveled. He had been digging through the mountainous amount of data for almost seven months. During those seven months he had worked several other cases, solved them and moved on. But he could not get the case of the missing computer hacker off his mind.

His cell phone vibrated. Wondering who would be calling this late, he glanced at the caller ID and quickly accepted the call. "Are you okay?"

"Yes, just exhausted. Sorry about the late call, I didn't know if you would still be up, so I was planning on leaving a voicemail." Stephanie's voice was strained, her normal cheerfulness missing.

"What's the matter, something's wrong?"

His answer was silence. Finally she said, "It's going to be another week before I can get back."

It was now his time for silence.

"Sean?"

"I'm here." He took a deep breath and let it out slowly. "We haven't seen each other in over a month."

"I know, I can't help it. We're having trouble finding franchisee's with solid financial backing. It's just taking time."

"This isn't working Steph."

"It's only temporary."

"It's late, I'm tired and you're tired. I don't want to discuss this right now. I'll call you tomorrow." He ended the call, stood and went to his bathroom to splash water on his face.

***

He woke up late the next day. Since it was Saturday, he started looking through the data again. By mid-afternoon, his patience growing short and his temper growing shorter, he saw a name in a document that caused him pause. He sent the document to his printer and grabbed it when it was done. He smiled, picked up his cell phone, scrolled through his favorites and pressed the call icon.

The call was answered on the third ring, "Well, well, I haven't heard from my favorite recruit for several months. How are you Sean?"

"I'm doing well Joseph. I talk to your nephew all the time, but not you. Since Alan's my boss, I prefer to talk to you."

Joseph chuckled, "Alan can be difficult. His mother was that way when we were growing up. So why the unexpected call?"

"When did you decide to get into computer security?"

There was silence on the other end of the call. "What do you mean, computer security?"

"Articles of incorporation, your name is plastered all over it."

Joseph was quiet again, "Uh—what are you working on Sean?"

"Searching for a missing fugitive. We have a theory he formed a computer company and I've spent the past seven months in my spare time going over article of incorporation from all over the country. I just ran across yours and since I'm tired of looking at this stuff, I decided to call you. Besides, we haven't talked in while."

Although Kruger couldn't see it, Joseph frowned. "What's the fugitive's name?"

Kruger told him, "We know he's taken on a new identity. From what we've learned, he's an expert hacker and has erased all traces of his digital existence." He chuckled, "So, you never told me why you started a computer security company."

"Oh, just a natural extension of my business. One has to stay current and relevant."

They talked for another hour, a little about the fugitive, but mostly two old friends, catching up on each other's life.

***

After the call ended, Joseph was quiet. He knew the name Kruger had mentioned early on in the conversation. It was from a long time ago and a different stage of Joseph's long and varied career with the United States government.

On Monday morning, Joseph caught the 6:00 a.m. Delta flight to Atlanta out of Springfield-Branson National Airport and arrived just before 9:00 a.m. Eastern time. Since he would be returning to Springfield later in the day, there was no need for any checked bags. After exiting the terminal, he sent a text message and waited next to the curb in the passenger drop-off area. After waiting several minutes, he saw his ride pulling to the curb. The driver was in his mid-forties with light brown hair, cut high and tight military style. His face was lined and weathered, and his biceps stretched the fabric of his desert BDUs, which bore no insignia or rank. The driver was silent as he accelerated the Ford away from the curb.

After a few moments, the driver said, "Good morning, sir. Did you have a nice flight?"

"Excellent. Thank you for picking me up, Sandy."

"No problem, sir. It's good to see you again." Major Benedict "Sandy" Knoll drove in silence for several moments. As they exited the airport, he said, "Per your request, I have a computer terminal ready for you in a private office at the facility. Do you mind if I ask what this is all about?"

Joseph looked out the window, "I'm checking on the background of an individual, that's all." He was silent for a moment then said. "He came through basic at Ft. Benning. Just want to see if the man is who he says he is."

Sandy gave him a quick glance and smiled. "Bullshit, sir. You could have done that without flying all the way to Atlanta." He paused and continued to stare out the front windshield. After a while, he said, "Just let me know if I can help."

Joseph nodded, "Okay, thank you Sandy."

An hour later, Joseph sat at a computer, his attempts to find information about the name Kruger had mentioned continuously blocked. Finally, after using his current status with the CIA, he found the file buried behind the military equivalent of a firewall.

The file was extensive and described a man trained in both computers and weapons. The man had been at the frontlines in various hotspots around the world. His skills included database hacking, denial of service attacks, computer virus creation, and small-arms and long-range marksmanship. He was also skilled in hand-to-hand combat. The file also contained a picture. A picture of a younger JR Diminski.

Joseph sat back in his chair and stared at the photo. "I'll be damned. It is him." He personally didn't care why JR had changed his identity. A man always had reasons. The only problem Joseph had was how to discuss this knowledge with JR.

As he examined the file, he found another potential

problem. Someone had accessed it seven months ago. It was the only time the file had been viewed in over ten years. Joseph frowned, scratched his goatee, and stared at the computer screen. The timing was correct; someone from JR's past had been trying to find him. He'd have Sandy check it out and get back to him. They had lunch and Sandy agreed to find out who had accessed the file. Afterward, Sandy returned Joseph to the airport.

Joseph caught the 4:00 p.m. flight back to Springfield and was at the Ozark Brewery by 6:15 p.m. Springfield time. JR was sitting next to him, sipping on a beer. Joseph was silent as he stared at the TV, still uncertain how to approach the topic he needed to discuss.

JR had asked him several times if anything was wrong, but Joseph just smiled. "Nothing, just thinking."

JR frowned. Joseph normally talked nonstop about sports during their so-called bar time while JR waited for Mia to get off work. But tonight, JR sensed something was wrong.

Finally he said, "Well, if you're going to be this much fun to be around, I'm going to the dentist and have some teeth pulled. At least he would talk to me."

"Sorry. I've got a lot on my mind tonight."

"Want to talk about it?"

Joseph looked at him. "It concerns you, but I can't discuss it here."

"I hate conversations that start with 'I can't discuss it here,' but"—he glanced at his watch—"Mia won't be off for another hour or so. Let's take a walk."

Joseph nodded and threw a twenty-dollar bill on the bar. He stood up and left. JR followed him out to the sidewalk and they started walking east toward the downtown area.

"JR, if I had something confidential to tell you," Joseph said, "how would you react?"

"I'd keep it confidential."

Joseph nodded and remained quiet for a few minutes. Finally, he said, "I know your real name isn't JR Diminski."

JR was quiet and stared ahead.

"I was in Atlanta today, refreshing my memory with some old army files. I confirmed my suspicions and read your official top-secret file."

JR's eye's widened. He looked at Joseph. "I didn't know I had a top-secret file. What's in it?" Realizing what he had said, JR frowned and stared ahead.

"Probably the only information left on the planet about a man named..."

"I couldn't get to it, otherwise it would be gone too." He stopped walking and stared at Joseph. "How the hell did you know to go looking for a file with that name?"

Joseph chuckled, "I wasn't always a gun shop owner my friend. At times during my career, I've recruited candidates for the FBI, CIA, DEA and ATF. I was the guy who used to get away from all the Ivy League colleges and ferret out good people who live in the middle of the country. I found and recruited, Sean Kruger, the FBI agent looking for you. I was also going to recruit a young man with computer and marksmanship skills from Fort Benning." He paused and glanced at JR, but he was staring ahead. "But, you were mustered out after a very negative review from your commanding officer. I didn't pursue the matter. And, quite frankly forgot about you, until Sean mentioned your old name the other day."

"Major Morton was a government-inspected, certified asshole. He encouraged me to leave. He kept talking about congressional defense cutbacks or some such nonsense."

"You were classified as one of the top computer experts in the army. Plus, you could shoot a flea off a dog's nose at five hundred yards. Not too many men have those skill sets. There were several individuals at the Pentagon who were not happy you chose not to re-enlist. In fact they severely chastised your commanding officer for letting you muster out. He was demoted back to captain." Joseph chuckled. "He put a note in your file about you being, and I quote, 'a malcontent, not fit for the army.' What did you do to cause that reaction?"

"I was smarter than he was." JR paused, looked at Joseph, "CIA?"

Joseph nodded. "I've met several Major Mortons in my career. They never think about improving the team. They're more interested in keeping the aggregate IQ level below theirs. If you're interested, he was killed by friendly fire in Afghanistan."

Diminski shrugged, trying to figure out what his next steps should be. He couldn't leave Mia. It was time to listen to Joseph and see what he had in mind. "Figures," he said. "Morton finally pissed off the wrong guy." He stopped walking. "Where is this conversation going, Joseph?"

"You have a problem bigger than that file, JR."

JR was quiet.

"I'm serious. The man I recruited to join the FBI is still looking for you. He's examining the records of incorporation for any computer related companies formed in the past nine months. It's tedious work, but, he is a very persistent individual. He's going to find you."

"My name doesn't appear anywhere. I incorporated under your corporate..." JR's eyes grew wide and his face pale.

"In his investigation, he just ran across the articles we submitted to form the computer security division of my company. Since we're old friends, he took a break and called me, to catch up."

JR was pale again, but said nothing.

"I'm just warning you this FBI agent does not give up. He'll find you JR." He paused to let that sink in. "There's also someone else looking for you. Your file was accessed seven months ago. Probably for the same reason. They're still looking JR. What did you do to cause so much attention?"

His eyes grew narrow, his face flushed and he said in a low menacing voice, "I was defending myself."

Joseph smiled. "That's what my friend Sean Kruger thinks as well. But, without talking to you, he has no proof, only the words of two very rich and powerful men. Men, I might add, who claim you were the aggressor, not them."

JR started walking east again, leaving Joseph several feet behind. After catching up he said, "Do you want to keep running the rest of your life? Or do you want to work with me and take care of the problem? Look, I don't know what you did. Nor do I care. I'm offering you help."

JR said nothing. He turned around and started walking again back toward the pub.

Joseph caught up. "I don't need an answer tonight. I didn't expect one. You don't know me well enough to completely trust me. But, right now I'm the best friend you could possibly have. I can help get this worry off your shoulders." Joseph smiled. "Then you and Mia can get on with your lives, have a family if you want." He paused. "Can you provide her that now?"

JR shook his head and stopped walking. Joseph looked him in the eye. "Think about it. If you want my help, be at the Ozark Brewery tomorrow night at six. I'll explain it to you then."

JR watched him walk away. After several moments, he said loud enough for Joseph to hear. "I'll think about it."

CHAPTER 13

Springfield, MO

When JR arrived at his building, he saw Mia's car parked in her spot. He hurried up the stairs to the second-floor apartment and stepped inside. The sound of her singing could be heard from the living room. She was standing at the kitchen counter tearing lettuce for a salad. She turned her head and smiled as he entered the room. JR rushed across the room and hugged her tightly.

The embrace lasted longer than normal. She pushed away. "What's wrong, JR?"

"Nothing," he said. "I just missed you."

"Right." She looked at him, her eyes narrowing. "How many beers did you have?"

He chuckled. "Just one. I didn't even finish it."

She smiled. "Okay." Returning to the salad, she started to say something but stopped. Her smile disappeared and she said, "JR, can I ask you a question?"

He stepped back and frowned as his stomach tightened. The beginning of a panic attack swept over him. He caught the edge of the kitchen table as he stumbled, but didn't fall. Had Joseph spoken to her?

She was startled at his reaction, "Are you okay?"

He nodded, "What did you want to ask me?"

"How do you feel about me?"

The sudden tension melted away and his smile returned. "I can't get up in the morning without wondering if you're up yet. The last thing I think about before bed is you. Plus, I spend most of the day imagining what you're doing." He paused briefly. "I'm falling in love with you Mia, that's how I feel."

She sighed deeply. "I've felt the same way about you for some time now." She sniffled, shivered slightly and took a deep breath. "Ever since my grandparents died, I've felt alone. My roommate in college was my best friend. After graduation, she got married and moved to the East Coast." She paused and wiped a tear with the back of her hand. "Everybody I've ever cared about is gone. First my mom left, then my grandparents died, and then my best friend moved away." She paused, buried her face against his chest and sobbed deeply, "I don't want to lose you too."

He felt wetness on his chest as his shirt absorbed her tears. She continued, "I'm falling in love with you too, JR, and it scares me. I know it sounds selfish, but if I give my heart to you, then something happens and you leave..." She was quiet for a few moments, then in a voice barely above a whisper, said, "I don't know—I might not be able to handle it."

In that instant, his decision was made. He would talk to Joseph in the morning and agree to meet with him at six tomorrow. "Mia, I don't know what the future holds for either one of us. I do know how I feel about you. I've had exactly one serious girlfriend in my life, and that relationship was more in my head than reality. She moved to Florida, supposedly to find a rich beach bum. I hope she found him." He paused. "Sorry, don't know why I'm babbling about my ex-girlfriend." He sighed. "For any relationship to survive, there has to be trust the other person feels the same way." He paused again. She kept her cheek against his chest and continued to sob. He said, "Since I've been here, I've met a lot of couples who have spent their entire married lives together. Can we? I would like to think so. I want to get married, I want a family, and I want to grow old with someone. That someone is you."

Mia lifted her head from his chest and held him tighter. He saw tears rolling down her cheeks. Her body shuttered and she took a deep breath, trying to suppress the crying. She didn't succeed. She put her head back on his chest and wept harder. He held her as tight as he could while her body shook. Finally after a minute she calmed down, looked up, reaching behind his neck and pulling him to her lips. They kissed. Then she pushed away, took his hand, and led him toward the bedroom.

The intensity of their lovemaking was beyond anything he had ever experienced. Afterward, they lay next to each other, sweating and holding each other tightly. She had not said a word since the kiss in the kitchen. Raising her head off his chest, she stared into his eyes. "If you ever leave me, you will never experience it that way again." She laid her head back on his chest. Her breathing slowed and became rhythmic as she drifted off to sleep.

JR continued to hold her. "Mia, I promise, I'll never leave you. Afraid you're stuck with me."

The next thing he knew, it was morning. Her side of the bed was empty, but the smell of coffee and her singing from the kitchen made him smile. He grabbed his cell phone and called Joseph. "I'll be there." He listened, "Yeah, six sharp. Thanks Joseph."

A few minutes later, she was back in the bedroom holding two cups of coffee. She smiled and handed a cup to him. She was wearing one of his old t-shirts, which he thought looked great on her. Sitting on the bed cross-legged facing him, she sipped her coffee and smiled. "And you're stuck with me."

***

Monday evening Kruger sat in O'Dowd's Irish Pub several blocks from his apartment drinking a beer and on the verge of feeling sorry for himself. He liked the place, but the few times he'd been there were with Stephanie. She had not answered or returned his calls on Sunday or today. As he was reaching for the phone to call her, it vibrated. He checked the ID and accepted the call as quickly as possible. "Hi."

"Hi back..."

"I'm sorry for what I said Saturday. I was totally out of line."

"That's why I called."

Kruger sat up straighter on the barstool, he blinked several times. "Oh..."

"I'm wrapping up early, I'll be home Wednesday. I'm sorry too, Sean. I shouldn't have called that late on Saturday. I was..."

"Lonely—so was I."

"Is this a good thing Sean? Missing each other this much."

"Yeah, it's a real good thing.

They talked for an hour.

***

Tuesday morning Kruger's cell phone vibrated again. The ID was blocked, but he accepted the call anyway. "Kruger."

"Sean, its Joseph." His tone was crisp and military.

"Aren't we a little formal this morning?"

"I need you in Springfield this afternoon. You owe me so many favors it's not funny. I'm cashing one in right now."

"Okay, when do you want me there?"

"No later than three. We need to talk before we meet someone."

Kruger was quiet for a few moments, "Who are we

meeting?"

"I will discuss it only in person."

Frowning at the demeanor coming across the phone, "I have to be back in KC on Wednesday, but I'll be in Springfield tonight."

"Good." The call ended.

Staring at the phone, Kruger said, "What the hell was that all about?"

***

JR sat at his usual spot at the bar, staring at the evening news on one of the TVs, and waiting. It was almost a quarter after six, and the weather report was starting. So far, no Joseph. He placed a napkin on the seat to his right for Joseph after a tall man had taken the seat to his left. JR glanced at him as the man ordered a Boulevard Pale Ale. JR smiled. One of his favorites too. After the man was served, he tried to engage JR in conversation. JR responded with clipped one-word answers until the man finally stopped talking. The absence of Joseph and the stranger on his left started to wear on his nerves. Where was Joseph? When he had spoken to him earlier in the day, Joseph had emphasized being at the pub no later than six o'clock. JR was ready to move forward with getting his life straightened out. Not making small talk with a stranger.

At 6:30 p.m., as a Cardinals baseball game was starting on TV, Joseph arrived and sat down next to JR. "Sorry I'm late. Got caught on the phone. So, have you met Sean Kruger yet?"

JR stared at Joseph. "What the heck are you talking about? I haven't met anyone." His eyes widen. He turned to his left and saw the man smiling.

The tall man and Joseph shook hands. The stranger said, "Nice to see you again, Joseph. Your friend here has been nervous, apparently not interested in small talk."

"He can be rude sometimes, under the current

circumstances. Please forgive him."

The man offered his hand to JR. "I'm Sean Kruger."

"Nice to meet you." JR limply shook the man's hand. "I think."

Joseph grew serious. "JR, this is the man I told you about. He can help you. I trust him explicitly. You should as well." He stood up, looked at JR in a stern, parental manner. "Listen to him, he's fair and can help you more than anyone else right now." He turned and walked out of the pub.

Kruger said, "Before you wet your pants, I'm not here to take you back to New York. I think you were defending yourself, I'm here to help."

Remaining quiet, JR stared at him.

Kruger nodded. "Okay, here's what I know..."

He proceeded to tell JR about the investigation and how they had lost track of him outside of the Westminster Hotel in New Jersey. JR realized the man knew a lot, but not the critical side of it: his side.

As JR listened, Kruger explained what Plymel had told the police and how he knew Plymel was lying. Finally, when the FBI man finished, JR said, "What do you plan to do with this knowledge?"

Kruger sipped his beer, stared at the TV, and said, "Nothing. I need someone like you to help me once in a while."

"Help you with what?"

"You know—computer stuff. If you want to help me, fine. If you don't, I'll walk out of here and you'll never hear from me again."

"How do you know Joseph?" JR asked.

Kruger shrugged. "Old family friend, he recruited me for the FBI. His nephew is my supervisor at the bureau."

"If I help you, what's in it for me?"

"I'll start the process of clearing your real name."

He stared at Kruger. If he and Joseph had been friends for years and they both wanted to help him, then it might be the best way to make good on the promise he had made to

Mia last night. If he could start their life together without looking over his shoulder, it was worth taking a chance. "What do you want to know?"

"How much money did Plymel have stashed away?"

"It was over sixty million, scattered across numerous accounts in the Caymans and Bermuda. Why?"

Kruger smiled. "With your skills, I hope you diverted some of that money."

JR laughed and nodded.

"Good, I'll need a copy of the files you acquired from Plymel's computer. Plus, I need you to hack into P&G's server to determine any measures they've taken to find you. I'll need to squelch those efforts immediately."

JR nodded and said, "I've already been in P&G's server. I've got a backdoor just in case I need it." He paused and said, "You're not like most FBI agents, are you?"

Kruger smiled. "I made a pledge to prosecute the guilty, not the innocent."

JR smiled and took a sip of his beer. He turned to Kruger. "I don't get it—why do you want to help me?"

Kruger laughed and took a gulp of his beer. "Good question. I read what P&G Global claimed in the police report; it didn't make sense. Too many time gaps—witness accounts too consistent with each other. They're covering something up. Bottom line, they lied to me. I don't like people lying to me."

"Thank you. I didn't think anyone would ever believe me."

Kruger frowned. "Don't thank me yet. I haven't done anything. When this is all over, you can thank me." He was quiet for a few moments. "I may need your assistance, but I'll try to keep you out of it as much as I can. Agreed?"

JR nodded. "Yes. Just let me know what you need."

He stood. "JR, I'm in your court. But if you lie to me in any fashion or manner, I will turn on you so fast."

JR swallowed hard. "All I can do is to tell you what happened. It's my word against theirs. I'm only one person against a bunch of very rich guys. You have to make the distinction."

Kruger smiled. "Let's go to your place and you can tell me everything."

***

Kruger walked out of the pub and headed toward his car. Joseph was sitting in the passenger seat when he got in behind the steering wheel. Joseph said, "What do you think?"

"I believe him. I'm not sure he has the ability to lie to anyone he trusts. He trusts you, therefore he trusts me."

Joseph nodded. "He was an exemplary soldier. But, unfortunately had a commanding officer who was scared of individuals with more intelligence. I need him in my little world, and I believe he would benefit you at times. Am I wrong?"

Kruger shook his head. "No, you're not wrong. Once I have the files from JR's transgression into P&G's server, I can go to the US attorney general and get a subpoena. Then I can bring in CPAs that carry guns. I'm kind of looking forward to that. It should be fun."

Joseph grew quiet. He stared out the passenger window for a moment then turned back to Kruger. "My biggest concern is there may already be someone else looking for him."

"You told me you found him after I mentioned his old name the other night. Are you starting to lie to me after all these years?"

Joseph shook his head. "No, I'm not lying to you. The point is, regardless of how careful JR has been, there are always trails. The more people looking for you, the more chances those mistakes will be found and acted upon."

Kruger nodded. He had the same concern.

***

JR sat on a sofa in his living room, Mia sitting next to him holding his hand.

Kruger sat across from him with a small digital recorder, and Joseph stood next to the fireplace. Kruger turned on the recorder and said, "It is September twenty-second, eight-thirty p.m., Springfield, Missouri. This is the testimony of the fugitive from an incident in New York City on February tenth of this year." He stopped the machine. "Are you ready?"

JR nodded. Kruger turned the recorder back on and leaned back in his chair.

PART 3

Springfield, MO

JR looked at Mia, took a deep breath, and said, "I met Tony Chien and Steve Wilson in college. We were all computer nerds. Tony and Steve wrote code and I debugged it. After college, Tony had the big idea, he asked Steve and I to join him. Those first few years, we'd work till two or three in the morning, crash, and start all over again at nine or ten the next morning. We had a blast.

"After our first program was released, Tony stopped programing and became our one-man sales department. Within six months, we had twenty people working for us. Steve was the genius behind all of the different products, and I was the guy who kept the programs working. We made a good team.

"About a year after we started, Tony had a meeting in Albany and bragged about me to some New York state senator. Not long after the meeting, I was asked to consult on the redesign of the state's revenue and licensing software. That's another story, I'll get into later."

Kruger said, "Is that how you were able to delete your driver's license file?"

JR nodded. "I'll explain it later, but yes, it was." JR paused for a second and said, "Everything went great for the next nine and a half years. We grew to about a hundred employees. Tony was a great individual to work for and with. He paid well and shared the profits with his people. We all had shares in the company. Since I had chosen not to get into management, the number of shares I owned didn't equal Tony's or Steve's.

"One day, Tony gathered ten of the individuals who had been with the company the longest, and had a meeting. Tony owned the majority of the stock and generally made most of the decisions. He would consult with Steve and a few others, but generally he made most himself. After he closed the door, he took a bottle of champagne from a small refrigerator and passed out plastic cups. He poured us all a small glass of the wine and said, 'We have just made the big time. P&G Global has agreed to invest in our company.' Steve shook his head and said, 'Why are we celebrating? I've heard about them. They'll destroy this company.'

"Tony shook his head and said, 'I have it in writing. They plan to leave current management in place and provide needed equity for our next expansion.'

JR stopped and took a sip of water. He continued, "It was probably thirty days after our little meeting when we were all called into the company's food court for a meeting. Did I mention how well Tony took care of his team? The food court was incredible. He contracted with ten local restaurants to operate satellite units in our building. We had everything: Italian, Tai, Chinese, pub food, vegan, and pizza. You name it, it was there. When I walked into the court that day, I kind of suspected something was amiss; all of the restaurants were closed. They never closed; we had people working all hours. Anyway, everybody was either sitting or standing around talking. We all grew silent when three guys in dark, expensive suits walked into the room. Tony was with them, but he wasn't wearing a suit. Everyone grew quiet. One of the suits was Abel Plymel. He walked up to a microphone and asked for everyone's attention. After the room was totally quiet, he said, 'Good morning. My name is Abel Plymel, one of the principals for P&G Global. We would like to welcome all of you this morning to our first meeting under the new ownership group of CWZ Software'.

"Plymel smiled and looked around the room. He continued, 'As most of you know, P&G Global purchased a majority of CWZ's outstanding shares thirty days ago.' After he said this, a murmur rose from the crowd. I looked at Steve Wilson, who was standing about five feet from me. His face lost all of its color and he had to steady himself by leaning against a table. Plymel droned on.

"This was when I looked at Tony. He was looking down at the floor as Plymel spoke. There was no smile on his face, just the look of a man whose soul had been ripped away. The only thing I could determine was that something had gone wrong when Tony signed the final papers.

"Plymel looked back at Tony and said, 'I want to thank Tony Chien for his leadership at CWZ Software since its founding. Tony will be promoted to a position on the board of P&G Global. This will be effective immediately. He will also be consulting on new products for CWZ.' Plymel started clapping and the room followed his lead. Tony managed a weak smile and waved to all of us.

"Plymel wasn't through with all of the good news. He continued filling us in on all of the changes. He said, 'Over the course of the next thirty days, we will be reviewing processes and strategies. We do know there are a lot of redundancies in the executive ranks. We will be making changes where it is deemed necessary. However, all of you out there are doing a magnificent job. We need you to keep doing what you do best.'

"With that statement, Plymel walked out of the room. He was followed by the other suits and Tony Chien. Funny thing, I never saw Tony again after that meeting. Several weeks later, it was announced that Tony had elected to resign from the board of directors and spend more time with his family. When I heard that, I laughed. Tony had been forced out, plain and simple. A week after that, Steve Wilson was gone. That was when I knew I needed to do something else.

"Two months after the gathering in the cafeteria, I was called to a meeting in the conference room next to the director of HR's office. By the way, she had been replaced a week before. There were three individuals sitting side by side on the opposite side of the conference table from where I had entered. I had never seen any of them before. The man in the middle wore a dark suit, was probably early fifties, bald, except for a strip of gray hair circling his head, and his expression was grim. He didn't smile or look at me. Two women sat on either side of him, their expressions were even grimmer. I don't remember much about them, except one was older than the man and the other was younger. There was a large cardboard file box sitting on the right of the older woman. She asked my name and I told her. She reached into the box and pulled out a file and handed it to the man. He motioned for me to sit across from them and I said, 'No thanks, I'll stand.' He stared at me and then referred to my file.

"He said, 'It has come to the attention of upper management that your position within the company does not produce revenue or develop new products. Is this correct?' I had already made the decision to leave, so I wasn't in a very good mood. I said, 'Yes, you're right. I don't sell nor do I develop. I just keep the programs we produce from screwing up and getting this company sued.' I leaned over the table and got in the man's face. 'By the way, who the hell are you?'"

JR chuckled, shook his head, and looked at Kruger. "I knew why I was there. The rumor mill was working overtime. I was getting fired, along with fifteen other people." He took another sip of water and continued, "The man stared at me like I was an infectious disease. He stammered and said, 'I'm an outside HR consultant. Our names are not important. Now, if you will sit down, I will go over your options within the company.'

"I laughed at him and said, 'What options? The midnight shift in Duluth?' Baldy shook his head. 'No, the position we are offering is in Atlanta.' I looked at him, he didn't get it. He really, truly didn't get it. I decided I wasn't going to play his game. So I said, 'Hey Baldy, I've been here since the company started. I don't need any shit from you or your two bimbos. Package me out and I'll get the hell out of here.'"

JR chuckled again. "The silence was deafening. All three stared at me with their mouths open. Baldy recovered first. He said, 'Well, I can see you want to be difficult. You will receive one week of salary for each complete year you've been with CWZ. You also have four weeks of vacation built up, which will be paid first. Do you have any questions?'

"I said, 'Nope,' and walked to the door. As I was opening the door, I looked back. They were already putting my file away and getting the next victim's out. A security guard met me at the door, and I was immediately escorted out of the building."

Kruger turned off the recorder, stood, and stretched. "That sounded pretty impersonal."

JR nodded. "It was. They were just hired guns. They didn't know us, nor did they care. Some of the employees at CWZ had given everything they had for ten hard years. Except for their stock, all they got at the end was a week's salary for each year they worked. The smart ones sold their stock immediately. They came out okay. The ones that didn't—well, let's say they got screwed a second time when the stock crashed." JR smiled. He got up and went to the kitchen for a cup of coffee.

They took a fifteen-minute break and then sat back down for JR to continue his narrative. Kruger turned the recorder back on, and JR picked up where he had left off. "What we didn't know at the time was that Tony had sold P&G Global ninety percent of his personal shares. What Tony didn't know was that Plymel had been buying publically traded shares for six months. By the time the sale closed, P&G owned fifty-two percent of all available stock. They had outmaneuvered Tony, and he lost his company. I haven't talked to Tony since. He never returned my calls.

"Over the next six months, CWZ was hammered by lawsuits and their flagship software program lost market share. P&G Global moved customer service to India and outsourced the programing. Within a year of buying the company, they had dismantled it and made their initial investment back plus a huge profit. From what I found in Plymel's computer files, they made a profit of over forty-million dollars by dismantling CWZ.

"Every single person I had worked with lost their job. Some went on to other careers; others found jobs with competitive companies. A few had their lives turned upside down." He paused and stared at his cup of coffee and took a breath. "Steve Wilson was devastated. His wife left him and took the kids. A few months later, he committed suicide." His eyes narrowed as he looked at Kruger. "That one event affected me more than anything else. Steve didn't deserve what happened. He was a really good guy. I still miss him.

"By selling my stock and combining it with my fourteen weeks of compensation, I had enough money to last a year. I was tired of the corporate scene, so I tried freelancing. That didn't work so well. While I was trying to figure out what to do, I found a job delivering pizzas." JR chuckled and shook his head. "I guess if I hadn't, I would still be in New York City. One night, I delivered five pizzas to an apartment in Manhattan. Plymel answered the door. I think I hid my surprise, but I really don't remember. He acted like a jerk and gave me a two-cent tip.

"After he slammed the door in my face, I didn't get mad. I decided I would make it my mission in life to fuck him any way I could, mainly for Steve Wilson. It took a couple of days, but I came up with a plan. After quitting the pizza job, I got a job with a locksmith. It's amazing how simple it is to pick a lock." Kruger grinned after JR made this statement, but he kept quiet. JR continued, "A month later, I knew Plymel's schedule—when he was at the apartment and when he wasn't. Exactly eight months after I walked out of the CWZ offices, I was showing my ID and work order to the doorman of Plymel's apartment building."

Kruger stopped the recording. "JR, are you going to admit to breaking and entering?"

JR nodded.

"Okay, the tape is officially off. In fact, I'm resetting the recorder." Kruger pressed a button, waited ten seconds, and put the recorder back in his backpack. "I really don't want a recording of you confessing to a felony. But, I still want to know what happened."

Kruger smiled, crossed his arms on his chest, and sat back. JR looked at Joseph, who smiled and nodded.

JR relaxed. "Plymel's door was equipped with a very expensive lock, a brand we sold where I worked, so I was familiar with it. I was in the door in less than thirty seconds. It was a little after nine in the morning and Plymel had been gone for two hours. I gave myself exactly thirty minutes to accomplish what I needed to do.

"The apartment had been professionally decorated and everything looked expensive. Even the light switch plates looked expensive. There were real oil paintings on the wall in the vestibule. I'm not real knowledgeable in the world of art, but I know who Picasso is. The living area was filled with Persian rugs, very uncomfortable-looking furniture and a wet bar. The kitchen and dining area were to the left of the living area. I found his office on the opposite side of the living room.

"The laptop was sitting on a solid walnut desk that was larger than the Toyota I drove in college. I sat at the desk, opened the laptop, and as expected, it was password protected. Guys like Plymel are very organized and they like to think of themselves as computer savvy. But they're usually not. I picked the computer up and looked on the bottom. Sure enough, there was the password. I took a flash drive out of my shirt pocket and slipped it into one of the USB slots. With a few keystrokes, a program I had written specifically for this occasion, downloaded. With a few more strokes on the keyboard, I erased all traces of the download. But, my program was still there, operating in the background. I closed the laptop's lid, put the chair back like I had found it, and carefully let myself out of the apartment. I was in the apartment less than ten minutes.

"The downloaded program was designed to record all of his keystrokes and save them to a file. Then every twenty-four hours, it would email the file to an account set up specifically to receive the data. All traces of the file and email would then be deleted from his laptop.

"It took several days before the stealth program could record enough information to be useful. First I found Plymel was skimming funds out of P&G Global and locating those funds in offshore accounts. Second, I discovered Abel Plymel had an exit plan."

Kruger stopped him and said, "An exit plan?"

JR nodded. "He had one more big deal to close. Once that deal was completed, he would have almost a hundred-million dollars sitting in offshore accounts. Once he reached that dollar level, he planned to retire and disappear. I don't have all the details on his exit plan, but in the emails I have, there's a hint he has an alternate set of identification papers."

Kruger frowned. "When will he execute this plan?"

Smiling JR said, "From what I could tell, he planned to be gone by the end of the year, maybe sooner."

Raising his eyebrows, Kruger leaned slightly forward in his chair. "I checked yesterday. He's still there. But, we can't risk him knowing we've found you. He could leave the country and disappear. I haven't spent the last seven months working on this to let that happen" Sitting back in his chair, he rubbed his face with his hands.

"I transferred all I could find, about sixty-million dollars. Those funds were transferred through various accounts in the Caymans until it was untraceable. Trust me; there is no way he will ever get the money back. It's gone."

Joseph laughed out loud. "What did you do, spend it?"

JR shook his head. "No, most of the money was donated to charities around the world. I also set up a trust fund for Steve Wilson's kids. His widow won't have to worry about paying for college. I kept a little bit of it. I figured the son of a bitch owed me."

Kruger stared at JR. "How much did you keep?"

"A little."

"How much, JR?"

"Not very much. Don't ask again, because I'm not going to tell you."

Kruger just looked at JR for a few moments, then nodded, "Okay, go on with your story."

"I have all of this information saved to a flash drive. I'll give it to you when we're done." Kruger smiled. JR continued, "There is a lot of information on the flash drive about Plymel conducting insider trading. That's how he screwed Tony Chien. It's also where most of the sixty million came from. Plus he's running a bit of a Ponzi scheme with some of his investors."

Kruger interrupted. "This information was illegally obtained. We can't use it in court, JR."

"I know that, but it gives you direction."

Kruger nodded. "Go on."

"Anyway, after I transferred all of his money. I started putting my own exit plan into place. I thought I might have a couple of weeks before I had to bug out. I was wrong."

CHAPTER 15

Springfield, MO

"My plan was to leave New York by the weekend, but on the Wednesday prior to my departure," said JR, "they found me. As I left my apartment building early that morning, a man fell into step next to me. The man was about my height and a lot more muscular. He was huge. I really don't remember much about him, except his size. He was slightly behind me as we approached the corner. A black Suburban screeched to a halt in front of me, just as I reached the crosswalk. The rear door opened and I was pushed into the vehicle. A much larger guy was already in the back seat and pulled me in as the shorter guy scrambled into the vehicle.

"I was now sitting between the two large men. I heard the guy on my left say, 'Go.' I looked at both of them and said, 'What the hell is going on here?' They ignored me. As the Suburban stopped for a stoplight, I tried to get up and exit the vehicle. The guy who had pushed me into the vehicle pulled a Glock out from under his suit coat, stuck it in my ribs, and said, 'Shut up.' So I did.

"I had no perception of time, so I can't tell you how long we were in the Suburban. I knew we were heading toward

Battery Park, but before we got there, the driver stopped in front of a very tall building. The shorter guy next to me got out, and I was shoved out the door by the taller one. He placed his hand on my back and pushed me toward the building. We got on the elevator after passing a security guard sitting in a booth, who only nodded at my two escorts and ignored my presence.

"I watched the floors count up on the panel. It stopped counting on the thirty-fourth floor. Once again, I was shoved and we exited the elevator into the lobby of an office suite. I was hurriedly escorted to a large office and forced to sit in front of a desk even larger than the one in Plymel's apartment. The owner of the desk was standing with his back to me, facing a large floor-to-ceiling window. My two burly escorts stood behind me.

"I really don't remember how long the man stood with his back to me. Probably wasn't very long, but it seemed like an eternity. Finally he turned and faced me. It was Abel Plymel. He said, 'You have something of mine and I want it back.' I just stared at him. He probably asked several times about the money, but I wasn't listening. I was weighing the options on how to get out of this mess. Not too many came to mind. His laughing brought me out of the funk. He said, 'I actually laughed when I saw the balance you left.' I tuned him out again. I had left a balance of two cents in each of his accounts. Probably not the smartest thing I've ever done, but it sure felt good at the time.

"He got my attention again when he showed the video recording of my excursion into his apartment. The last thing on my mind that morning was security cameras. I watched myself download the program to his laptop and leave the office. The quality was poor, but you could tell it was me."

"Is there a copy of this recording, JR?" said Joseph. He had straightened from leaning on the mantle, his composed expression gone, in its place a look of apprehension.

JR shook his head. "A week after I arrived here, I hacked back into P&G's corporate server. I found the video file, deleted it, and renamed another security file to the original file name. If anyone looks at it again, all they will see is five minutes of an empty hallway." Joseph chuckled, relaxed, and again leaned against the fireplace mantel.

JR took another long drink of water. Placing the bottle of water on the coffee table, he started his narrative again. "At this point, Plymel leaned over the desk and said in a low growl, 'Now, do you want to tell me where the money is?'

"I stared back into his eyes and said, 'You'll never find it.' That's when Plymel straightened and sat down at his desk. He leaned forward in his seat, put his elbows on the desk, clasped his hands together, and made a steeple with his index fingers. Tapping them against his lip, he said, 'Tell me now where the money is, or I will not be responsible for what happens to you.'

"I chuckled slightly, stared back at him, and said, 'That's the trouble with guys like you. You never take responsibility for your actions.' His faced turned crimson. I thought he was going to stroke out. But just as fast, he calmed, looked at both of the gorillas standing behind me, and nodded. They grabbed under my arms and yanked me to my feet. As I was being pushed toward the door, Plymel said, 'Tell me where the money is. It will be less painful.' I turned my head back toward him and just before I was shoved through the door, I said, 'Go to hell.'"

Kruger smiled and leaned forward in his chair. He said, "There's the threat of bodily harm I was looking for. I'll call Alvarez in the morning. He can start pressuring the guard who survived, then we'll have collaboration on what Plymel said. Sorry, JR, go on with your story."

JR nodded and said, "We rode the elevator to the ground floor, and I was pushed out just behind the short one. I noticed the bulge under his suit coat on his right hip. He was slightly ahead of me to my left. The taller guy was slightly behind me on the right. I noticed the Suburban waiting at the curb through the front glass of the lobby. I knew if I got into the vehicle, I was dead. I'd never get out of it alive.

"I really didn't make a decision. I just acted. My instincts and training from the military took over. To this day, I don't really remember much about it. I do remember seeing the shorter guy with a bullet hole just above his right eye. The next thing I can really remember is running, turning a corner, field stripping the Glock, and stuffing the various pieces into pockets of my jeans. I walked a few blocks and devised a plan. I had sixty-thousand dollars and my computer backup files in a safe deposit drawer at a bank. The money was an emergency fund in case something like this might happen.

"After walking several blocks from the building, I hailed a cab and took it toward the bank. I got out seven blocks from it and discretely threw the pieces of the Glock into storm drains and trashcans. I figured I had less than an hour to accomplish what needed to be done. There was a sporting goods store about two blocks from the bank, so I ducked in and bought a Swiss Gear computer backpack. With the new backpack, I entered the bank and gained access to my box. I kept a rotation of thirty-two-gig flash sticks as backups for my laptop and the sixty-thousand dollars in the box. It took less than a minute to pack everything. Once that was accomplished, I took another cab to a public library about eleven blocks from the bank.

"Thirty minutes after the incident, I was using a public computer to access my personal laptop at my apartment. Once I was into the computer, I executed a program that basically destroyed the hard drive of the laptop. Trust me. No one was going to get any data off that drive.

"Once I had my computer destroyed, I left the library and hailed a cab. I wanted this guy to remember me, so I gave him a hundred-dollar bill from my stash. As I handed the money to him, I said, 'Get me to Newark by one and I'll give you another hundred.' The guy was from some Middle Eastern country. He had the keffiyeh and a seven-day-old beard." JR chuckled. "I'll never forget his look. It went from bored to euphoria in microseconds. His greenish-hue grin revealed several missing teeth. The taxi screeched away from the curb as he tackled the midday traffic. We made it to Newark International with a minute to spare. I handed him the other hundred and without a word slipped out of the cab and ran into the airport.

"I stopped inside the vestibule, turned, and watched as he slowly pulled away from the curb. Once the cab joined the multitude of vehicles exiting the airport, I walked into the terminal. Inside, I looked around and found a souvenir shop. Taking my time, I meandered into the store and started looking. I found a dark windbreaker, sunglasses, and a New York Knicks hat. After my purchase, I looked at some magazines and finally left the store ten minutes later. The down escalator was close to the store. Taking the moving stairs down, I went to the lower-level taxi queue, caught a cab, and went to the Westminster Hotel in East Hanover. I figured the cabbie wouldn't remember dropping me off at a hotel. But he would remember dropping someone off at a Best Buy. Anyway, I walked the quarter of a mile to the store, bought a new computer, an electric screwdriver, a T-Mobile hotspot device, and a bunch of prepaid minutes. It had been four hours since the incident, and I was relatively sure I was ahead of the police. But I needed to keep moving.

"It took me an hour to set up the laptop and clean the crap that comes with a new computer off the hard drive. Afterwards, I used the coffee shop's free Wi-Fi to find nearby used car dealers. The smart thing would have been to take a bus, but I didn't feel I had any extra time to waste. So I tipped one of the Baristas to call a cab for me, mentioning that my cell phone battery was dead. The cab arrived and within twenty minutes I was talking to a guy about a ten-year-old Honda Accord with one hundred and twenty-six thousand miles on it. I paid him in cash and drove off the lot.

"I filled the car with gas at a Seven-Eleven, bought a heat-n-eat sandwich, a bag of Doritos, a couple bottles of water, and a big coffee." JR smiled. "Road trip food. The Honda drove good, didn't squeak, and the tires looked like they had at least another fifteen thousand miles on them.

Which was fine. I didn't plan to keep the car any longer than it took me to get to the middle of the country. I found I-78 and started driving west toward Allentown. Lehigh Valley International Airport was about seventy miles away, and it would take me at least ninety minutes to get there. To my surprise, the Honda's cruise control worked, so I settled down for the drive and relaxed for the first time since early morning.

"Eighty-five minutes later, I was circling the long-term parking lot at the airport and found what I was looking for. A Honda Accord. It was the same year and color as mine. It had Missouri license plates on it, and since Missouri was one of the states I was considering, it was a no-brainer. I found an open slot several rows from the car and pulled in. After retrieving the new power screwdriver from my computer bag, I casually walked over to the Honda from Missouri. As I approached the car, I determined where all the security cameras were located and found I had lucked out. The car was parked next to a large SUV, which obscured the view of the closest camera. I knelt down next to the car's front license plate and reversed the screws and took the plate. Calmly walking back to my car, I got in and drove away.

"I had not been in the parking lot long enough to get charged, so I left and got back on West I-78. About five miles later, I pulled off the highway and put the Missouri plate on my Honda. Now if a highway patrolman called the plate in, it would come back as the same color, make, and year car, but registered in Missouri. The only problem I might have was if the person I had stolen it from came back and noticed the license missing. If that happened, I'd be screwed, but I didn't have any other choice.

"Eventually, I got to I-70. From there, it was a straight shot west to St. Louis, where I would need to make a decision. I ran out of steam when I got to Columbus, Ohio, around nine. All of the day's adrenalin was gone and I couldn't keep my eyes open any longer. On the west side of town, I found a group of small low-cost motels surrounded by chain restaurants. I paid cash for a ground-level room in the back, drove around the building, and backed into the parking slot in front of my room. Since I didn't have any luggage, unpacking didn't take a lot of time. A pizza and a two-liter Diet Coke from the Domino's next door was my dinner. I used the T-Mobile device to check news from New York City. There was nothing about the morning's event. Which was kind of surprising. A shooting close to Wall Street would normally warrant mentioning, apparently not this time. Next, I checked a map of Missouri and after a few Google searches, decided on my destination.

"My destination was over seven hundred miles away, and I was determined to get there by the next evening. After a long hot shower, I was asleep as soon as my head hit the pillow. Six the next morning found me back on I-70 with a big cup of coffee and an Egg McMuffin from a nearby McDonalds.

"At seven that night, I checked into the Baymont Suites on the south side of Springfield. I was in the middle of the country, in a city large enough to start a new life, but small enough no one would think to look. At least, that was what I thought at the time.

"The hotel was situated in an area with shopping centers and a bunch of chain restaurants. It was perfect, I bought supplies and clothing at a nearby shopping mall and ate at the Outback Steakhouse within walking distance of my hotel. It was my first decent meal in two days. Life was good again. The only problem was, I didn't have an ID. Plus, I couldn't use my real name without leaving a trail. It had been thirty-six hours since the incident, and I was over twelve hundred miles away without leaving a paper trail. I felt somewhat safe, but not until I could change my identity, which I did the next day."

JR took a deep breath, let it out slowly and said, "That's it. Now you know the truth, not the BS made up by Plymel."

CHAPTER 16

Springfield, MO

Kruger leaned back in his chair. He looked at Joseph, who nodded. He then returned his attention to JR. "That corresponds to what we knew about the case. You confirmed my suspicions about the physical threat. Did you find all of his diverted funds?"

Diminski shook his head. "No, I don't think so. He probably had a few accounts he didn't access while the program recorded keystrokes. But I got a lot of them."

Kruger was silent for a few moments. Then he said, "As far as I'm concerned, I still haven't found the fugitive from New York City. But I am concerned about who else is looking for you and who accessed your military file?"

Joseph said, "I have someone looking into the matter."

Kruger nodded. "You mentioned you still have a backdoor into Plymel's computer."

JR said, "I have one into P&G Global. His laptop is invisible. They changed the access codes after they found the security camera recording. He has a new email account, which I'm sure will be easy to find when I go back into the corporate server."

"If we needed to, could you bring their system down for a few minutes?"

JR smiled. "I can bring it down for hours or days if we need to. They still haven't spent a lot of money on security. If their investors knew how susceptible they are to a computer breach, they'd be screaming."

Kruger smiled. "How fast could you set it up?"

JR looked at the floor and was silent for a few moments. He turned his gaze to Mia, who squeezed his hand. He returned his attention to Kruger. "It can happen pretty quick. I've had a DOS attack ready for several months. I just haven't implemented it."

"What's a DOS attack?"

"Sorry, it means denial of service, basically thousands of computers trying to access their system simultaneously. This causes the system to overload and shut down. They're easy to set up, but they're a bitch to defend against. Particularly if you don't know what you're doing. P&G's team doesn't have a clue."

"I take it you know how to keep them from finding the source of the attack?"

JR smiled. "They'll never find the source. The attack will appear to be coming from overseas."

Kruger nodded. "Good. Do you still have the files from his laptop?"

JR tossed a flash drive to Kruger, who grabbed it. "It's yours, I didn't make a copy."

Glancing at his watch, Kruger said, "It's late. I'm spending the night in town, but I have to leave for KC by late morning. Joseph and I will be back first thing tomorrow, hopefully with a plan. I need to think about it tonight." He stood and moved toward the front door, Joseph right behind him.

Just as he was opening the front door, JR said, "Agent Kruger. Why did you decide to help me?"

Kruger turned and looked at JR. "Plymel lied to me in New York City. I don't like people lying to me. Besides, his partner, Alton Crigler, was a deputy attorney general and was on my case the entire time he worked at the Justice Department. Crigler pulled in a few favors to get me assigned to this case. Now he wants me fired. So to answer your question, I wanted the truth. Now I have it. Besides, I don't like rich guys screwing the rest of us." Kruger smiled, turned, and walked through the door. Joseph winked at JR, turned, and followed Kruger.

As soon as the door was shut, JR turned to Mia. "I'll understand if you walk out and never want to see me again."

Mia frowned and pointed her index finger at JR. "Don't even go there. It's going to take a lot more than this to make me walk."

***

Kruger found a hotel close to JR's Condo; he needed time to think before he met with Joseph the next morning.

Joseph was an old friend, the man who had originally encouraged Kruger to join the FBI. The man's past was still a mystery to Kruger. He knew Joseph still worked for the government, in some fashion, but every time he asked Joseph what he did, the man would smile and not answer. Kruger had his suspicions, but respected his friend's wishes to keep it confidential. Over the years, their collaboration had resulted in a lot of very dangerous people being removed from society.

Once settled in his room, Kruger pulled a legal pad from his computer bag, propped himself up, and leaned against the headboard. This was his normal way of working through a problem. He made a line down the middle of the page and started making bullet points on the left side, rebuttals on the right. By midnight, he had the beginnings of an idea.

After putting the legal pad back in his backpack, he called Stephanie to find out when her plane would arrive from San Francisco tomorrow. They talked for an hour. After the call, he turned the lights out.

The next morning, after checking out of the motel and having breakfast with Joseph, the plan had taken shape. Their discussion had resulted in several modifications. After both were satisfied, they headed to JR's.

***

Kruger handed the flash drive with the files from Plymel's computer back to JR. "I need this information sent to me via an email address that can be traced back to a personal account of Alton Crigler. Make it hard to trace. Next, we need to know who was trying to access your military file."

JR nodded and typed on a small laptop.

Joseph said, "We should know that by the end of the day."

Kruger said, "As soon as the file is received, I'll called my boss and asked for a forensic accountant to be on standby. At that time, the case in New York City will be reopened. "

Smiling, JR continued typing.

"I'll be heading to KC in a few hours. I'll be in back in New York in a day or so to meet with my team. Charlie Craft will be my forensic technician; he was with me when we first started this little expedition. The forensic accountant will be Sharon Crawford. She's good and not easily intimidated."

JR said, "When do you want the DOS attack to begin?"

"Once I have the team in place, I'll let you know. I need to get a few things organized before we pull the trigger. When we pull it, events will happen fast."

Joseph's cell phone vibrated. He noted the ID, accepted the call, and said, "Good morning, Sandy. How are you?"

"Fine, sir. I just found out who accessed the file you were interest in."

"Who accessed it?"

"The ID used is assigned to a Sergeant Major George Morris, currently a hand-to-hand combat training specialist at

Bragg."

"Interesting, just a moment, hang on." Joseph looked at Kruger and said, "A sergeant named George Morris accessed the file. Does that name mean anything to you?"

Kruger shook his head and looked at JR.

Shaking his head, JR said, "No, but I've been out for a long time. Who is he?"

Joseph said, "Hand-to-hand combat trainer at Fort Bragg."

JR looked puzzled. "I never was at Bragg."

Kruger frowned, "Ask him to find out all he can about this Sergeant Morris. I doubt he decided all of a sudden to look up JR's file on his own. Someone's paid him to find the information."

Joseph nodded. He said into the phone, "Sandy, find out what you can on Morris." After the call ended, Joseph said, "Sandy looked him up. He's a twenty-five-year veteran, multiple deployments, commendations too numerous to mention and deep in debt. He has two ex-wives who take more than half his salary in child support and alimony. He's being watched by Army CID, but they can't pin anything on him."

Kruger looked at Joseph. "Can Sandy pay him a visit?"

Joseph nodded.

JR said, "Get me his email address. I can see if anything's there."

Kruger smiled. "Even better."

Over the next two hours, Kruger laid out the remainder of his plan. When he was through, he said, "JR, things might get a little dicey once Plymel is under arrest. We know they're still trying to find you. Once I start working on Crigler, they might double their efforts. You and Mia might need to take a long vacation."

"How long?" asked Mia.

Kruger shook his head. "Don't know, could be awhile."

JR shook his head. "I'm not running anymore."

"I'm not asking you to run away," said Kruger. "Just be

unavailable for a while, that's all."

Looking at Mia, JR said, "We've been talking about going to the mountains. What'd you think?"

She nodded. "I hear it's beautiful this time of year."

JR turned back to Kruger. "When do you think we should leave?"

"Do you have to monitor the DOS attack?"

"No, I can start it from anywhere."

"Then if you can arrange it, leave the day after tomorrow. The fireworks will start not too long after." He turned to Joseph. "Can you arrange someone to watch this place while they're gone?"

Joseph nodded. "I was thinking about that myself. Consider it done."

"Then we're all set." Kruger handed JR a business card. "Buy several throwaway cell phones, with cash, and keep in touch."

JR laughed. "Sorry, I'm way beyond that. I can call you from anywhere in the world through my computer and no one would be able to trace the call."

Kruger smiled. "When we're done with this little mess, you'll have to share that tidbit of knowledge."

"It will be my pleasure."

CHAPTER 17

New York City

Adam Weber read the email from Sergeant George Morris for the second time. He sat back in his chair and tapped his index finger on his lips. Why had the sergeant been questioned earlier in the day about accessing the fugitive's file seven months ago? Why now? In his experience, most individuals on the run made mistakes. Had the man finally made a mistake and the army was now after him? Something had changed.

His cell phone was on his desk. He reached for it and did a search for Morris's number. He needed to know details the email left out. The call was answered on the fourth ring.

"Sergeant Morris."

"Can you talk?"

"No, sir. Not at the moment."

"Okay, call me when you can."

"Yes sir. Thank you, sir."

Half an hour later, Weber's phone vibrated. He glanced at the caller ID and accepted the call, "Who's asking questions?"

George Morris said, "I had a visit from Army CID this

morning. They wanted to know why I was accessing, without authorization, a classified file."

"How did they know you accessed it?" Silence was his answer. "Sergeant, are you there?"

"I'm not sure. They didn't tell me."

"What did you tell them?"

"Not much. I told them I accessed the file by mistake." Weber had the feeling Morris was lying. He said, "And they bought that?"

"I have no idea, major. Look, you never told me this guy was radioactive. Why are they pissed off about me looking at a file that's been closed for fifteen years? Who is this guy?"

Weber was silent. It was a legitimate question. Why was CID involved? "Sergeant, tell me, who exactly came to see you?"

"A lieutenant and a staff sergeant did all the talking. There was a major with them. He wasn't CID, and he didn't say anything. He just stood back and listened."

"What was his name?"

"He wasn't introduced and I didn't ask. But his name patch said, Knoll."

"What did he look like?"

"Big guy, bigger than me, short sandy-brown hair, built like a funnel, you know, wide shoulders, narrow hips. His biceps looked like my thighs. The funny thing about him, he wore BDUs with just his oak leaves and name patch, no other identifiers. To me, he looked like Special Forces."

"Is this going to be a problem for us, Sergeant?"

There was silence on the other end of the line. Finally, Morris said, "You know my memory isn't what it used to be, but a couple more thousand would really help me forget."

Weber closed his eyes and shook his head. "I see. I'll make sure your memory continues to be poor. Good night, Sergeant." He ended the call and sat back. Who was this Major Knoll? And why was he interested in the fugitive? Weber could understand if just CID showed up, but a major with no insignias—something wasn't right.

***

Caroline Welch was a recent graduate of Amherst. While not the homecoming queen, she considered herself attractive. She also considered herself smarter than the other recently hired female associates at P&G Global. Unfortunately, she was still classified as an intern. After searching for a job for six months, without success, she had taken the internship. Hopefully to learn more about hedge funds and high finance. Her current project was so far from that goal, she was livid. Finally, at her limit and ready to quit, she stormed into Alton Crigler's office and threw the file onto his desk. She said, "This is not why I was hired."

Crigler looked up at Welch, took off his glasses, and reached for the file. "Ms. Welch, you were hired to do research. Why don't you sit down and take a couple of deep breaths. We'll talk about it."

His calm demeanor dissipated her anger like a fall wind scattering leaves. She took a deep breath and sat in a leather chair in front of his desk. She was quiet as he read through the file.

"This is good work, Ms. Welch. Tell me, what are your conclusions from this data?"

"Thank you, Mr. Crigler. My assignment was to identify start-up computer companies the firm might be interested in funding. When I joined the firm…"

Crigler held up his hand, palm toward her. "Ms. Welch, let's be clear on your status. You are not officially a member of this firm, yet. You are a paid intern. We are evaluating your worth and will make a decision within six months. However, I like your initiative, and your work. So, please, go on."

"I'm very much aware of my status, Mr. Crigler. However, as I was saying, when I started my internship, I was told I would be doing research for possible acquisitions." She pointed to the file in his hand. "The companies I'm researching are small start-ups. How am I supposed to learn the big picture? All I'm doing is wasting my time with companies that aren't even profitable."

"I assure you, Ms. Welch, you are not wasting your time, as you so enthusiastically put it."

She frowned, but remained quiet. Crigler continued to read the contents of the folder. After five long minutes, he pulled ten sheets of paper from the file and set them aside. He opened a file drawer on the left side of his desk and dropped the file into a slot. Looking back up, he took the ten sheets of paper and said, "You've done a nice job on this, but"—he handed them back to her—"I need you to dig further into these ten. We need to know more about the individuals who started the company and their background, particularly if they were ever in the military. Can you do that, Ms. Welch?" She nodded. "Please make a copy of each of those pages and give them back to me. It's important to the company, Ms. Welch, trust me."

She stood and clutched the papers to her chest. For a second, she appeared ready to say something, but instead walked out of Crigler's office.

He smiled as she left and reached for his cell phone on the right side of his desk. His call was answered on the second ring. "Why don't you come to my office around five. There's been a new development."

***

Adam Weber finished reading the pages Caroline Welch had returned to Crigler. He handed them back to Crigler, and said, "I think you have a valid idea here. What next?"

Smiling, Crigler said, "What did your military friend tell you about the fugitive's military training?"

"He confirmed what we suspected; he had a lot of hand-to-hand combat and weapons training. Plus he was being groomed to be in a cyber-warfare unit." Weber stopped, his eyebrows rose, and he flipped through the pages again. "Each one of these companies was started by someone with military training and knows computer security." He paused. "And, each one was started in the past eight months."

Crigler nodded, "Very good, Adam, very good. One of those companies is here in New York City. I doubt it's him, but you need to check it out. The others are scattered across the country. Why don't you take a road trip?"

Weber nodded, stood, picked up the ten sheets of paper, and placed them in his inside suit coat pocket. "I believe I will."

***

The first company, outside of New York, was located in an old house a few blocks from Wrigley Field in Chicago. Adam Weber sat in his rental car and double-checked the address with the file. It was the same. He parked the car at the curb and walked to the front door. After ringing the doorbell, he waited. After the third time, the door barely opened and a small man about five foot six peaked out. He said, "May I help you?"

Weber was tired and knew after he saw the man he was wasting his time. He pushed the door open. "I'm looking for this man." He had the picture of the security camera cropped so it did not show the security guard. The small man wasn't intimidated, which surprised Weber.

Without looking at the picture, the man said, "Nope— never seen him before. Now get the hell out of my office."

"Mind if I look around, make sure you don't know him?"

"Yeah I mind, I have work to do, now get *out!*"

Weber turned around to face the man who was still standing by the door holding it open. He pulled out his H&K and said, "I'm looking around. Shut the door."

The man stared at the gun, shook his head, and bolted out the open front door. Weber holstered the gun and started rummaging around in various offices. All he could see was computer equipment in various states of disrepair. In a filing cabinet, he found a file containing the business organization and structure. The man was listed as a sole proprietor. Weber closed the file and walked back to his rental car. Several blocks later, he saw a patrol car speeding in the opposite direction. Smiling to himself, he headed back to the airport.

Over the next couple of days, Weber had similar results at companies in Minneapolis, Dallas, Little Rock and Kansas City. The next to last company he needed to check was south of Kansas City in Springfield. Since there were no direct flights, he drove the three hours and arrived shortly after six-thirty in the evening. The business was located in a strip center surrounded by dentists, accountants, hair salons, and payday-loan offices. The sign on the door identified the business as Ozark Security and Computer Consultants, LLC. The hours of business were stenciled on the glass front door, plus there was an after-hours contact number. The door was locked and no lights were on inside.

Back in his car, he dialed the number listed on the door. A female voice answered and said, "Ozarks Security, how may we help you?"

"Yes, my name is Alex Volmer," said Weber. "I'm taking bids on having our computer system upgraded. Who would I speak to in your company?"

"I'm afraid he is out of town for a few days. I can transfer you to his partner."

"Oh, no need. When do you expect him back?"

"I'm not sure, sir. This is an answering service. He only tells us when he's out and lets us know when he returns."

"I see. Well maybe you should transfer me to his partner."

"Just a moment, sir. I'll transfer the call."

The phone was silent for a few moments. Weber was curious why a computer specialist would still be using an answering service. But his thoughts were interrupted by the phone being answered. "This is Joseph, may I help you?"

"Yes sir, my company is taking bids to have our computer system upgraded, and I wanted to speak to someone in your organization who could give us a bid. The answering service indicated he was out of town."

"Yes, he is. I can take your contact information. When he gets back, I'll have him call you. Would that be sufficient?"

"Well, I was hoping to have this process done by the end of the week. Will he be back in a day or so?"

"No, he's out till the end of the week."

"Okay, thank you."

***

Joseph ended the call with a frown on his face. It was a fishing expedition—of that, he was certain. Someone was looking for JR. First, the area code of the call was from New York; JR refused to do business with anyone east of the Mississippi River. Second, the man wouldn't leave his contact information. He walked to a laptop and entered the phone number in a reverse directory website service and found it unlisted. Smiling, he went to another search engine JR had designed and entered the number. The results showed the number belonged to an Adam Weber of New York City.

The name sounded vaguely familiar, but he couldn't place it. But he knew someone at the Justice Department in Washington DC who might be able to help. It was after eight on the East Coast, so he dialed her cell phone number. The call was answered immediately. "Joseph, I was thinking of you the other day. When are we going to take that trip you keep promising me?"

Smiling, Joseph said, "I'm ready anytime. You just have to tell me when." The two of them had been talking about a trip to New Zealand for years. In reality, they would probably never take it, but it was fun to talk about.

"What do I owe the pleasure of this call, Joseph?"

"I need some information. Have you ever heard of a man named Adam Weber?"

Silence was his answer. He was beginning to think the call had been dropped, when she said in a questioning tone,

"Why do you ask?"

"I'm just doing a little background check, that's all."

"Are you thinking about hiring him for some reason?"

Now it was Joseph's turn to be quiet. Finally he said, "You sound hesitant. Do you know him?"

"Yes, if it's the same Adam Weber. He's an ex-US Marshal, who left under a cloud of suspicion. There were rumors, rumors he was selling the locations of several individuals in the Witness Protection Program. Those individuals disappeared suddenly. If I remember correctly, nothing was ever proven, but his career was essentially over after the allegations were made."

Joseph frowned. That was why the name sounded familiar. "Mary, I need to know more. How hard would it be for you to get me more information on this guy?"

"Not too hard, but it will cost you."

He smiled. "How much?"

"You'll have to come to town and take me to dinner. We can talk about the rest of the payment after we eat. I have a sexy new dress I was saving to wear for just such an evening."

"You're on, my dear. Our last night out was most memorable."

"Good. I'll see what I can find, then get back to you. I'll expect immediate payment."

They both laughed and said their goodbyes. Joseph's next call was to Sean Kruger.

***

After deciding Colorado was their vacation destination, Mia found on the internet, a moderately priced Bed & Breakfast in Boulder near the base of the Flatirons. It offered Wi-Fi, which was JR's only request, so he thought it was perfect. They drove straight from Springfield to the B&B. Fifteen hours and eight hundred miles later, they were pulling into the parking lot. Their room was on the top floor of the building, with a window facing the west. It was already dark when they walked into the room, and as soon as their heads hit the pillows, they were asleep.

JR and Mia spent the first day hiking and enjoying the breathtaking scenery. Dinner was at a small brew pub within walking distance of their B&B. JR forgot about what was happening on the East Coast and relaxed for the first time in almost a year. But later that night, after making love and listening to Mia's gentle breathing, all JR could do was lay there and worry. Finally at one in the morning, he got out of bed, shut the door to the bedroom, sat at the small worktable in the living area, and signed onto the internet. He programed the denial of service protocol to start at noon Eastern Time later that day. Then without a specific plan, he started attacking the P&G Global server.

An hour later, just before shutting down his intrusion into the P&G Global system, he stumbled onto a gaping hole in their network security. Smiling, he started rapidly typing.

When he completed his incursion, he sat back and stared at the screen. The end result would be several catastrophic events occurring at the same time of the DOS attack. Recovery would take days. He removed the indicators of his excursion into the P&G Global system and broke the connection. Returning to bed, he dosed off around four.

The next thing he knew it was nine in the morning. The curtains in the bedroom were open, and Mia was standing in front of the sliding glass door with a cup of coffee in her hand. She was apparently mesmerized by the view of the mountains. The thin white t-shirt and the light from outside outlined her body, leaving very little to the imagination. He said, "Beautiful aren't they?"

She turned. "I've flown over them, but I've never seen them up close like this." She got back in bed and removed her t-shirt. It was afternoon before they left the room.

CHAPTER 18

New York City

"Interesting," said Kruger. "Did they ask for him by name?"

"No," Joseph replied. "The guy asked who he could talk to, no specifics. The caller said he needed a computer upgrade. I wouldn't have thought much about it, except the New York area code."

"So they didn't know who to ask for, that's good. It means they're searching various computer companies, just like I did." Kruger was quiet for a few moments. "When Charlie did a search of newly formed computer businesses, the results were overwhelming. I wonder if they found a way to narrow the search."

Joseph said, "Wait a minute. What if they used the information Morris gave them and only checked companies founded by veterans in the last eight months. When we incorporated, I identified myself as a veteran, but not JR. It would have narrowed their search field."

"You may be right, Joseph, it makes more sense. It also explains why they didn't have a name to ask for."

"If JR had answered, I bet the conversation would have led to a face-to-face meeting. Do you think they have a photo?"

"Almost assuredly. They'll have the security photos and possibly a HR photo from the company P&G Global bought." Kruger paused for a few moments. "It doesn't change my plan. Tomorrow morning, the article in the *New York Times* will be published. Once Sharon Crawford arrives with the search warrant, we'll serve it and she can start stripping away the layers of deception. It should be fun. By the way, where is JR?"

"Not here. They left yesterday, just like we asked them to. I've put a twenty-four-hour watch on their apartment. If we see anyone parked outside, you'll get pictures and details."

"Good."

Joseph said, "When are you going in?"

"As soon as Sharon and Alvarez arrive, probably before nine. It depends on when Plymel gets to the building. I want him to have time to read the New York Times."

"Be careful, Sean. I don't want to be the person telling Brian something happened to his father."

"Damn, you can be such a little girl sometimes. I'll be fine. Besides, I have the federal government behind me. On second thought, I'll be careful."

They both chuckled and the call ended.

***

Meanwhile, Abel Plymel sat at his desk waiting. It was a little before 5:00 p.m., and his attorney had still not called. Final negotiations were taking place in Cincinnati for P&G Global to buy out a dominant Ohio healthcare provider. The healthcare's board of directors had met earlier in the afternoon and rumors were spreading on the internet that the offer from P&G Global of thirty-one dollars per share had been accepted. The profit potential was tremendous. A cash buyer for one of the subsidiaries of the company was already in place. In essence, when the transaction closed, P&G Global would already have a contract in place to recoup the original cash outlay for the healthcare company. He was in a great mood, even Alton Crigler had stopped by to congratulate him.

His phone rang at five minutes to five. It was his assistant. "Mr. Plymel, Bob Walters with the *Insider* is on line two. He'd like to speak to you about some breaking news."

Plymel smiled. So, the word was out about the deal. "Okay, I'll take the call." He pushed the button with the flashing light. "Plymel here."

"Mr. Plymel, my name is Bob Walters with the *Insider*. We want to get your comment about a story we're publishing online and appearing in the *New York Times* tomorrow."

"Okay, go ahead."

"We have information accusing you of insider trading. The documents we have in hand, point to several acquisitions made by P&G Global over the past five years. These documents explain how you personally started buying stock in the target companies through a shell entity prior to the announcement. In fact, we have documentation that shows where you personally delayed announcing the acquisition so you could increase your stock holdings. These activities are in strict violation of SEC regulations. We also have information that the incident earlier this year, where a security guard was killed, was staged. Do you have any comments, sir?"

Abel Plymel was silent, his mind racing on how anyone could have found this information. He finally regained his composure. "Mr. Walters, these so-called documents you have are inaccurate and pure fiction. If you decide to publish, I will pursue legal action against you and your company."

"That's what I thought you would say. We have independently confirmed the facts, sir, and we will publish. I suggest you contact your legal counsel about your own defense. Good day."

Plymel sat stunned. Why now? He had calculated this day would come, but not for a few more years. By then, he would have left the country and be sitting on a beach somewhere in the southern hemisphere that didn't extradite individuals to the US.

He picked his cell phone up from the desk, found the number he needed, and hit send.

***

The next morning found Kruger watching the building where P&G Global was located. He had been sitting in a Starbucks across the street since seven. His view was unobstructed as he watched the building's daytime inhabitants arrive. Most arrived on foot, some arrived by cab and a few of the high rollers arrived by chauffeured car. Abel Plymel was one of those individuals. Just before eight, a black Mercedes sedan, its windows tinted dark to preserve the privacy of the occupants, pulled to the curb in front of the building and stopped. Kruger watched as a man emerged from the right rear passenger side, stood for a moment, and then leaned over to say something to the driver. Plymel then shut the car door, turned toward the building, and walked inside.

From his seat in the café, Kruger used a digital camera to take several pictures of Plymel as he emerged. After Plymel disappeared into the building, Kruger reviewed the pictures on the small Nikon. One picture had a clear shot of the license plate of the Mercedes. Another one showed the driver after he had rolled down the window just before driving the car back into traffic. He removed the SDHC memory card from the camera, inserted it into his laptop, and proceeded to email the pictures to Charlie Craft. Hopefully Charlie would be able to determine the owner of the car and the identity of the driver.

Kruger sipped his coffee and opened a file on his laptop. The information contained in the file included P&G Global's official resume on Plymel. It was the non-official information Kruger wanted and Charlie had found quite a bit. Plymel was one of the founding principals of P&G Global. Prior to appearing on the high finance scene, he had led an obscure

128

life. There was only a brief mention of his parents and where he went to high school. An editorial note from Charlie indicated the information could not be independently confirmed. Kruger frowned when he read this part. After earning a degree in finance and banking, Plymel took a position with Kohlberg Kravis Roberts, Co. in the early eighties. After his involvement in KKR's leveraged buyout of RJR Nabisco in 1989, he left and founded P&G Global in 1990. Originally, P&G Global was a venture capitalist firm. The company grew and profited during the nineties, focusing on emerging internet-based companies. After the dot-com bubble burst, Plymel took his funds and transformed P&G into a company specializing in leveraged buyouts. Estimates of his personal net worth ranged from five hundred million to over 1.2 billion. Kruger didn't really believe that figure, after his discussion with JR.

He sat and stared at the building, thinking. *Why would a man worth over five hundred million have over sixty-million dollars in a secret cash fund? And, why would he be embezzling those funds from the company?* It didn't make sense to Kruger, but then he wasn't versed on high finance. However, he did understand basic greed. According to JR, Plymel had other secret cash funds that JR was not able to access. *How much were in those funds?* He glanced at his watch. Sharon Crawford would arrive with the search warrant in less than an hour.

His laptop dinged with the receipt of a new email. It was from an email account he knew to be JR. The message contained the link to the *NYT* article and an online news service called the *Insider.* Kruger smiled.

When he finished the *NYT* article, he clicked on the link to the *Insider* and found basically the same information. In essence, they both summarized the first round of files JR had supplied from Plymel's computer. The plan was to release the stolen files over the course of several days. The first round accused Plymel of insider trading and staging the incident in front of his building seven months ago. The *NYT* article implied there was a connection, but did not speculate on the why. It merely stated that their ongoing investigation would determine any ties. The reporter at the *NYT* also noted an attempt had been made to get a statement from Plymel. But he had refused, threatening a lawsuit if the article was printed.

Kruger smiled. The plan was coming together.

Sharon Crawford entered the café, saw where he was sitting, and walked to the table. Kruger stood and gave her a brief hug. "Thanks for getting here early, Sharon."

"No problem, Sean. The paperwork is here in my briefcase." She smiled, gazed at Kruger for a few seconds and sighed. "Has he arrived this morning?"

"Yeah, about thirty minutes ago. He was later than usual. He probably had a sleepless night."

Sharon Crawford was in her mid-thirties, a ten-year veteran of the FBI's forensic accounting department. She and Kruger had worked several cases together over the years and knew each other quite well. He found her to be intelligent and highly skilled at her job. A job he would have found tedious and boring. She was slender and tall, an inch shorter than Kruger. She wore her dark-brown hair short, which accentuated her slightly oval face and hazel eyes. During work hours she was professional, wore little make up, and had a stern demeanor with blocky unflattering glasses.

One night, after successfully concluding a case, they had had dinner together. The glasses were gone; she wore a hint of makeup and was fun to be around. When asked about the contrast, she said, "When I first started with the agency, I wasn't taken seriously. After all, who ever heard of a female forensic CPA? A friend suggested I change my appearance to fit the stereotype of an accountant. It worked and I've been doing it ever since."

Since then, Kruger and Sharon had seen each other socially whenever he was in the Washington DC area. With his growing feelings for Stephanie, he wasn't sure where the relationship with Sharon was headed. Today, she was in her accountant disguise: dark-gray pantsuit with an open-collar silk blouse, black low-heel shoes, and a black leather computer bag on her shoulder.

She handed him the search warrant, which he reviewed and placed in his left inside suit coat pocket. He checked his emails one more time to see if Charlie had replied to his inquiry on Plymel's car. He had.

The car was registered to a leasing company owned by P&G Global. Okay, nothing there. The driver was identified as an ex-cop, currently working for a multinational security company. Kruger was familiar with the security firm; they were professional and expensive. Apparently Plymel was taking no chances after the incident seven months ago.

He looked back out the window of the café and saw the final members of his party arriving. NYPD Detective Preston Alvarez walked into café, followed by two uniformed officers. Alvarez saw Kruger, waved, turned to the uniformed officers, and said something. Both nodded and left the coffee shop. Alvarez looked weary. His slightly wrinkled dark-blue suit indicated he had been at work for awhile. Kruger shook his hand, "Thanks for coming Preston. Want some coffee while we go over our plan?"

Nodding, Alvarez said, "Yeah, I would. It's already been a long day."

As they sat down, Kruger introduced Sharon to the detective. "Preston, would you review your findings about this case for Sharon?"

Alvarez spoke with a slight accent Kruger couldn't place. Perhaps a combination of the variety of New York City's cultures—it was hard to tell. Alvarez nodded. "I thought the story we were getting from Plymel was BS from the start. So I did a little checking. The two ex-military guys he said were his guards weren't licensed to carry. Both had Glock nine-millimeters. I found a few witnesses who said they saw a man pulled from a Suburban and pushed into the building. This was about thirty minutes prior to the shooting. But they couldn't identify him from the security camera picture. Both witnesses were too far away. Then we had the security guard at the front desk tell us about the guy being pushed into the elevator. Two hours later, he has amnesia and can't remember? Give me a break."

"Well that confirms what my source told me," said Kruger looking back at the building. "Adds more credibility to his story."

Alvarez said, "Did you find the guy, Sean?"

Kruger nodded.

"Where is he?"

Pointing to the west, Kruger said, "Out there somewhere. I've promised him I would keep his location confidential for the moment."

Alvarez smiled. "Okay, I can live with that. You mentioned on the phone about new evidence?"

Sharon Crawford said, "Plymel's source of funding for many of his buyouts is questionable. Preliminary data shows he's been using shell companies to buy up shares of his target companies prior to announcing the takeover. Once the announcements are made and the target company shares skyrocket, the shell companies sell the shares. He uses those profits to help pay for the takeover. The SEC defines that as insider trading. There's more money involved, but the source of those funds are suspicious."

Alvarez looked at Crawford and then at Kruger. "What do you mean *suspicious*?"

Kruger shrugged. Crawford shook her head. "We don't know. The only information we have is circumstantial. But, the insider trading gave us enough to get a search warrant for their computer records."

"Is Crigler involved with this?" said Alvarez.

"We have no evidence or even a suggestion anyone else at P&G Global is involved, but that doesn't mean anything at the moment," said Kruger. "I've known the guy for a long time. He's an asshole. But, a criminal?" Kruger shook his head. "He still had enough political pull to get me assigned to this case. My guess is he suspects Plymel's doing something illegal and using us to take him down. Crigler would want to keep his image clean, staying above the fray. He'd be the shining knight who saved P&G Global from the scoundrel Plymel. Afterward, he'd take control of the company."

Alvarez laughed and shook his head. "Sounds like those soap operas my wife likes to watch."

Kruger didn't laugh but frowned. "Crigler can be dangerous, and he's not above hiring someone to find our fugitive. We have reasons to believe he already has. A sergeant at Bragg was caught looking into the fugitive's military file. One the fugitive couldn't get to when he was erasing his past. It was highly classified." Kruger glanced at his watch. "Well, we're wasting daylight. Let's get this done."

CHAPTER 19

New York City

Even before the elevator doors were completely open on the thirty-fourth floor, Kruger was out and walking purposely toward the reception desk. He was followed by Sharon Crawford, Detective Alvarez, and four uniformed NYPD officers. The receptionist looked up from her desk, her eyes widening as Kruger shoved his ID in her face.

"I'm agent Sean Kruger with the FBI. We have a search warrant for these premises. Please back away from your desk and leave everything as is. Everyone within these offices will immediately assemble here and remain here." Nodding at the uniformed officers, who stood on both sides of him, he continued, "These officers with the New York Police Department will assist in gathering everyone and escorting them to this location."

Leaning over her desk, Kruger said in a calm, stern voice, "You will accompany me to Abel Plymel's office." She blinked several times and lifted a handset from a phone on her desk. Kruger took the handset from her hand. "Now"— he looked at the nameplate on her desk—"Cynthia." She continued to stare, wide eyed. Finally after a few moments, she stood and walked to a hall on the left side of the reception area. Kruger turned to the uniformed officers. "Gentlemen, please help everyone find their way to the lobby."

Kruger, Sharon, and Alvarez followed closely as Cynthia walked down the hall. She stopped at a large door and raised her fist to knock. Before she could, Kruger stepped in front of her, opened the door, and proceeded inside. Plymel was sitting behind his desk, deep in discussions with two men sitting in wingback chairs facing him.

Kruger walked quickly to the large desk, his credentials out. "Sean Kruger, FBI." Reaching inside his suit coat pocket, he pulled out an envelope. "I have a search warrant for this office and all computer files. Please stand and step away from the desk."

Plymel stood. "How dare you. This is a private meeting. My lawyer will need to be involved before you can search this premise."

Kruger held the search warrant in his hand and shook his head. "Doesn't work that way. A federal judge signed it this morning. If you resist, Detective Alvarez will place you under arrest. Now stand back from the desk." He turned to the other men and said, "You two need to go directly to the reception area." Both men stared at Kruger with the same wide-eyed expression as the receptionist. But without a word, each rose from their chairs and hustled out of the office.

Alvarez stood next to Kruger and smiled slightly, enjoying the moment.

Plymel glared at Kruger. "Get out of my office. I'm calling my attorney." He picked up the handset on his desk phone and started to punch in numbers.

Kruger stepped up to the front of the desk, turned, and nodded at Alvarez, who proceeded around the desk with his handcuffs ready. Kruger leaned across the desk, grabbed the handset from Plymel just before Alvarez grabbed his other arm and applied the cuffs.

Kruger said, "You are now under arrest for resisting a

dutifully served search warrant." He turned to Sharon. "Start looking for the laptop and related files." Watching Plymel's reaction, he noted a slight widening of the eyes, which darted to the left then returned to stare at Kruger.

Plymel's face grew crimson red, and he said through clinched teeth, "You have no idea who you are dealing with, agent. You are making a seriously huge mistake."

Leaning forward and placing his palms on the desk, Kruger said, "Is that a threat, Mr. Plymel? Did you just threaten an agent of the Federal Bureau of Investigation?"

Glaring at Kruger, Plymel shook his head. "No, but you are making a mistake. I have nothing to hide. This could have been handled in a much more civil manner."

"Doubtful. You would have delayed the investigation indefinitely with lawyers."

Alvarez led the now handcuffed man to a corner of the office. Kruger watched Plymel as Sharon searched the desk. His eyes did not deviate from her as she retrieved the laptop from a drawer in the huge desk. Kruger could see Plymel stiffen when Sharon gained access to the files on the computer. "I have access. Sean."

Alvarez leaned in and whispered in Plymel's ear, "I found out who your dead security guard was. His background wasn't what you claimed, was it?" Plymel turned to face him and stared hard. A slight smile came to Alvarez's lips. "You lied to a police officer. Not a very smart thing to do, Abel."

Plymel's breathing grew rapid as he turned his head and once again stared at Sharon working on the laptop. Alvarez's smile broadened. Plymel was furious, so he pushed him a little further. "What are they going to find on that computer, Abel? Something you don't want the world to know? That you're a fraud and this company is just a house of cards ready to collapse?" Alvarez felt the man stiffen. Plymel didn't turn around this time but continued to stare at Sharon.

Ten minutes later, she raised her head from the screen, smiled, and said, "I believe this is what we need. Detective, could you ask a couple of your officers to box up the contents of this desk?" Alvarez, nodded, made Plymel sit on one of the sofas in the office, and left to retrieve a pair of the uniformed police officers. She said loudly to Kruger, who was in the adjacent conference room, "Are there any filing cabinets in there?"

Kruger walked back into the office and shook his head. He saw Plymel sitting on the sofa and walked over to him. As he approached, he noticed Plymel breathing rapidly. His face was crimson and he was focused on Sharon. Standing directly in front of Plymel, to block his view, Kruger said, "I read the article about you in this morning's *New York Times*. It had a few unflattering things to say about you. Care to comment?"

Plymel shook his head. "I want my lawyer. This is an outrage. He'll have your badge, agent—so help me, he will."

Kruger laughed. "Do you know how many times I've heard that cliché? Guess what? I still have it." He paused and turned to see Sharon placing the laptop into a storage box one of the uniformed officers had found for her. Turning his attention back to Plymel, he said, "I was going to take the cuffs off and leave you here. But, I changed my mind. I can just image how embarrassing it will be for you as we pass through the crowd of associates gathered in the reception area. Then we'll have to stand there while we wait for the elevator. Glad I'm not you." Plymel now focused his attention on Kruger. His eyes grew wide as he realized the situation was real.

A tall man in his sixties appeared at the office door. "What is the meaning of this invasion?"

Kruger looked at the newcomer. Alvarez and two patrol officers appeared behind the man. Kruger said, "Don't get involved sir. This only involves Mr. Plymel."

Alton Crigler stared at Plymel and then at Kruger. "Why is Mr. Plymel in handcuffs?"

Kruger handed the search warrant to the man. "I will repeat myself only one more time. Do not get involved."

Crigler scanned the search warrant and handed it back to Kruger. "Your paperwork does not appear to be in order.

Leave everything where it is and remove yourselves from this office immediately."

Kruger smiled. "Nice try. The search warrant is in order. If you continue to interfere, I'll have you placed under arrest as well. Are you sure that's what you want to do Mr. Crigler?"

Knowing his bluff had been called, Crigler shook his head and left. Alvarez and his two officers reentered the room. The two patrol officers went to the desk and started loading storage boxes with the content of Plymel's desk. Alvarez stood next to Kruger and said in a low voice, "Sorry about that. He claimed he was with the attorney general's office at one time, demanded to know what was going on."

Kruger chuckled. "He was. At one time he was the deputy attorney general, maybe five or six years ago. That little display was for show only. He knew the warrant was legit. He's probably in his office laughing his ass off right now."

As Plymel was led through the reception area toward the elevators, the associates of P&G Global grew quiet. Plymel's hands were cuffed behind his back and his head was down staring at the floor. Crigler was nowhere to be seen. Kruger figured he was on the phone with the firm's lawyers. As one of the patrol officers held the elevator door open, they all got in for the ride to the first floor. No one spoke during the descent as Plymel just stared at the floor.

As the group exited the elevator, two men crossed the lobby rushing toward them. Kruger said, "Lawyers. Everyone just keep moving." Two of the officers moved in front of the group trying to run interference. Alvarez and the two remaining officers were carrying evidence boxes while Kruger and Crawford held each of Plymel's arms.

The older lawyer stopped in front of them. "What is the meaning of this?"

Kruger did not break stride and kept leading the group toward the front entrance of the building. The younger lawyer tried to stop them by placing his hand on Kruger's chest. Kruger looked the younger lawyer in the eyes and with a menacing tone said, "Are you sure you want to do that, son? Remove your hand or you'll join him in cuffs." He watched as the younger man swallowed hard and his eyes grew wide.

The older lawyer placed his hand on the younger ones shoulder. "We're Mr. Plymel's attorneys. Please explain why he is in handcuffs."

Sharon said, "He threatened a federal officer and is now under arrest. If you wish to know more, you can discuss it after he is booked. Now, I suggest you both back off and stop interfering." Both lawyers backed away and the group walked out of the building into a crowd of reporters.

Kruger smiled. His plan was working. He had sent JR an email just before they left Starbucks. JR was to inform his contact at the *Insider* that Plymel was to be arrested that morning. Then the natural order of a media circus would take shape in front of the building.

Plymel groaned as they walked into the crowd. Questions were being shouted, but Plymel kept his head down and ignored all of them. The din of the reporters was deafening, but it was not Kruger's first time to navigate through this type of crowd. He stared ahead, remained quiet, and kept moving forward. Cameras flashed and microphones were shoved in their faces, but they kept their silence and led Plymel to one of the waiting patrol cars, its light bar flashing. Once Plymel was secured in the back seat, Kruger closed the door and tapped the ceiling twice. After Alvarez got in the front passenger side, the car sped away. Kruger and Sharon walked to the black Ford Taurus, which had been parked behind the patrol car. The reporters calmed down, backed off, and started dispersing.

One of the uniformed officers handed her the box containing the laptop and she placed it in the back seat. Kruger settled into the passenger seat while she got behind the steering wheel. After touching a switch, the bureau car's hidden emergency lights started flashing. She eased the car from the curb and followed the patrol car toward Manhattan Central Booking.

Staring out the window, she was concentrating on maneuvering through traffic. After a few moments, she said, "Well, everything happened just like you said it would."

Nodding, Kruger smiled. "Yeah, we should find out if Plymel's in this by himself. I doubt it. Were you around when Crigler worked at the Justice Department?"

"Yes, but I never had any contact with him."

"You didn't miss anything. I always wondered why he and the director were so tight. I just learned this week they were college buddies. I really expected a more convincing protest from him about Plymel's arrest." Kruger paused and said, more to himself than Sharon, "He definitively wants Plymel out of the way."

"What's next, Sean? We really don't have anything to hold Plymel on except resisting arrest, and that charge is pretty flimsy. His lawyers will probably beat us to Central Booking."

"I'm counting on it. We have forty-eight hours to hold him without pressing charges." He glanced at his watch, "Which should give us plenty of time to turn up the heat."

CHAPTER 20

New York City

After his feeble attempt to stop Plymel's arrest, Crigler returned to his office and waited an hour before placing a call to the company's law firm. He was connected to the managing partner without delay.

"Good morning, Alton. What can I do for you today?"

"I will assume you have already heard about the incident we had here this morning."

Wesley Elliot paused only a moment before answering, "Yes and I read a very disturbing article this morning in the *New York Times*. Very unpleasant. Is this call about engaging our services to handle Abel's indiscretions?"

Crigler smiled. "No, we need to divorce ourselves from Mr. Plymel on these matters. P&G Global, and any company associated with P&G Global, cannot be seen as endorsing his behavior in any way."

"I see."

"Good."

"How would you suggest Elliot, Elliot, and Brimmer handle any request by Mr. Plymel, should he call us for representation? I need to mention, one of our partners was already involved this morning."

"I understand, but I'm sure you have agreements with various other law firms in town to handle, uh, let's say, conflicts of interest."

"We do."

"Good, when Abel calls, please use your discretion and suggest one of those firms."

"Very well. That's how we will handle it. I appreciate your call, Alton. Several of the partners were concerned about how we could handle his—"

The phone went dead. Silence. Crigler frowned, laid the phone down on his desk, stood, and walked out of his office. Outside in the cube farm, voices could be heard cussing. Heads were popping up, looking around, and asking if their neighbor's phone was working. His assistant rushed to his side. "Our computer system just went down. Since the phones are tied to our network, they're down as well. No email or internet connections. I'm going to IT and check. Hopefully they can tell us how long it will be."

Crigler nodded. "Thank you, Bob. Make sure they understand that our business depends on communication with the market. The longer we're down, the more money we lose." His assistant turned and practically ran toward the IT department.

Returning to his desk, he stopped and realized too many incidents had occurred too close together. The *New York Times* article about Plymel, the search warrant, and now the computer system going down—was it the work of the man Plymel was looking for? His office door opened and Bob leaned in. "IT department just told me we're having a denial-of-service attack on our server, whatever that means."

"How long before they can fix it?" said Crigler.

"He didn't say, he was too busy."

Crigler stood and moved toward his office door. "Maybe he'll talk to me." He left his office and walked to the IT department. As soon as he opened the door, he knew the situation was grim. The glassed-in room where the company's rows of servers were kept appeared to have a thin cloud floating within its confines. He noted several men rushing from server to server, opening panels and disconnecting cables. He saw the head of the IT department at his desk on a cell phone, furiously writing notes on a pad. Walking over to the desk, he stood in front of it and remained silent as the man finished the call.

Looking up, Irving Greer raised one finger indicating he was almost done with the call. "Okay, I think I have it. I'll call you back after we do this." He ended the call and looked up at Crigler. "System's fried. Whoever did this was good, very good. That was our tech at Microsoft. He's only heard of this type of attack once or twice."

Crigler didn't like what he was hearing. "How long before they're working again?"

Greer shook his head. "I don't know. Could be awhile. We have to replace a lot of equipment and rebuild the system. It might be two or three days."

"That's unacceptable, Irving. We lose money every second those machines don't work."

"It may be unacceptable, but there isn't a lot we can do except install all new servers and work all night to rebuild the systems. That's if you want it back by late tomorrow."

"Do it. Bring in extra help if you need to. How many transactions were lost?"

"Everything from today. We back up a little after noon and once again after the market closes. The attack hit just before the noon backup."

Crigler was silent. This had to stop. "Very well, keep me informed on your progress. Just get it done as rapidly as possible." He walked back to his office, shut the door, and started making calls on his cell phone informing the board of directors. By the time he was finished, he had the board's support and was named acting CEO. Plymel was suspended and after an audit could face possible criminal charges.

His next call was to Adam Weber.

***

Upon his arrival, Weber was shown into Crigler's office at three in the afternoon. By 4:30 p.m., Plymel's assistant had been interviewed and escorted out of the building. At fifteen minutes before five, all associates, except those in the IT department, were called to a meeting in the main conference room.

Crigler stood at the head of the main conference table. The chairs around the table were occupied by senior vice presidents and their assistants. Everyone else stood against the walls. The room was eerily quiet. Crigler smiled slightly, his normally booming voice low and dripping with concern as he said, "I will make this as brief as possible. There are a lot of rumors floating around about the events of today. Mr. Plymel has been arrested on suspicion of insider trading. Our computers have been attacked by outside sources, and maintaining contact with our clients is a challenge. Suffice it to say, all of these events threaten the very existence of our company. However, the board of directors has been kept informed and made several management changes effective at five this afternoon."

He glanced over his shoulder at Weber, who had been standing behind him. "Adam Weber will be the new head of security. I've known Mr. Weber for over twenty years. He was a US Marshal for fifteen of those years and now owns his own security company. He will be responsible for making sure we do not repeat the events of today going forward. The board also made several top management decisions. Abel Plymel will be taking a leave of absence while the accusations against him are addressed. In the meantime, I have been named acting CEO until Mr. Plymel's issues are resolved. Finally, we expect the computer systems to be operational again in the morning. Please continue to use your personal cell phones to maintain contact with your clients until our phone system starts working again. Are there any questions?"

The question was answered by a deafening silence. Of

the forty individuals sitting and standing in the room, no one spoke. Crigler looked around the room, nodded, and said, "Thank you for your support during this period. Be careful on your way home tonight. We will see everyone tomorrow." With that statement, the meeting ended and everyone quietly ambled out of the room. Crigler returned to his office with Weber following.

As soon as he closed the door, Crigler said, "Find out what the FBI knows and what the charges are against Plymel. The lead agent is Sean Kruger. I didn't recognize the woman. Also, see if you can find out who's been feeding the information to the *New York Times*. My guess is, our missing computer expert. He's probably responsible for the computers crashing today as well."

Weber nodded.

Crigler frowned. "I doubt Plymel bothered to look at the man's background before he was fired. Have you made any progress on finding him?"

Weber shrugged. "I just got back from checking the companies your intern found. They all turned out to be dead ends. I have one left, but the guy I need to see is out of town."

"Where is this one located?"

"Missouri."

Crigler was quiet for a few moments, then said, "Kruger lives in Missouri. I wonder…" Crigler turned and stared out the window in his office, his finger tapping his lips. Several moments passed. The only sound Weber could hear was the hiss from the air-conditioning vent. Crigler turned back around and said, "Go back to Missouri and dig around a little. It may just be a coincidence, but I doubt it. Kruger's probably found the guy and is using him against us."

"It's a possibility."

"What do you know about him?"

"Works in the Criminal Investigation Division as a profiler. He's not a team player and has a reputation for being a cowboy. He works alone most of the time and reports directly to an assistant director. He also has a tendency to bend the rules, sort of like me."

Crigler smiled. "Do you know anything about his personal life?"

Weber shook his head. "No, all I know is his wife abandoned him and their son when the boy was about a year old. That was eighteen years ago. I've never heard anything about his getting married again. Like I said, he's a loner."

"See if you can find out what he knows. Stay in touch, I need to be updated on your progress daily."

Weber nodded and left.

Crigler turned the chair back toward the window and stood up. After walking over to it, he clasped his hands behind his back and stared at the Manhattan skyline. Five minutes later, he smiled and returned to his desk.

CHAPTER 21

Washington DC

Tall and slender, Mary Lawson's heritage was Jamaican, French, and for attitude, a bit of Louisiana Cajun. After graduating in the top ten from Columbia University Law School, she had spent her entire career at the Justice Department. Now as the deputy director of the Office of Violence Against Women, she was at the pinnacle of her career.

There was only one man in her life, and they had both chosen career over family. Her career was time consuming, as was his. They saw each other when he was in town, which recently had been an infrequent event. While it wasn't a perfect situation, she accepted it as their reality.

She had not heard from him for several weeks and it always brightened her day when they spoke. But the call from Joseph yesterday had been a surprise. While the information he had requested was easy to find, she was concerned about the purpose of his request.

She was sitting at her desk trying to decide what to tell Joseph, when her cell phone chirped. She smiled. "Two calls from you in as many days, I love it."

Joseph laughed. "I need to call more often, don't I?"

"Yes you do—but life gets in the way sometimes."

He was silent for a moment. "I know. I hope we don't regret we allowed it to do so."

"We probably will…" She hesitated for a moment. "I made a few phone calls. Exactly, why are you interested in Weber?"

"Doing a little research for a friend. Why?"

"Before I tell you, have you ever heard of an individual named Abel Plymel?"

Joseph hesitated and said, "I've heard of him. Why?"

"He's the CEO of a very large investment company called P&G Global located in New York City, very well connected politically, likes to hire retired Washington insiders. Plus he's very rich. There was a story in the *New York Times* this morning accusing Plymel of various federal crimes, including insider trading, fraud, and murder for hire. My source tells me Weber is currently working for P&G Global as a consultant."

"Interesting."

"Interesting? Really, Joseph, that's all you can say? I've known you a long time, so don't give me *interesting*. What's going on?"

Immediately regretting not being truthful with her, he said, "I apologize. I'm more familiar with Plymel than I care to be, and I'm aware of his transgressions. But I didn't know about Weber's association with P&G Global. It explains a lot."

"Remember, you called me. What does it explain, Joseph?"

Joseph was silent for a moment, trying to determine how much to tell her. "I can't tell you everything, but I've learned that Weber is trying to find a friend of mine. My friend has a history with Plymel. Not a good history either. You just connected several dots in a very big puzzle."

"Who's the friend, Joseph?"

"I'm afraid I can't tell you."

Mary was a quick study. "Your friend wouldn't be the man who killed the security guard in front of Plymel's building and then disappeared, would he?"

"That's part of what I can't tell you."

"Harboring a fugitive is a federal crime, Joseph."

"I'm aware of that, but there are always two sides to every story, Mary. I have evidence my friend was acting in self-defense. It's complicated."

"Indulge me."

"Very well, pick me up at Reagan National at seven. We'll have dinner and I'll explain everything."

***

Something was wrong. Kruger looked at his watch. It was past four in the afternoon and Plymel's lawyers had not arrived at Manhattan Central Booking yet. He and Sharon were in a conference room waiting. Sharon was using the time to examine Plymel's computer, while Kruger paced. What the hell was going on? Experience with high-profile criminals always included lawyers showing up before their clients were processed. Plymel's hadn't. His cell phone vibrated. "Where are you?"

Joseph said, "I'm flying to Washington DC to meet someone who might be able to help us. I should arrive by seven or so. What's going on there?"

Kruger smiled and said, "Tell Mary hello for me. Plymel's lawyers haven't showed up yet. I think P&G may have cut him loose and he's on his own. We have less than forty-eight hours to find what we need, or we have to release him. Sharon's working on the laptop, but it's going to take time to build a case against him."

"Can you meet me in DC tomorrow?"

"Yes."

"I'm in Chicago changing gates right now. Tonight I'm meeting Mary for dinner; she found some very interesting information, which may help us. Let me know where you're staying and I'll pick you up in the morning."

The call ended and Kruger stopped pacing. He turned to Sharon, "I need to go to DC. Are you good by yourself here?"

She looked at him and shook her head. "Yes, Dad, I'll be fine."

Kruger chuckled. "I deserved that. Sorry. I meant to say: I need to go to DC, keep looking into the laptop, and call me if Plymel's attorney shows up."

"That I can do. I'll email you a summary of my findings. Be careful, Sean. From what I'm finding in this computer, these people do not respect authority."

He stared at her, trying to decide if she needed to accompany him or stay in New York. Finally, after several moments, he said, "I'll be careful. You do the same."

She nodded and went back to the laptop. As he left the room, he had a nagging feeling about the situation. As he walked down the hall, he stopped, briefly undecided about Sharon staying in New York. Shaking his head at the premonition, he left the building and took a cab to the airport.

***

Joseph sipped his coffee and smiled. "Dining with you is one of life's great pleasures. Tell me again, why we don't do it more often?" They had just finished eating at one of Joseph's favorite places, a bistro near the Chevy Chase, Maryland–District of Columbia dividing line. He liked it because it reminded him of Paris. The place was small and intimate, the food was excellent, and they had one of the better wine lists in the area. It was also out of the mainstream DC circuit, and he felt comfortable no one would see him.

Mary Lawson said, "You know why Joseph." She patted his hand and changed the subject. "I've done a little more inquiring into P&G Global."

"Oh." He smiled. "Enlighten me."

"Did you know that Alton Crigler was now the CEO at P&G?"

Joseph's eyebrows rose. "Since when?"

"Late this afternoon. It seems the board of directors are embarrassed about the allegations surrounding Plymel. They're distancing the firm from him and cutting all ties."

Joseph sipped his coffee. "Did you ever hear why Crigler left the attorney general's office?"

"No, but the general consensus is he was passed over for the top spot too many times. He left for the private sector and more money." Mary shrugged. "Good riddance. I didn't care for the man. He had a mean streak, especially toward women."

Joseph was silent. He stared into the now empty coffee cup. "He's a devious man."

It was now Mary's turn to be silent. After a moment she said, "Do you know him?"

He shook his head. "Not personally, but Sean Kruger knows him and called him that several times. He was glad to see him leave."

She nodded. "Most men in this town are either deceitful or stupid, present company excluded."

Joseph smiled and raised his recently refilled cup of coffee to her. "I'll take that as a compliment."

"Good, it was meant that way. What did Sean mean about being devious?"

"I'm not really sure. He wouldn't go into detail, he just said, the man had a narcissistic personality and the country was safer without him in public service."

Mary laughed. "I love Sean's simple explanations. He said more in those few words than most politicians say all year."

Joseph nodded. "He does have a way of cutting through the BS." Pausing briefly, he continued, "I need you to do something for us, Mary."

She smiled. "Time to pay for dinner. What would you have me do, my love?"

He smiled back. "We need everything you can find out about Abel Plymel before he started P&G Global."

"What am I looking for?"

Joseph shrugged. "Not sure, Sean wouldn't elaborate, but he said there's a gap in the man's background."

She frowned. "A gap. Really? What kind of gap?"

Shaking his head, he said, "Don't know."

"How much time do I have?"

"As quickly as you can. Plymel can only be held forty-eight hours. Sean thinks events will start escalating rapidly tomorrow."

She looked at him and smiled mischievously. "Do we have time to go back to my apartment? Or—do I need to start right now?"

"I believe we have time."

***

"Thanks for waiting, Brittany." Sharon Crawford smiled as she signed the transfer of evidence form the young female police officer had handed her.

"Not a problem. We've been shorthanded and I needed the overtime. Are we still on for dinner?"

Sharon smiled and nodded. "Definitely, I need a little downtime after today."

Brittany Hardy was a seven-year veteran with the NYPD doing temporary desk duty in the evidence room after recovering from injuries sustained in a shoot-out with would-be bank robbers. Her partner had been killed, and she suffered a bullet in her left thigh. She stood and grimaced slightly.

Sharon said, "Does it still hurt?"

Brittany chuckled. "No, but when I sit for long periods, my leg protests. Doctors tell me the hitch may never go away. I can live with it. Better than the alternative." Brittany was several inches shorter than Sharon Crawford and had barely met the height requirement for the department. She wore her shoulder-length brunette hair up while on duty. After she returned from locking Plymel's laptop up in the evidence room, she said, "Where do you want to eat?"

"There's a really nice bistro across from my hotel. You could be a dear and drive. That way I don't have to take a cab."

Brittany's hazel eye's sparkled and she said, "Let me change out of this uniform and we'll get out of here."

An hour later, they were sitting at the bistro's bar, sipping wine as they waited for a table to open. Sharon said, "How long has it been since we worked together, Brittany?"

"Couple of years. Time flies, doesn't it?"

Sharon nodded. "Yes, it does."

"Are you still seeing Sean Kruger?"

Sharon was quiet for a few moments. "No."

"That's too bad. He's cute."

Smiling, Sharon nodded. "That he is. But, it's hard to maintain a relationship when you're twelve hundred miles apart. Are you seeing anybody right now?"

Brittany nodded. "Yeah, he's an EMT with the fire department."

"Is it serious?"

"Maybe." She held up her hand and showed Sharon the engagement ring.

Sharon smiled brightly and leaned over to hug her friend. "Congratulations. Have you set a date?"

Brittany shook her head. "No, I'm still trying to decide if I'm going to stay with the department." She patted her leg. "This got my attention and I would really like to have a more consistent schedule. We barely see each other some weeks. He's on, I'm off, or the reverse."

"Yeah, you sometimes have to wonder if it's worth it."

Brittany frowned and looked at her friend. "Regrets?"

She shrugged. "Maybe. I think Sean and I could have made it. At least I would like to have tried." She stared ahead at all the liquor bottles behind the bar, not seeing any of them.

Brittany was quiet for awhile. "I'm sorry."

Sharon smiled, then turned her attention back to her friend. "No worries. It just didn't happen." She paused. "I'm really happy for you, Brit."

It was close to ten before Sharon stood in front of her hotel room door. She slid the keycard into the door lock, heard the click, and started opening the door.

A strong hand clamped around her mouth as the hotel room door was shoved in by her assailant's other hand.

CHAPTER 22

Washington, DC

Kruger's phone vibrated just after eight the next morning. Normally immediately alert when he woke, his dream about Stephanie left him disorientated. Barely able to open one eye, he saw the caller ID was Sharon's cell phone. Smiling slightly, he said, "Kruger."

A gravelly voice said, "Your friend wasn't very helpful last night. I hope you're smarter. Drop the inquiry into Plymel or you'll end up like your friend."

Kruger eyes widened and his heart raced. "Who is this?" Silence. He looked at the phone's screen. The call had ended. "Shit," he mumbled as he hit the "last call" icon. It went straight to voice mail. He repeated the call—again, voice mail. He did a quick internet search on his phone and called the hotel were Sharon was staying.

"It's a great day at the Marriott, how can I direct your call?"

"Sharon Crawford, room fourteen-oh-five."

"One moment please."

The phone rang twenty times without an answer. Kruger ended the call and redialed the Marriot. When it was answered, he said, "My name is Sean Kruger. I'm with the FBI. I need to speak to the day manager immediately."

Silence was his answer. Finally, the young lady said, "Just a moment. I'll get her."

Less than fifteen seconds later, a voice said, "This is Marilyn Kramer. How may I help you?"

"Ms. Kramer, my name is Sean Kruger. I'm an agent with the FBI. A fellow agent is staying in room fourteen-oh-five. She's not answering her cell phone or her room phone. I must insist you go to her room and check on her safety."

"Just a moment."

The phone was silent as he waited. After several minutes, Marilyn Kramer returned to the phone. "Mr. Kruger, I'm not getting an answer. Are you sure she's in her room?"

Shaking his head, Kruger said, "No, I'm not sure she's in her room. That's why I'm calling. She may be in danger. Ms. Kramer, I really need you to check her room. Take an assistant, knock on the door. If she doesn't answer, open the door and make sure she's okay. If everything is fine, I'll apologize for the inconvenience. Otherwise, you might be a big help."

"Very well, Mr. Kruger. Please give me your number. I'll call you back. It might take me a few minutes."

Kruger gave her his cell phone number and ended the call.

His next call was to Joseph, postponing their meeting. An excruciating hour later, Kruger's cell phone vibrated. "Kruger."

"Sean, its Alvarez. Are you in New York?"

"No, DC. Why?"

"Get back to New York as fast as possible?"

***

The hallway was empty, except for police tape and uniformed police officers. After showing his badge and ID, Kruger was allowed within the perimeter and escorted to the room. Preston Alvarez appeared at the door and stopped him. "Sean, you don't want to go in there."

Kruger glared at Alvarez, pushed him aside, and entered the hotel room. His first impression was total chaos. Sharon lay diagonally across the mattress, sightless eyes wide open, fixed on the ceiling. She was fully dressed, except for what appeared to be rips in her clothing from a struggle. The contents of her suitcase were scattered across the bed, with the suitcase ripped and cut apart. The sofa was overturned, cushions cut, and thrown against the wall under the window. Her computer case was lying on the floor, the contents scattered, but no computer.

Kruger looked at the body on the bed. She was a friend, a co-worker, and at one time a lover. Someone he had been intimate with. He took a deep breath, slowly let it out, and said in a low, barely controlled voice, "Was she raped?"

Alvarez shook his head. "No, she doesn't appear to have been. The ME said her neck was broken. She probably died instantly. This wasn't about her, Sean. She had something the killer wanted."

Kruger's eyes widened. "Where's her computer?"

"Not here."

"Abel Plymel! Damn. When was he released?"

Alvarez cocked his head to the side. "Didn't think of that. I'm not sure. Last I knew, he was still in custody."

Kruger took his cell phone out of his jacket pocket, searched for a number, and pressed the call icon. When the called was answered, he said, "This is Kruger. When did Abel Plymel's lawyers get him out?" He listened for a few moments then said, "Really? They didn't get there till nine this morning?" More silence as he listened. Finally he said, "Did Sharon place a computer in evidence?" He nodded. "Thanks." After ending the call, he turned to Alvarez. "Someone was looking for Plymel's computer. They didn't find it and killed her because of it. That's why I got the phone call this morning."

Alvarez said, "What phone call?"

Kruger took a deep breath. He let it out slowly and in a slightly shaky voice said, "The reason I called the hotel this morning was a phone call. A gravelly male voice said, 'Your friend wasn't very helpful last night. I hope you're smarter. Drop the inquiry into Plymel or you'll end up like your friend.'"

Alvarez nodded. "The hotel didn't call us. The station got a similar call, only the voice said an FBI agent needed assistance. We got here just as the hotel manager returned from the room. Apparently, she's not taking this well. They took her to the hospital just before I called you." Alvarez grew quiet and glanced at the body. Returning his attention back to Kruger, he said, "How long did you know her?"

Kruger's hard expression softened, his shoulders drooped, and he smiled slightly. "About five years. We worked a few cases together. I considered her a friend."

"Is there anyone we need to call? A husband or parent?"

Kruger shook his head. "She wasn't married." He paused. "She has a sister in California and her mom lives in Florida. Her mom's phone number should be in her cell phone. Not sure about the sister. They weren't very close. If you don't mind, I'll contact the mother. It's the least I can do."

Alvarez nodded. "Okay, I hate those calls anyway. But we haven't found a cell phone."

Kruger frowned and nodded. "My call originated from her cell phone. Whoever did this, took it." He paused and looked back at Sharon's body. "Someone's playing with us, Preston."

Alvarez nodded and looked toward the hotel room's door. "They're here, Sean." He took his friend by the arm. "Let's let them do their job."

Kruger glanced toward the door and saw the coroner's team in the doorway of the hotel room. They looked like they had somewhere else to be, so Kruger allowed Alvarez to lead him out of the room.

Once outside, he glanced down the hall and saw the

floor's exit door. He smiled at Alvarez. "I'll take the stairs." As soon as the door to the stairwell closed, he walked down half of a flight and leaned against the wall. His head slowly moved back until it touched the cinder block wall of the stairwell. He closed his eyes and a sudden wave of exhaustion and grief swept over him. He wiped away a tear with the back of his hand and just stood there. Whoever did this had made a mistake, a serious mistake. Now it was personal.

He stood there for several minutes not moving, just staring up the stairwell and thinking. Finally he started down the stairs, a determined look on his face.

***

Plymel sat in one of the interview rooms, his orange jumpsuit two sizes too large. A man in uniform stood by the door until Kruger entered. The guard left and closed the door behind him. Plymel's eyes grew wide, but his expression quickly changed to a glare and a slight smirk. "Come to apologize for the mistake?"

Kruger shook his head. "No."

"My lawyer was here. He said I'll be out this afternoon. Now if you don't mind, I have more important things to do than talk to you."

As Plymel stood, Kruger smiled. "I'm here to let you know that someone killed my partner last night." Plymel's expression remained neutral. "Currently, we don't have a suspect, but I've filed paperwork naming you as a person of interest in her death."

Plymel stared at Kruger, his eyes narrowing. He took a deep breath, spread his arms wide, and grinned. "I was here last night. A pretty tight alibi wouldn't you say, agent?"

"Oh, I didn't mean you personally killed her." He shook his head. "No, a man of your position has many ways of having it done for him. That's actually what I should have said."

Plymel laughed. "You're grasping at straws agent. I'm

just a simple businessman. I don't have those types of individuals working for me. Nor do I know any."

It was Kruger's turn to smile. He extracted a file from his computer bag, placed it on the desk, and opened it. Extracting the picture of JR and the security guard, he turned it around so Plymel could see. "Remember this man?" He said, tapping the image of JR with his finger. "He stole a lot of money from you. Money you'd stolen in the first place. The gentleman on his right was escorting him to a waiting SUV." Kruger stood so he could look Plymel in the eye. "What were your instructions to the big man? Take him out for coffee and a bagel? I don't think so."

Plymel stared at the photo, remaining quiet.

Kruger continued, "I know the background of the guard. He was a suspect in a murder case several years before this picture was taken. Yet you hired him. Why did you do that, Abel? You just said, you don't have those types of individuals working for you."

Plymel said, "I believe I'm done talking to you, agent, without my lawyer present."

"You really don't need your lawyer," said Kruger. "I'm done asking questions. You see, this isn't an interview. I'm just taking the opportunity to inform you of several important pieces of information. One, I know the truth about you. I know how much money you've stolen from your company and how you stole it. I also know it's no longer in your possession." He paused to watch Plymel's reaction. The man did not disappoint. Plymel blinked rapidly for several moments, but settled into a blank stare. "Two, the death of Agent Crawford was a big mistake. It's now personal. You don't know me, but I'm not someone you want looking into your affairs." He leaned forward and got within inches of Plymel's face. "Because, I'll find all the dirty laundry and you won't like the consequences."

Plymel's reaction to this information was more important to Kruger than anything the man could say. He watched closely as he finished talking. Once again, Plymel didn't disappoint. His eye's widened briefly, his breathing rate increased, and his cheeks flushed. But he recovered just as quickly and a bored expression appeared. "Really, agent, that's all you have? Just empty accusations with no evidence. I believe it is time to have my lawyer present and end this discussion."

Smiling, Kruger said, "Oh, I'm done." He paused and opened his computer bag. "My suggestion would be for your lawyer to check the new charges I filed against you this morning: conspiracy to commit murder and fraud." Smiling, he said, "Have a great day." He placed the file back in the computer bag and walked out of the room, leaving Plymel by himself. As he walked out, he nodded at the guard. "Thanks, I believe it worked. Keep me posted." The guard nodded and went in to escort Plymel back to his cell.

CHAPTER 23

Boulder, CO

"When did it happen, Joseph?" JR stared out the window of the bed and breakfast, the mountains in the distance unseen, his cell phone pressed tightly to his ear.

"Last night around ten. She was attacked as she opened her hotel door," said Joseph. "At least that's the prevailing theory. Her neck was broken and the room ransacked."

"They were looking for Plymel's computer, weren't they?"

"It appears so."

JR covered his eyes with his hand and was silent for a few moments. "Did they find it?"

"No, she'd checked it back into the evidence room. Her personal computer and cell phone are missing."

"Damn. Too many people are dying because of me. This has to stop, Joseph."

"JR, this wasn't your fault."

"Yeah, well, tell that to her."

Joseph was silent for several moments. "JR, I'm going to give you a little advice. This isn't a game anymore. These guys are playing for real. You can choose to blame yourself and whine about it, or you can get mad and do something. I've only known you for a short time, but I believe you'll do the right thing and help us stop them."

"How can I help?"

Joseph paused for a few moments. "Sean wants you to examine Plymel's laptop. He believes there's something incriminating to both Plymel and P&G Global on it."

"Makes sense. Do I need to go to New York?"

"No, we'll get the laptop to you. Sean and I both believe it's in everybody's best interest for you to stay where you are. As I told you earlier, someone figured out how to find you. My guess is the business license."

It was a logical assumption. Joseph and JR had formed a business arrangement based on JR providing computer security for Joseph's clients. Both companies shared the same office address. "It wouldn't have been that hard to find me. It's no secret I work with computers. You narrow it down and check out the business. I didn't think about it until just now."

"Don't beat yourself up about it, but we're not taking any chances. What do you need from the laptop?"

"The hard drive. A copy won't do."

"Okay, we'll get it to you. I'll let you know when it's on its way."

The call ended and JR continued to stare out the window. P&G would have to rebuild their computer system from backups, and it would take a day or so. If his guess was correct, they might be testing the rebuilt system fairly soon. Time for a nap, a little hiking with Mia, and then he would work through the night.

***

Exhausted from the day's activities, Mia fell asleep shortly after eleven. Quietly leaving their bed, JR went to the living area of the suite and opened his laptop. Five minutes later, he was in the newly rebuilt P&G Global server system.

As he suspected, they had used backup and his backdoor was still active. He wasn't sure how it reflected on their IT department, but he was glad they had missed it. First thing was to open a new backdoor and close the old one. As he examined the newly rebuilt system, he found more security holes. His already low opinion of their IT department declined further with each new security problem he discovered. Once his survey of the system was complete, he posted the security holes to a hacker blog site. P&G's IT department would be busy once the hackers attacked like sharks the next day. The one piece of information he did not share was his new backdoor.

Around three in the morning, he stumbled onto a file with a time stamp prior to his original incursion, over a year ago. The file did not have any recent updates, and from what he could tell, it had not been accessed for a long time. There was a strong possibility the old file had been resident on an old backup. After reviewing the file, he copied it to a flash drive and renamed it on the main system with an innocuous data-file name. The content of the file was the Rosetta Stone of Plymel's indiscretions at P&G Global. He sat back and smiled. Without thinking, he dialed Kruger's cell phone.

A croaky voice answered, "Yeah—this is Kruger."

"It's JR."

"Do you know what time it is?"

He glanced at the clock in the lower right-hand corner of his laptop. "Well, it's three-sixteen in the morning here. That would make it five-sixteen there."

"What's up?"

"Found something in the P&G Global computer system a few minutes ago, a file somebody deleted and for some reason is back on their system."

"And?"

"It contains spreadsheets and memos about how P&G is utilizing investor funds to pay dividends to other clients. One of the memos is from a senior accountant claiming he found discrepancies in several big-dollar client accounts. The memo was sent to Abel Plymel. A quick search of the company's personnel records indicates the accountant is no longer employed at the firm. There's a termination letter in his personnel file dated the same day as the memo."

Kruger was silent. Finally he said, "Send me the accountant's contact information. What else did you find?"

"More money."

"How much?"

"Remember, this file is more than a year old. There's at least another thirty million sitting in various accounts scattered around the world."

"Can you access the money?"

"From the information in this file, yes, if he hasn't moved it."

Kruger was silent again, probably thinking about what needed to be done next. JR remained quiet. Finally Kruger said, "Okay, here's what I want you to do: see how much you can find, cut off his access, and get back to me. Don't move any of it yet." Kruger stayed silent for a few seconds. "I'm curious, was Plymel the only one skimming money?"

"Nope, there's a managing director doing the same thing."

Kruger laughed. "Alton Crigler. I always knew he had a streak of larceny in him. I'm going to enjoy taking him down."

"How'd you know about him?"

"I knew him when he was the deputy attorney general. He made a feeble attempt to stop us from arresting Plymel the other day. The attempt was for show, nothing more. Now I know why Plymel didn't have a lawyer immediately. Good work, JR. See how much of the money you can freeze, and get back to me."

Several hours later, JR discovered there was now over forty-nine million stashed in the various offshore accounts. Once he felt he had found all of the accounts, he changed the user names and passwords on each one. An email to Kruger summarized his accomplishments. He went to bed at 6:00

a.m., more comfortable with his situation than he had been in a long time.

***

Kruger was waiting in the interview room when a guard opened the door and Plymel entered, followed by a heavyset man in his sixties. Plymel was still in his orange jumpsuit furnished by the great state of New York, and the heavyset man wore an expensive suit.

As the guard shut the door, the heavyset man said, "Mr. Plymel will not be speaking to you today, Agent Kruger, so this will be a short meeting."

Kruger nodded. "Who are you?"

"Felix Benson, Mr. Plymel's attorney."

"Well, Mr. Felix Benson. I'm not here to ask Mr. Plymel any questions. I came merely as a courtesy to inform both of you of new details recently learned in our investigation."

"We're listening."

Plymel was sitting with a smug look on his face. Kruger stared at him. "Our investigation has discovered some very disturbing activities involving your client. In fact, I have notified the SEC about these activities." Plymel's arrogant demeanor remained. Kruger stared hard at the man and continued, "We have evidence of Mr. Plymel defrauding his investors of millions of dollars. An internal P&G audit discovered the fraud and was reported to Mr. Plymel. The accountant who conducted the audit and sent the memo was terminated. Funds totaling forty-nine-million dollars have been found in offshore accounts owned by shell companies controlled by Mr. Plymel. Effective this morning, the federal government has frozen those assets."

Plymel did not disappoint Kruger; the self-righteous look was temporarily replaced with a look of horror, then just as quick, anger. Plymel started to stand. "How dare you..."

Benson grabbed his arm. "Sit down, Abel, and keep quiet. I'm sure there is a more logical explanation about these assets than theft."

Kruger shrugged and stood. He stepped toward the door. "Not according to our evidence, counselor. You'll get a summary of it in your discovery packet." He stopped just before exiting the room and turned to Plymel, "As I mentioned the other day, I'm not someone you want looking into your business." He walked out of the interview room, closed the door, and smiled for the first time since learning about Sharon.

***

Abel Plymel stared at the closed door. The FBI agent's statement about the money was devastating. First, the hacker had taken sixty million. Now the government had found the rest of his money. How did they find it? The incriminating audit memo had been deleted long ago. He leaned over and supported his head with his hands.

While his attorney was rattling on about change of venue, illegal searches, and other benign topics, he wasn't listening. All he could think about was the last few words the agent had said; the government had frozen access to the money. He had to get out of here and find out what was going on. He turned to Benson. "Shut up. Why am I still in this hellhole?"

Benson's eyes grew wide, and he looked at Plymel in silence. After a few moments, he said, "If you would listen to me occasionally, you would know, probably this afternoon."

"I have to get back to the office and see what kind of damage these meddling police officers have done—"

"First of all, they are far more than just police officers. They represent the Federal Government. And second of all, you are no longer welcome at your office."

"What?" He stared at Benson, his eyes blinking rapidly. "What do you mean, I'm no longer welcome?"

"Exactly as I said. You are no longer associated with P&G. You have been dismissed and replaced as CEO. They are distancing themselves from you, due to the severity of the charges. As I told you earlier, my firm has never been associated with P&G Global. Your case was referred to us, and at this point I'm not sure how long we will maintain the relationship. For the moment, I'm your attorney. However, I will not tolerate your lack of cooperation or your attitude. Once you are released, I will reevaluate our association and let you know if we will continue to represent you. Good day, Mr. Plymel." Felix Benson stood, grabbed his briefcase, and left the interview room, leaving the door open. A guard immediately appeared and motioned for him to follow.

***

Benson was good on his word; Abel Plymel was released on bond at four-thirty that afternoon. His attorney was there and accompanied him through the crush of reporters to a waiting car. Questions were screamed at both Plymel and Benson, neither answered. After the car drove away from Manhattan Central Booking, Benson said, "Where do you want us to drop you off?"

Plymel stared out the passenger window. "My apartment will be fine."

Shaking his head, Benson said, "Probably not a good idea. There's still a team of FBI agents searching it. Plus, the media was told of your release. There's a swarm of reporters and television cameras camped outside your apartment building waiting for your arrival."

Unable to comprehend all of the events of the past few days, he lashed out at Benson. "Just what the hell are you doing to earn your substantial legal fees?"

"Apparently you have no idea of the legal ramifications against you at the moment. You are accused of fraud, conspiracy to commit murder, and numerous other felonies. If convicted of any of these accusations, you're looking at a possible life sentence in a federal prison. So far, all you've done is whine and tell me I'm incompetent and unworthy of representing you. If you wish to terminate my services, I can find plenty to do that will not require listening to your complaining." Benson sat in the back seat of the car next to Plymel. His attention focused straight ahead, once he was finished, he turned and stared at Plymel. "Your decision, not mine."

"I'm innocent."

Benson shrugged. "Immaterial. I could care less if you're guilty or innocent. My job is to defend you in a court of law. I can't do that if you refuse to acknowledge the situation. So far you've denied the fact there is mounting evidence against you. Plus, you've been terminated from P&G Global. Not exactly an image of innocence."

Plymel stared out the window on his side of the back seat, and was silent. He had never experienced this level of helplessness. Always being in control was how he managed his life. Now events were occurring too rapidly for him to adjust and overcome. "Take me to the Midtown Carlton; I'll stay there for a few days."

"Very well. I will be by in the morning to discuss your defense. But only if you'll cooperate."

Plymel nodded but remained quiet. He had to talk to Crigler tonight and find out the details of his dismissal. Afterwards, he would start planning his comeback.

***

After being told the president's suite was unavailable, Plymel presented his American Express Black Card and was immediately shown to the room. He was now accessing the internet on the in-room laptop. It took only five minutes to confirm his forty-nine-million dollars was unavailable. He sat back in the desk chair and tried to think. How could they have found it? He had deleted that information a long time ago. Unless Crigler…

The phone on the desk rang. He stared at it, momentarily undecided whether to answer or not. Shaking his head, he picked up the receiver. "Yes?"

"Mr. Plymel, this is the hotel manager Fred Barnes. I hope you found your room comfortable and to your satisfaction. If there is anything we can do to make your stay more pleasant, please let me know?"

"Yes—yes, everything is fine." He hesitated, suddenly remembering he didn't have any clothes or toiletries with him. "Do you have a professional shopper on staff?"

"Why, yes we do. Can she be of assistance?"

"Actually she can. Please send her up, I need to give her a list."

***

After the fourth attempt to reach Crigler by phone, Plymel concluded he was being ignored. If Crigler wasn't going to take his calls, there was only one way to find out what he needed to know: confront the man face to face.

The personal shopper had performed admirably. Plymel now had several new suits, shirts, ties, shoes, items of lounge wear, and all the personal items needed to keep him groomed and presentable. The few moments of self-doubt he had experienced earlier in the day were long gone.

After locating a smaller fund that was still available, he immediately transferred the money to an account he could readily access. With the discovery of the money and a new wardrobe, his self-confidence returned. Dressed in one of his new suits, he dialed a memorized number on the hotel desk phone.

"Covergirl Escorts, this is Marie. How can I help you?"

Plymel smiled. "Yes, this is Abel Plymel. Is Darby available tonight?"

CHAPTER 24

Atlanta, GA

The man waited patiently, watching passengers disembark flight 1172 from Dulles International Airport. He wore black jeans, black Reeboks, a white button-down oxford shirt, and a navy blazer. Except for his size, he would have blended into the background of business travelers and been invisible.

His patience was rewarded as the tall black man walked through the gate and paused for a brief moment as he scanned the crowd. Their eyes met for the briefest of moments. The black man then walked quickly to the main hallway and turned to his right, hurrying toward his connecting flight.

The large man in the navy blazer waited a few moments before grabbing the duffel bag at his feet. Without hurrying, he walked in the same direction as the taller man. There was no need to catch up; he knew where the man was going.

As he approached his destination, he saw the taller man standing in the gate area examining his boarding pass. Major Benedict "Sandy" Knoll walked up to him. "Nice to see you again, colonel."

Joseph smiled and turned to his friend. "Good to see

you too, Sandy. Let's dispense with the titles."

"Yes sir. Thank you for the invite. I've never been to the Ozarks. I hear it's a beautiful part of the country."

"It is, but I'm afraid we have a storm brewing. I need some extra boots on the ground."

"My pleasure, sir. All the equipment you requested is checked and will arrive with us."

"Good, thank you."

"You were a little vague on the phone, sir. How bad is this storm going to be?"

"With you there, I'm sure its intensity will be lessened."

Nodding, Sandy understood it wasn't appropriate to discuss the matter in public. He remained quiet and waited for their flight to Springfield.

Just before boarding, Joseph handed Sandy an eight-by-ten envelope. In a low voice, he said, "There's a driver's license, credit card, hotel reservation, and a brief summary of our objectives in this envelope. Read it over. When we get to Springfield, we'll depart separately. You have a SUV with a GPS unit reserved under the name on the ID. Go to your hotel and wait for me to call you."

Sandy nodded and remained quiet.

"Once again, Sandy, I appreciate your help with this matter. The man we are trying to protect will make an excellent addition to our team."

Sandy looked at the picture from the envelope. "I remember this guy. It was a long time ago, but I competed against him in several marksmanship tournaments. He kicked my ass every time. I don't remember his name, but damn, he could shoot."

Joseph smiled. "He's even better with a computer."

It was Sandy's turn to smile. "Well then, I'll just have to make sure this storm doesn't do any damage."

***

JR's phone chirped at five minutes after five in the

afternoon. Quickly noting the caller ID, he accepted the call. "Yeah."

Joseph said, "Have you ever thought about just saying hello?"

"Yes, but I dismissed it as being pedestrian."

"Where are you?"

"Halfway between Topeka and Kansas City. Should be back in town a little after nine tonight. Why?"

"Can I convince you to stay in KC tonight?"

"Why?"

There was a pause before JR heard him say, "We may have a small problem. We believe someone will be arriving in Springfield in the next day or so looking for you. He may already be here; we're not sure. Another day would give us time to check."

"What do you mean *us*?" Joseph was quiet for a long time. JR said, "Are you still there?"

"You don't miss much, do you?"

"Try not to. So who is the *us*?"

"I asked an old friend to help out."

It was JR's time to be quiet. For almost eight months, no one knew anything about his past. Now more and more individuals were involved. "One person has already died, Joseph, someone I didn't even know." His voice rose in volume, "Now you're telling me you're dragging more people into this. How many more, Joseph? How many?"

"He has certain talents we can use."

JR was quiet, he took a deep breath and said, "Give me a better reason to stay in KC."

"Kruger believes a very dangerous man knows your location. This individual may be on his way to Springfield. We need time to set up surveillance without you being in the way."

"How long do you want me to stay?"

"One night should do it. Go to a Royals game or something."

JR turned to Mia. "Want to get a room in Kansas City

tonight?" She had been watching him during the phone call, understanding the direction of the conversation. She stared at him with unblinking eyes, a tight smile, and finally a nod of her head. JR said, "Yes—we'll stop in Kansas City."

"Don't tell me where you're staying—that way, I can truthfully say I don't know where you are. Plausible deniability. Keep you cell phone charged."

"Okay. Call me when you know more."

"Will do."

The call ended and Mia said, "What's going on, JR? Is something wrong?"

"I don't know for sure. Joseph was vague at best. He said he needed some time to set up surveillance, whatever that means." He paused and looked at Mia. She stared at him, her arms crossed and her left hand rubbing her throat.

He tried to maintain an upbeat attitude. "So, where do you want to stay?" She continued to stare at him. Pausing briefly, he said, "Let's go to the Plaza—great hotels and lots of good food. We'll try to get hold of Kruger; he lives somewhere around there. We can ask him what's going on."

She turned toward the front window and stared out at the highway.

"Try not to worry. Joseph has everything under control." As he said it, he wasn't sure if he believed it.

***

Joseph ended the call to JR and immediately called Sandy, who answered on the first ring. "Yes."

"Did you find your accommodations satisfactory?"

"I'm a little disappointed. Only two rooms and I haven't seen the scantily clad maid yet."

Chuckling, Joseph said, "Budget constraints. Let's meet at my office as soon as you can get here."

"How far is it?"

"About ten minutes, if you use the freeway next to your hotel. The address is in your envelope."

"Already in the GPS. See you in ten."

Sandy walked through the door of Ozark Computer Security eleven minutes later. "Okay, give me the details."

By nine in the evening, Sandy was up to speed and Joseph felt better prepared for any possible visit by Adam Weber. JR's apartment would be under surveillance by early morning. Also, the security for Joseph's shop had been upgraded by some of the equipment Sandy had brought from Atlanta. The only item missing was a picture of Weber. A Google search had failed to provide one, so Joseph called Mary. She provided one via email fifteen minutes after his call.

Once the image was saved to the main server, Joseph said, "I think you'll be impressed with JR's facial recognition program. It's faster than anything the government has." Just as he said that, one of the monitoring laptop's pinged. Joseph looked at the message. "Apparently Mr. Weber has found us." He pointed to the split screen on the laptop. The left side was a live shot of the parking lot in front and slightly east of their location, and the right side was the newly saved picture of Weber with his name and current bio underneath the image.

Joseph's shop was located in a commercial development that was designated as multi-use. The neighboring businesses varied, ranging from dentists and attorneys to restaurants and fitness centers. The complex was long, extending a half-mile from east to west. Joseph's office was on the western side next to a fitness center and several high-end restaurants, so at this time of night, the parking lot was still busy.

Weber was standing next to a sedan several spaces from a light pole. The driver-side door was open, and he was holding what looked like an open file tilted toward the light pole. As they watched, Weber would look at the file and then the building. He did this several times before closing it and tossing it back into the vehicle. He surveyed the office complex, looking east and then west. Finally, he lifted a small digital camera to his eye and started taking pictures.

Sandy walked over to a laptop and typed in several instructions. The surveillance camera that was focused on Weber zoomed in and started recording. "He's doing recon. Not very subtle about it, is he?"

Joseph shook his head but remained quiet as he watched the man taking pictures.

Sandy typed on the laptop keyboard again and said to the screen, "I wonder what you're planning to do next, Mr. Weber."

Finally, after several minutes, Weber got back in the sedan and left the parking space slowly. The camera tracked the car's movement until it disappeared around the corner of the office complex one hundred yards to the west. Sandy said, "Bet he's driving around to check out the rear entrance."

They were in the workshop located at the rear of the office. On the back wall, a steel door led directly from the room into the service alley. Joseph walked to the wall and flipped off the light switch. He said, "No need to advertise someone's here."

Sandy typed more instructions on the laptop. The image on the laptop was now from cameras covering the alley. The split-screen format showed the view from cameras facing west and east. As they watched, the automobile driven by Weber appeared around the west end of the complex and slowly drove down the alley toward their door. Weber stopped the car next to the back door and got out again. He stood looking at the door and then concentrated on the roofline of the building. They could see him concentrating on a particular spot. He took the digital camera from his pocket and started taking more pictures. He pointed the camera directly at two of the security cameras secured in the back alley. Smiling, Weber got back into the car and drove on down the alley.

Joseph smiled and nodded. "He spotted the old cameras, not your new ones. That's good."

Sandy watched the image. "Why is he being so obvious taking pictures of the building and cameras?"

Joseph shook his head. "Not sure." He paused for a few moments. "Unless he's planning on coming back later and doing a more thorough job of looking around."

Smiling, Sandy said, "I hope so."

CHAPTER 25

New York City

The FBI investigative team looking into Sharon Crawford's murder had so far found very little forensic evidence. Basic facts were all they had. She had died from a broken neck after a brief struggle.

The killer must have worn gloves, because the only prints in the room were Sharon's and the cleaning staff's. She had not been sexually assaulted and she had not been able to scratch her assailant—no DNA evidence under her fingernails.

Stray clothing fibers were found on her business suit as the killer grabbed her from behind and rubbed his clothing against her during the struggle. Analysis of the fiber matched it to a thousand identical suits sold at JC Penney. Her motel room had been turned inside out as the assailant searched for something. All the forensics team could determine missing was her laptop, cell phone, and her wallet.

Sean Kruger read through the reports, studied the crime scene photographs, and then repeated the process. Viewing the pictures of Sharon was the hardest. As he worked, something troubled him. Something was missing. He couldn't place it, but he felt something was wrong with the scene. He turned to one of the technicians working in the room. "How tall was the assailant?"

Beverly Castro was a twenty-year veteran of the New York Crime Lab, mid-forties, black hair streaked with gray pulled back in a ponytail and twenty pounds overweight. She looked at him over half glasses. "Not sure," she walked over to a desk in the lab, opened a notebook, and read for a few moments. "Tall, angle of the bruise marks on the victim's neck—"

"Her name was Sharon," said Kruger.

"Sorry, the bruises on Sharon's neck indicate her assailant was a lot taller than she was."

"The report says the carpet had been vacuumed before she arrived back at the hotel. There's only one set of footprints leading to the bed. Did he carry her?"

"There were signs of a struggle. We think her neck was broken after he carried her to the bed."

Kruger nodded; he had guessed as much. "Did you find any hair samples of the assailant around the bed?"

Beverly consulted the notebook again and shook her head. "Nothing conclusive, mostly just Sharon's hair."

Kruger was silent as he stared at his copy of the report. Finally he said, "There's mention of several short gray hairs found on her clothing. Have they been sent off for analysis?"

She nodded. "Yes, but the results really won't help us until we have a suspect. Why?"

Kruger thought for a moment. "Check them against US Marshal personnel records, active, non-active, and retired."

Tilting her head to the side, Beverly said, "You know something we don't?"

"Just a hunch, I'm probably wrong." He gave her a weak smile. "But—you never know."

"Okay, if you feel it's important, I can push it through faster."

Kruger nodded. "Yeah, I feel it's important."

***

Standing outside the evidence locker at Police Headquarters at One Police Plaza, Kruger handed the transfer-of-evidence paperwork to the officer at the reception desk. She looked at his ID, then the paperwork and nodded. She wrote something on a pad of paper and handed it to a young officer sitting behind her. She said, "Bobbie, please get this and I'll finish up here."

As soon as the young officer was gone, she looked up at Kruger, a small tear in her eye. "I'm Brittany Hardy, I knew Sharon. We worked a case together several years ago and became friends. Whenever she was in town, we'd have dinner."

Kruger nodded. She was in her mid-thirties and slightly overweight. She was pretty in a simple way, with hazel eyes and shoulder-length light brown hair she tucked behind her ears. He said, "She was a special person."

Brittany looked down at her desk and was quiet. "Did you know her very well?"

Kruger hesitated. He nodded. "Yes, we worked a few cases together. I considered her a friend."

Brittany's eyes suddenly grew wide and her hand went to her mouth. "You're Sean, aren't you?"

He nodded.

"I'm sorry. I just now made the connection. She spoke of you often."

Frowning, Kruger said, "What do you mean she spoke of me often?"

"You know, just girl talk. When we chatted about the men in our lives, she would always mention your name, no one else. I think she was still in love with you."

Kruger stared at Brittany, struggling to keep tears from forming. Finally, he found his voice and said in a low whisper, "We were close at one time."

Changing the subject, Brittany said, "Do you know where she'll be taken?"

He nodded. "I spoke to her mother. Sharon's service will be in Florida. She grew up in Orlando."

Brittany nodded and was about to say something when the other officer handed her the box containing Abel Plymel's computer. She took it out and checked the information against Kruger's paperwork and signed his copy. He signed her copy and placed the computer in his backpack. He placed one of the pack's straps over his shoulder and turned to leave. The young woman said, "Did you and Sharon have plans for the future?"

He nodded. "At one time, yes…"

He left, not trusting himself to say anymore.

***

His appointment with the ex-accountant for P&G Global was scheduled for eleven the same morning. Upon arriving, he was shown into the man's office without delay. Robert Hill was in his early thirties and currently working at a CPA firm in mid-Manhattan. Kruger had avoided telling the receptionist he was with the FBI to keep the rumor mill quiet. As they stepped into Hill's office, he said, "I appreciate you not identifying yourself, Agent Kruger. Please sit down. Is this about P&G Global?"

Kruger nodded as he took a seat in front of Hill's desk. The office smelled of Brut aftershave, dust, and musty files. The young man was slight of build, prematurely thinning hair, green eyes behind rimless glasses, and a rather sharp nose. Kruger said, "How long were you there after sending the memo about discrepancies?"

Hill chuckled. "I was gone that afternoon. They told me I'd made several errors in an account that cost the company millions. Apparently, Plymel used me as an excuse for the missing funds."

"How much was missing?"

"Over five million from three accounts, all of which were worth more than a hundred million each, and those were just the easy ones to find. I knew of at least twenty other accounts with discrepancies, but I wasn't able to examine them before I was dismissed."

Kruger made a few notes and was quiet for several seconds. "Why did you send the memo directly to Plymel and not your boss?"

Hill shrugged. "The organizational chart was a little odd; everybody in the accounting and auditing departments reported directly to Plymel. He was my boss. I always thought it was to streamline communications, but now I realize he was keeping tabs on anyone discovering the transfer of funds."

"What was Alton Crigler's roll in all of this?"

"That's a great question. He was supposed to be the managing partner, but was seldom there. He spent four to five days a week in Washington. I was responsible for auditing his expense account. Every Monday I would receive one from the preceding week. Like clockwork, it would be on my desk before I arrived in the morning. My instructions were to check the math, correct any errors, approve it, and send it to accounts payable. All of this had to be done by noon on the day I received the report. He had no limits on expenditures, and I was not to question any of his expenses. Which should have been a red flag for me, but I had just passed my CPA exam and was a little green."

"What were his expenses like?"

"Hugh, minimum of four figures and sometimes five on a weekly basis." He paused, stared at this desk and continued, "One time I questioned a five-thousand-dollar restaurant bill without a receipt. I was told to pay it and shut up." He sighed. "The whole place felt like that."

Kruger frowned. "What do you mean?"

"I don't know. It was like everything we did was for the pleasure and compensation of Mr. Plymel and Mr. Crigler. We were all there just to make sure they kept their lifestyle."

Kruger made more notes. "Did you ever find any discrepancies with any of the accounts Crigler managed?"

Hill shook his head. "No, I wasn't involved with them. He was more of the handshaking and backslapping guy for the company."

They spoke for another thirty minutes as Hill described his overall duties in more detail. Kruger finally said, "Mr. Hill, I appreciate your time. Here is my card. If you think of anything else, please call me."

He stood and walked to the door. Just as he was about to open it, Hill said, "One more thing, Agent Kruger."

He turned around to look at Hill. "Yes."

"There are some good people in the auditing department, but you need to know they're scared."

Kruger nodded. "As well they should be."

***

Kruger pulled into his parking slot at the condo a few minutes after eight that night. He was tired and frustrated. Over an hour ago, he had returned Joseph's message to call him as soon as his flight landed in Kansas City. Now Joseph wasn't answering. In his message, Joseph had told him that JR would be in KC, but no specifics on where. Plymel's computer had to be in the lab in Washington sometime tomorrow, or questions would be raised.

With his computer backpack slung over his shoulder and his overnight bag in his hand, he walked up the one flight of stairs and went to his door. There was a small yellow Post-it note at eye level next to his apartment number—no words, just numbers. He unlocked the door and took the note inside. There were nine digits with no spaces, parentheses, or dashes. After depositing his luggage in the bedroom, he stared at the numbers and suddenly smiled. After punching the numbers into his cell phone, the call was answered on the second ring.

"You must have gotten my message?"

"Not much of a message, JR, but yes, I did. I have something for you."

"Good, I'll be right there." The call ended without

another word.

Fifteen minutes later, JR and Mia were in Kruger's condo. JR sat at the breakfast bar examining Plymel's laptop, and Mia stood next to Kruger as they watched him work. She said, "Are you going to be able to help him?"

Kruger nodded. "Yes, I believe I can."

She looked up at him and smiled. "I hope so. He's a good man." She paused, took a deep breath, and sighed. "I'm falling in love with him."

Looking at her, Kruger remained quiet. She was staring again at JR, her arms crossed tightly across her chest. "He's determined to get through this so we can have a future together. I have to help him in any way I can."

Kruger didn't respond.

She continued, "Did you know he was in the military?"

Kruger nodded.

"He was a member of a group of men trained to start the first Cyber Warfare unit, but he and his commanding officer had a disagreement, so he quit."

This was news to Kruger. He wondered why Joseph had failed to mention this fact.

She continued, "When those two men escorted him out of the building, he knew if he got in the SUV, he'd never get out of it alive, so he defended himself." She looked up at Kruger, a tear in her eye. "If he hadn't defended himself, I'd never have met him. I'm sorry someone died because of it, but I'm glad it happened. Is it wrong for me to feel that way?"

Kruger shook his head. "No."

She turned her attention back to JR. "I'll do whatever it takes to help him."

JR looked up from the computer. "When do you need to take this computer back?"

Kruger said, "I have to have it in Washington by tomorrow afternoon. Can you analyze the disk by then?"

JR shook his head. "I don't have the right software with me. I need to do it in my computer room."

"We don't have that kind of time."

"What if I clone the drive and put the clone in the computer? That way I have the original?"

Kruger said quietly, "Why is the original so important?"

JR shrugged. "Personal preference. From what I can see on first glance, the disk is heavily segmented, which means a lot of data has been deleted recently. I can recover the deleted information as long as I have the original disk."

"Would someone else be able to tell the original was replaced?"

"Not when I'm done."

Kruger nodded and smiled.

JR and Mia left his condo just after ten, planning to return in the morning. JR knew a place in Overland Park where he could buy a duplicate hard drive. He would then clone the original and install the clone in the laptop. Afterward, he and Mia would drive back to Springfield.

Kruger walked down the condo hall and knocked on Stephanie's door. It took several knocks, but finally he heard the dead bolt being released, and the door opened. Stephanie smiled as he walked into the living area. They hugged and she said, "Hi, stranger. When did you get back?"

"Couple of hours ago. I hope I didn't wake you."

She smiled. "No, just finishing up some paperwork."

He suspected she was lying; her hair was pulled back and she wore a baggy sweatshirt. "I know it's late, but I wanted to see you before I leave again."

The smile on her face disappeared briefly, but she recovered. "That's disappointing. When do you have to leave?"

As he stood there, weariness spread through his body. He took a deep breath. "I was planning on leaving tomorrow afternoon. But I just decided to postpone the trip for a day."

She smiled. "I'm in town till next week. I was hoping you'd be home this weekend."

"I'll make sure I am."

CHAPTER 26

Springfield, MO

Determined not to make the same mistakes he made in Chicago, Adam Weber surveyed the security cameras and rear door of the business. Gaining entry was not going to be difficult. He had no plans to steal anything; he just wanted to see the personnel files. Utilizing skills learned from the many characters he had encountered while a US Marshal, he would be able to gain access easily.

After visiting a Walmart store several miles from the office complex, he returned around midnight. He parked his car several blocks away in a residential area and approached the back door to the business under cover of darkness. Weber was now attired in black jeans, a black long-sleeved t-shirt, black gloves, black walking shoes, and a black watch cap. He crouched outside the lighted zone of the security lights and aimed the paintball gun he had purchased at one of the security cameras. It took two shots, but he hit the lens with a dark-red ball, effectively rendering it blind. He repeated the process on the second camera. Placing the paintball gun in his new duffel bag, he quickly walked up to the back door of the office. Working with improvised tools, he had the door unlocked, opened, and closed within thirty seconds. He found the security system panel, recognized the brand, opened the front panel, and disconnected two wires. There would be no alarm.

Satisfied his intrusion was undetected, Weber turned his flashlight on and surveyed the room. Rows of metal shelving held inventory for the business. After studying the contents of the shelves, he frowned. State-of-the-art surveillance and alarm equipment were on every shelf. In addition, the workbenches were occupied by laptops in various states of repair.

He stared at the shelves, then at the door, and back at the shelving. After several moments of indecision, he said, "Fuck it. I'm already here."

Without hesitation, Weber left the room and walked down the hall. The second office door was labeled "Helen Meyers, Purchasing and HR." He tried the doorknob and found it locked. Twenty seconds later, he was in the office and looking through the filing cabinets. His search discovered several files of interest, which he photographed with his cell phone.

He glanced at this his watch. Of the ten minutes he was allowing himself inside the office, only six had passed. He kept searching. Finding nothing else of interest, he returned to the back door, reattached the wires on the security system and slipped out.

Weber walked back to his car, opened the driver-side door, and sat behind the wheel. After several deep breaths, the rush of his late-night incursion subsided. He started the engine, powered down a window, and listened. The night was quiet; no police sirens could be heard converging on the area. His concern about a silent alarm, after seeing the sophisticated equipment in the storage room, was unfounded. Smiling, he turned on the headlights and drove out of the neighborhood.

***

Waiting in a darkened alcove several doors east, Joseph stood watching his back door. He also was dressed in black. He smiled as he watched Weber close the back door, quickly walk across the darkened alley, and disappear into the shadows behind the office complex. He checked his watch. The man was in the office for only nine minutes. Unconsciously, he nodded in appreciation. Sandy appeared out of the shadows and crossed to Joseph's location. "Found it. He was parked about two blocks away on a residential street. Device is safely tucked under the driver's-side rear bumper."

"Good, let's find out where he's staying."

***

Sandy Knoll pulled into a parking space at the twenty-four-hour diner next to Adam Weber's hotel. The Ford Focus with the tracking device was parked on the side of the hotel, several spaces from its north entrance. It was a little after four in the morning as Knoll stepped out of his rental car and looked back at the diner. There was a table next to a window with a perfect view of Weber's car. He smiled and entered the diner.

Two hours, seven cups of coffee, and an early-morning breakfast special later, Knoll observed Weber exit the hotel. He watched as the man threw a suitcase into the trunk of his rental car and got into the driver's seat. Knoll looked at his bill, placed a twenty on the table, and headed for his car.

Weber drove toward the interstate, a quarter of a mile north of the hotel. He took the westbound exit and headed toward the airport. Knoll followed five cars behind. Twenty minutes later, he was parked in the airport's short-term parking area with a clear view of the rental car lot. Weber had returned the car to the rental agency and was now walking into the terminal. As Knoll entered the airport building, he caught a glimpse of Weber walking toward the security area.

He paused next to a coffee shop, watched as the man went through security and proceed toward his gate.

After showing his military ID and a brief discussion with the head of the local TSA contingency, Knoll gained access to the gate area. He spotted Weber talking on his cell phone at an American Airlines gate, from which a 7:45 a.m. flight to Dallas was scheduled to depart. The flight appeared to be full as the waiting area was crowded. Knoll found an empty chair several rows away, with a clear view of Weber. He watched and waited until the flight to Dallas was announced. When the second boarding group was called, Weber ended the call, stood, walked to the gate, and handed his boarding pass to the attendant. Once he was through the gate entrance, he disappeared from Knoll's sight. Twenty minutes later, the jet bridge rolled away from the plane.

Once the commuter jet was pushed away from the gate and rolling toward the runway, he quickly walked toward the security area exit. It took several minutes to leave the terminal and locate the rental car Weber had been driving.

Knoll glanced around, bent down, and retrieved the small device he had placed inside the driver side rear fender the previous evening. As he slowly walked back to his own rental, he watched the commuter jet lift off, gain altitude, and disappear into low-lying clouds headed southwest.

After paying the parking fee and exiting the airport grounds, Knoll dialed a number on his cell phone. It was answered on the second ring. "He just took off on a flight headed for Dallas."

Joseph was silent for a few moments. "That was too easy. Do you think he found the device?"

"I can't say. It didn't appear to have been disturbed."

"Okay. We won't assume he's finished here. We'll keep the watch going on JR's condo. In the meantime, go on back to your hotel and get some sleep."

"Sounds good, I'll be back midafternoon."

***

Alton Crigler listened as two senior vice presidents heatedly argued the true value and profitability of a company P&G Global was preparing to buy. His cell phone vibrated. He glanced at the caller ID and answered the call. "Just a moment." He cleared his throat. "Gentlemen, I believe we have debated this topic to death. Put your arguments on paper, and we'll reconvene this afternoon. I need to take this phone call." He stood and walked out of the conference room and returned to his desk. "Good morning, Adam. Where are you?"

"Dallas."

"Do you have any news for me?"

"Yes—I found him."

"In Dallas?"

"No, Springfield, Missouri."

"Never heard of it. Is it close to St. Louis?"

"No, it's in the southwestern corner of the state, close to Arkansas and Kansas."

"Still haven't heard of it. Does he know you've found him?"

"No." Weber paused, trying to decide how much to reveal at this point. "There could be a few complications."

"How so?"

"He has help."

"What do you mean *help*?"

"At this point I haven't actually seen him, but all indications point toward this being the correct location."

Crigler didn't say anything for several moments. "Then why are you in Dallas?"

"While I was examining the company's personnel records, someone planted a tracking device on my car. I let them follow me to the airport and watch as I left for Dallas. I'm switching to another ID and flying back in a couple of hours."

"I'm not going to ask how you examined their records; I can only imagine. Confirm the fugitive is there and get back to me."

***

The call ended abruptly. Without comment, Weber stood, placed the phone in his pocket, and headed toward an exit and the ticketing counters. He would be back in Springfield by early afternoon.

At 4:00 p.m., Weber was parked on a residential street across from the office complex containing Ozark Computer Security. A busy street separated his location from the complex, and the elevation was higher. Through high-powered binoculars bought at a nearby Bass Pro Shop, he watched the entrance to the office. Now it was a simple matter of watching and waiting for someone to leave.

At fifteen minutes after five, a woman exited the office door and walked quickly to a five-year-old Honda Accord parked fifty feet from the entrance. Weber recognized her from several pictures in the office where he had found the personnel records. This was Helen Meyers. He watched as she backed her car out of the parking slot and drove to an exit leading to a busy east–west artery of the city. Weber started his car and was about to follow her when a large man, whom he recognized from the airport earlier in the day, stepped out of the building followed by a tall black man. The black man held the door open as the two conversed. They shook hands and the larger man walked to a parked GMC Denali. The black man closed the door and remained in the building.

Weber's first instinct was to follow the woman, but at the last second he decided to follow the SUV. If it was a dead end, he'd wait until tomorrow and follow the woman. The Denali turned out of the parking lot and headed east. Weber stayed several cars behind and was almost stopped by a traffic light, but blew through it just as it turned red. The GMC turned off the busy thoroughfare and headed toward the center of the city. Fifteen minutes later, the SUV pulled into the parking lot of a three-story building near downtown. The big man exited the vehicle and entered the building.

Weber waited patiently and finally after an hour, a gray Toyota Camry pulled into a parking spot near the front entrance to the building. The passenger side was facing Weber, and a petite oriental woman stepped out, stood, and stretched. A man emerged from the driver's side. Weber trained his binoculars on the man as he turned his face toward the woman. Weber smiled. As he watched, the big man came out of the building and shook hands with the fugitive. The two of them walked back to the trunk of the car, where the fugitive said something to the girl, who shook the hand of the big man. Luggage was taken from the trunk and they all entered the building.

Weber pressed the send icon on his cell phone; it was answered on the first ring.

"Where are you?"

"Back in Springfield."

"And…"

"Found him. I just watched him enter a building."

Crigler was silent for a few moments. "How many people are helping him?"

"I'm not sure, at this point. I know of at least two. One looks military. There's also a girl. What do you want me to do?"

More silence. Finally Crigler said, "Find out the name he's using, plus everything you can about him. Then we'll talk again." The call ended again without another word.

Weber got out of his rental car, which was across the street from the three-story building in a larger parking lot. Several restaurants and small shops were located north of where he was parked. It was approaching dusk as he entered one of the restaurants and found a seat by the front window. The location gave him a view of the fugitive's building. He ordered a beer, sat back, and waited for it to get dark. An hour after sunset, he paid for his beer and left the restaurant. Casually crossing the street to the parking lot containing the

Camry, he used his cell phone to take a picture of the license plate. After returning to his car and writing down the building's address, he backed the car out of the parking slot and left the area.

***

Sandy Knoll stood looking out one of JR's apartment windows, drinking a beer while the couple unpacked from their trip. He watched a man cross the street at the north edge of the building's parking lot. The man stopped, looked around, and stared up at the building. After a few moments, he calmly walked up to JR's gray Camry, took a cell phone out of his pocket, and pointed it at the back of the car. Knoll quickly said, "JR, do you have security cameras watching the parking lot?"

JR walked into the living room from the back part of the apartment. "Yeah, several, why?"

"I can't be sure. It's too dark out there, but I think the guy who broke into Joseph's office last night is back. He just took a picture of your car's license plate."

JR disappeared into the computer room as Knoll stayed at the window watching the man cross the street to a car in the parking lot across from the condo. JR returned and handed Sandy a sheet of paper with a picture on it. The shot was from above, but it caught the man's face as he surveyed the building. Sandy nodded. "Yeah, that's him. It appears we screwed up and lead him right to you JR. Sorry."

"Who is he?"

"His name is Adam Weber. We believe he was hired to find you."

JR was silent as he stared at the parking lot.

After a few moments, Knoll said, "We need to get you two out of here and set up surveillance."

JR shook his head. "No, I'm done running. It's time to make a stand."

Sandy looked at JR and smiled. "Good, let's call Joseph."

Later that night, as JR lay on his back in bed staring at the ceiling, he felt Mia stir. She was sleeping restlessly, but at least she was sleeping. Joseph had arranged for a security company he had worked with in the past to do surveillance on his building and the surrounding area. Knoll had told him it was temporary. He would have his own team in place by morning.

The lights from the parking lot normally didn't bother him. But tonight, they did. The shadows cast on the walls of his bedroom morphed into images of his last day in New York City. For the first time since escaping, he was scared—not for himself, but for Mia. The digital clock on the nightstand displayed three minutes after one when he finally slipped out of bed and headed to his computer room. Once seated at his desk, he stared at the hard drive from Plymel's laptop. He picked it up, smiled and turned it over in his hand. "Let's see what secrets you hold."

After attaching it to a cable connected to a custom-made laptop computer, he typed in several commands. Using a program he had designed several years earlier, he accessed the data on the hard drive. Like a surgeon, he discovered and reconstructed deleted segments one after the other. A little over an hour later, he found what he was looking for. He saved all of the discoveries to a flash drive and transferred them to a powerful desktop computer. It took two hours, but when he was done, he found the last of Plymel's funds.

Once found, he transferred the money through various offshore accounts until they were untraceable. He smiled as a thought occurred to him. Hacking into the American Express website, he located and canceled Plymel's Black Card account. When he had completed his night's work, it was fifteen minutes after six in the morning. Abel Plymel was now essentially broke. The man's last remaining funds were beyond his grasp, and his credit cards were useless. All it would take to finalize the long night's work was to press a key on the computer. Weary from the lack of sleep over the last forty-eight hours, JR sat back in the desk chair and swept his hair back with his left hand. His fingers hovered over the keyboard. As he pressed the enter key, a faint smile came to his lips and he whispered, "Showtime."

CHAPTER 27

Kansas City, MO

The Mustang was parked in the same long-term parking lot he always used when flying out of Kansas City International Airport. Kruger walked back to the car's trunk, opened it, and stared at his travel and computer bags for several seconds. *Here we go again*, he thought as he lifted them out of the trunk. After setting them on the pavement, he was about to use his key fob to lock the Mustang when his cell phone rang.

The caller ID displayed only a number, but it was a New York area code. Frowning, he accepted the call and said, "Kruger."

An excited female voice on the other end said, "How did you know the hairs we found would be from an ex-US Marshal?"

"Who is this?" he said.

"It's Beverly Castro from the crime lab. We got a hit on that DNA we submitted."

He stood in silence watching a shuttle bus leave the waiting area closest to his parking space. Finally he caught up with the conversation. "Do you have a name?"

"Yes, his name is Adam Weber, left the US Marshal's

office several years ago. The individual I spoke to wouldn't go into detail, but apparently his departure was not voluntary. He started his own private security company right after he left. Someone said he was named head of security at P&G Global a few days ago. Do you know him?"

Kruger was silent again. Finally he said, "I've heard of him. Are you sure?"

"Yes, the thirteen-loci DNA profiles match exactly. It doesn't get much better, Sean."

"I need a picture. Do you have one?"

"Yes, we have a copy of his personnel file from the US Marshal's office."

"Scan the file and send it to my email address. Thanks, Beverly. You did good work on this."

"Thanks, Sean."

He ended the call and stood silently. The sun was starting to break through the thinning clouds, and a gentle breeze stirred the crisp fall air. Was this the guy Joseph had called him about last night. The one that broke into Joseph's office two nights ago and then was seen taking a picture of JR's car?

He glanced at his watch. It was twenty minutes to eight, and his plane left at eight-thirty. The importance of being on the flight quickly faded. Returning his luggage to the trunk of the Mustang, he took out his cell phone after sitting down in the driver's seat. As he backed out of the parking slot, he made a call.

Joseph answered on the third ring. "Good morning. Thought you were flying to DC?"

"New plan. I'll be there in three hours. We got a hit on the DNA found in Sharon's room."

"Anyone we know?"

"Yeah, how sure are you about your nocturnal visitor?"

"Depends on how much you trust JR's facial recognition software."

"Do you trust it?"

"Yes."

"A hair sample found on Sharon was matched to Adam Weber, ex-US Marshal."

Joseph was silent for several moments. "Then we have a bigger problem than we originally thought."

"Yeah, I'd say so. Do you know where he is?"

"No, we didn't have any assets available to follow him after he showed up in JR's parking lot last night." He paused briefly. "We screwed up. Our Mr. Weber knew we were watching him. Damn."

"It happens."

"It won't happen again."

"Good, I should be there before eleven." He ended the call as he pulled up to the exit gates for the parking lots.

***

Mary Lawson's cell phone vibrated as she was walking back to her office from a meeting. She glanced at the caller ID, smiled, and accepted the call. "I've spoken more to you in this past week than I have for a year. How are you this morning, my love?"

"I'm well, but missing you."

"How sweet. I hope this isn't a business call and you're going to talk dirty to me."

"Regrettably, it is a business call," Joseph said, with a note of sadness.

She chuckled. "Is it time for me to pay for the wonderful evening we had earlier this week?"

"No, you already settled that account. Remember our conversation about Adam Weber?"

She was silent for several moments. "Yes, why do you ask?"

"Kruger just called; he's the prime suspect in Sharon Crawford's murder. Plus he was photographed by a security camera last night here in Springfield."

"Oh, dear."

"Yeah, oh dear."

"Joseph, what's going on? Weber was named head of security at P&G Global by Alton Crigler the same day Abel Plymel was arrested."

Now it was Joseph's turn to be silent.

"Joseph, are you there?"

"Yes, just thinking."

"Joseph, the man left the US Marshal under suspicious circumstances. During his time there, he had numerous complaints filed against him for unnecessary force. He also had several prisoners die while in his custody. However, no charges were ever filed."

"How do you know so much about him?"

"After you returned to Springfield, I called a friend at the Justice Department. Charges of sexual harassment and assault were being prepared. After he left the service, the charges were dropped. I'm sure it was an arranged departure."

"Wonderful, now he's the prime suspect in Sharon Crawford's murder."

"He's a dangerous man, Joseph." She paused for a few moments. "I did a little more digging into Abel Plymel's background like you asked."

"And..."

"Sean was correct. He has a few gaps in his past."

"What do you mean by a few gaps?"

"Well, you would think someone like that would have a solid resume. I called the university where he claims to have a degree. There's no record of him ever attending. He also doesn't appear to have held a job for several years after he claims to have graduated. In addition to all of this, I contacted the Social Security Administration. There are no records of his contributing prior to 1981."

"What do you think, Mary?"

"I don't think he's who he says he is."

"How would you prove it?"

"I know someone over at Homeland Security. They can do a more thorough investigation into his background." She paused for a few moments. "That is, if you want me to."

She couldn't see it, but Joseph was nodding, deep in thought. "Mary my dear, you always have the proper resources. By all means, have your contact find out all they can about this man. It's time someone did."

***

During his drive south, Kruger received a call from Joseph suggesting they meet at a restaurant before going to JR's apartment building. Walking into the café, he saw Joseph and a large man sitting at a table with a view of the parking lot. Joseph smiled and stood to shake his old friend's hand. "Sean, I'd like for you to meet a colleague of mine. This is Sandy Knoll."

As the two men shook hands, Kruger did a quick assessment of the big man. His first impression was career military, but he kept the thought to himself. He sat next to Joseph at the table and kept his eyes on the big man. "Nice to meet you, Sandy. Joseph mentioned on the phone you're in charge of JR's security. Bring me up to speed and then I'll tell you what I've learned."

Knoll proceeded to summarize the events of the previous night. After he was finished, Joseph said, "We had a team arrive early this morning from Fort Benning. They've taken over security and surveillance as of seven hundred hours."

Kruger smiled and raised his eyebrows. "Joseph, am I to assume you're still working for the CIA?"

Knoll laughed.

Joseph, frowned and shook his head. "I'll explain later."

Kruger returned his attention to Knoll. "DNA analyses of hairs found in Sharon's hotel were matched to Adam Weber. He's now our prime suspect in her murder. A federal warrant will be issued for his arrest by noon our time." Knoll nodded. Kruger thought for a second and added, "Out of curiosity, what is the status of your team? Are they military police?"

Knoll shook his head. "No sir. They're better than MPs."

Kruger stared at Knoll for a few moments and then realized what the man was saying. "Okay, I won't ask."

Joseph said, "Probably a good idea."

A slight smile came to Kruger's lips. "I take it your team has been trained for infiltration and detention?"

A big grin was Knoll's immediate response. "Plus a few other specialties."

"I want to emphasize, I need Weber alive." Kruger paused for a few seconds. "If possible."

Both Knoll and Joseph nodded.

Kruger changed the subject. "Where's JR and Mia?"

Knoll answered, "JR's still asleep and Mia is in the apartment telecommuting."

"I need to know what's on that hard drive as soon as possible."

Joseph nodded. "He worked on it last night." Pausing briefly, he looked at Kruger. "We've discovered more information about Plymel."

Kruger half smiled. "Mary?"

Joseph nodded. "Your suspicions about his past were correct. His degree is fictitious and he made no contributions to Social Security until six years after he claims to have graduated."

"I'm getting all kinds of goodies to stick up Crigler's ass. What else?"

"Mary is talking to a contact at Homeland Security. We might know more about Plymel later today."

"Good, let's go wake up JR."

***

JR stood in the kitchen, hair disheveled, eyes red, drinking coffee, and listening to Kruger summarize the situation. After he was finished, JR nodded. "Plymel's broke. I canceled his American Express Black Card last night and found the rest of his money. He'll be desperate when he finds out. My guess is he'll lash out at Crigler."

Kruger said, "How much did he have left?"

JR shrugged. "There's now a scholarship fund in my mom's name where I went to college. Full rides for a couple of gifted computer nerds each year. I also set up a trust fund for Mia in case something happens to me." He smiled ever so slightly.

Kruger laughed. "I'm going to enjoy working with you, JR. But nothing's going to happen to you."

JR shrugged again. "Hope not. We'll see."

Mia walked into the kitchen. "JR, I have to go to the office. I forgot about a quality control test I have to do today. There's no way I can do it from here."

JR shook his head. "Not today, Mia."

She crossed her arm against her chest. "Yes, JR, today. I'll be fine."

Knoll stood, pulled a cell phone out of his pants' pocket, and walked out of the room. Thirty seconds later, he walked back to the kitchen where JR and Mia were arguing. He said, "I can have someone drive you. Will that work?"

Mia stared at Knoll, then at JR, then nodded. "I need to leave in five minutes."

As she walked out of the room, JR said, "Call me as soon as you're there."

JR watched from one of the living area windows as Mia got into the passenger seat of her red Ford Fusion. Knoll stood on the opposite side of the car next to a tall man dressed in jeans, sweatshirt, and running shoes. His hair was cropped short, and he wore wraparound sunglasses on an oval face. The man nodded several times. They shook hands and he sat down in the Fusion's driver seat. Knoll closed the door, walked around to Mia's side, leaned in, and said something to her. He laughed and stepped back as the car backed out of the parking space. Two minutes later, he was back in the apartment. "Mike will call me when she's at the office. He'll stay with her car until she's done."

Kruger stood. "I'm going to find a hotel and call Alan. I'll be back before three." As he walked down the stairs to the parking lot, Kruger wondered what Weber's next move would be.

CHAPTER 28

Springfield, MO

"He's going by the name JR Diminski. He owns a computer consulting business that was started eight months ago. He has a reputation for designing very secure websites for banks and manufacturing companies. The girlfriend's name is Mia Ling. She's a computer chip designer for a local tech company." Weber paused, waiting for Alton Crigler to respond.

"Interesting. Who's helping him?"

"Not sure. There's an older black guy and a big white guy. The white guy looks military."

"Don't you think it would be important to know who these people are, Adam?"

Weber chuckled. "Look, Crigler, I'm the one in the field, not you. Don't try to micromanage me at this point. I can walk away from this little enterprise just as fast as I started it."

Crigler was silent for several moments. "Is that a threat?"

"No, it's a promise. I do this my way or you can find someone else. It's very simple."

Once again, there was silence on the other end of the cell phone call. Finally Crigler said, "Very well. What's your plan?"

"I'm going to watch the apartment for a while, see who comes and goes. But, I need to know what you want done with Diminski."

"Find out where the money is. Once we have this information, his usefulness ceases. Would you agree?"

"Yes."

"Good, glad we agree on something. As you just said, you're the one in the field. Make it happen."

As usual with Crigler, the call ended without another word. Weber stared out the window of the empty loft apartment. The lock on the second floor loft had been easy to pick, and it provided an excellent location to survey the fugitive's apartment building and the surrounding area. By five in the morning, he had located three teams of two men, all of whom were too interested in the fugitive's building.

At seven, all three teams left the area. While he hated to assume anything, the possibility of another group of watchers taking over seemed very likely. If they had, he couldn't spot them.

At eleven forty five, two cars pulled into the parking lot of the fugitive's building. The black man and the big white guy stepped out of one car and waited for someone to get out of the other. Weber smiled as he focused on the man who stepped out of a dark gray Mustang. FBI agent Sean Kruger stood, surveyed his surroundings, closed the car door, and followed the two other men into the building.

Thirty minutes later, the woman emerged from the building, followed by the big man. As she got into the passenger side of a Ford Fusion, Weber realized she was being driven somewhere. He left the empty apartment and quickly returned to his car several block away. Having driven by the building where the woman worked, he drove to an intersection along the route. As he suspected, the woman was being escorted to her place of work. The Ford passed by the intersection two minutes after he arrived. Turning right out of the intersection, he followed at a discrete distance. As they pulled into a convenience store, five blocks from their destination, Weber drove past and continued on until several blocks beyond her office building. He turned around and drove back, just in time to see Mia get out of the car next to the building's entrance. Weber watched as the driver escorted the woman into the building and returned to the car. After positioning the car in a parking space on the far side of the parking lot, he shut the engine off and stepped out.

***

The young man driving Mia to the office was pleasant enough, but spoke very little, except to tell her his name. When they arrived at S&W Technologies, it was twelve forty and the parking lot was busy with employees coming and going to lunch. He parked in front of the main entrance, quickly ran around to the passenger side, let Mia out, and followed her to the front door. As she was walking into the building, he said, "What time should I pick you up?"

"I should be done by three this afternoon. Anytime it's convenient for you afterwards."

"I'll be here at three."

Mia smiled. "Thanks, Mike."

As soon as she was safe inside, he parked the car and called Major Knoll. "Sir, she's in the building. I'm to pick her up at three." He listened for a few moments. "Yes, sir."

***

At three o'clock, Mia's Ford pulled up to the front entrance and she hurriedly walked down the stairs and got into the passenger side of the car. As she shut the door, she turned to the driver, and with a little surprise said, "Where's Mike?"

As the driver pulled away from the curb, he turned to her. "Mike's not feeling well. I'm your driver."

Mia looked at the big man now driving her car; she knew

if there had been a change in plans, JR would have called her on her cell phone. She said with cool detachment, "You're the man looking for JR, aren't you?"

"Very good—you catch on quick." He pulled onto the street and headed east, accelerating to the posted speed limit. "Now, we can make this easy for all of us, or we can make it difficult. It's very simple. My employer wants to know where the money is."

"I have no idea what you're talking about. Where's Mike? Did you hurt him?"

"I don't have time for playing games, lady. Your boyfriend stole a lot of money, and it's time to give it back. The man who drove you this morning is fine. He'll probably be stiff and sore for a few days, but he'll survive."

Weber turned right onto a major north south artery of the city and headed south. His destination was thirty miles south of town in a remote rural area. Several years earlier, he'd been to the location for advanced firearms training. After checking with the owner, he knew no one would be at the facility for the next ten days. There would be plenty of time to complete his plan.

***

At four in the afternoon, JR's concern for Mia intensified. She was due back at the apartment no later than 3:30 p.m., but no one had heard from her. Knoll had made several calls to Mike, which went unanswered. JR had called her cell phone numerous times with no answer, each call going straight to voice mail.

Finally at four fifteen, his cell phone rang. It was Mia's cell phone number. "Where are you? I was getting worried."

"That's good," said a gruff male voice. "You should be worried."

JR froze and was silent. He put the phone on speaker and motioned Kruger and Joseph closer to the phone. "Who is this?"

"Who I am is immaterial. What is important is you have something that my employer wants back."

"I have no idea what you're talking about. Where's Mia?"

"She's with me."

"If you hurt her…"

"She's healthy, for the moment. Now shut up and listen."

Kruger wrote a quick note, handed it to JR. It said, "Can you trace phone location?"

JR nodded. "Okay, go ahead, I'm listening."

The voice on the phone said, "I saw an FBI agent enter your apartment this morning. Let me talk to him."

JR looked up at Kruger, handed the phone to him.

Kruger took the phone. "I assume this is Adam Weber."

There was silence on the other end of the call. Finally the voice said, "I was told you were good."

JR went to his laptop and started typing. Kruger watched him. "What do you want?"

"I'm going to make this very plain. Do not get involved. If you do, the girl will never be seen again. My business is with the man calling himself JR Diminski. Do you understand, agent?"

"Yeah, I understand. But, you need to understand something as well. If any harm comes to the girl, I will make finding you a national pastime. You won't be able to hide anywhere. Do you understand me, Weber?"

"I'll call back in thirty minutes."

The call ended and Kruger looked at JR, who smiled. "Mia turned on the GPS function on her cell phone last night. Normally, I don't feel it's necessary for the phone company to track you. But in this situation, both our phones have it turned on. Her phone is thirty miles south in Christian County, just off Highway 160 on State Highway 5 heading west.

Kruger looked at Joseph and then JR. "What's down there?'

JR shook his head. "Don't know, lots of hills and trees I

assume."

Knoll walked to the door. "I need to send someone to check on Mike. I'll be right back."

***

Thirty minutes later, JR's phone chirped. It was Mia's phone again. "Yeah."

"Where's the money?"

"I don't have it on me, but it's safe."

"Okay, here's how this is going to work. I want the location of the funds, the account numbers, and passkeys. You have to bring them in person. Then, once I verify the information, I'll tell you where the girl is located."

"What if I give you the information and you forget to tell me where Mia is?"

"Guess you'll just have to trust me. Now, I'm going to give you some directions. If you're not here in an hour, the girl dies." Weber gave JR the information and ended the call.

JR showed the directions to Joseph, who nodded. "I believe I know where he is. There's a police and civilian firearms training facility located there. It's owned by a friend of mine. The place is very remote and secluded. He'll be hard to find once he's on the compound." He turned to JR. "Can you find this on Google Earth?"

JR nodded.

Kruger said, "Call your friend and tell him what's going on."

Joseph shook his head. "Nobody's there. The compound is unoccupied. He takes his vacation this time of year."

"Damn."

"These directions take you to the north side of the property." Joseph went to the laptop JR was using and pointed at the screen. Displayed was a Google Earth shot of the compound. He placed his finger on a road labeled Molly Avenue and said, "This is the main entrance." He moved his hand to the right, tapped another road named Stoops Lane, and continued. "Sandy and his team will insert here. JR, you will drive to the first dirt road on your left. Make the turn and follow till it ends. Have your cell on, so we can keep track of you, plus give you updates."

JR nodded and made sure the small Bluetooth ear bud was properly inserted in his right ear. He checked to make sure the GPS function on his cell phone was turned on. "Guess I'd better get going." He turned to Kruger. "Whatever happens, I appreciate your belief in me."

Kruger smiled and put his hand on JR's shoulder. "We've got a good plan, we'll find her. Now let's go."

They walked to the parking lot and met Knoll who was talking to the remaining three members of his surveillance team. A fourth member had been sent to check on Mike. Each man was dressed in camouflaged hunting outfits, purchased the previous evening at Bass Pro Shops, several miles from JR's apartment.

Knoll said, "We got a call from David. Mike is awake and talking. While he was waiting to pick up Mia, a large man walked up to his car and claimed to be from security. The guy wanted to know what he was doing in the parking lot. As Mike lowered the window to talk to him, the guy pulled a Taser and shot him in the stomach from about two feet. He was pulled out of Mia's car and dumped on the grass. Mike lay there until someone found him and called an ambulance. He's got a severe burn, but otherwise is okay. Dave will stay with him. The rest of us are good to go."

Joseph said, "Do you have everything you need?"

Knoll nodded. "JR gave us an iPad that will track the GPS signal from Mia's Ford. We'll locate it first and improvise from there."

"Good. Stealth is the word today. I don't want him to know we're there."

Forty minutes later, Kruger drove Knoll's rented GMC Denali west on Missouri Highway 5 toward their destination. Knoll sat next to Kruger and his three companions sat in the back. Brian, a twenty-seven-year-old staff sergeant watched the iPad with intensity. Two miles after turning off Highway 160, he said, "I've got a fix on the Fusion."

Kruger said, "Where?"

"Southwest of the compound. It's in what looks like a clearing when I superimpose it on Google Maps."

"I'll drop you off at the southwest corner. You guys can find it from there."

Knoll nodded. "Pop the back lid when you stop. I have to get a few things."

Kruger stopped the SUV at the junction of Stoops Lane and Highway 5 and let Knoll's team disembark. He watched as they disappeared into the Missouri countryside. Knoll had retrieved an M110 semiautomatic sniper system from the back of the GMC and followed his men into the thick growth of oak and cedars trees native to southwestern Missouri. Kruger accelerated the SUV toward the main entrance of the compound, a half-mile to the west. His role was to set up surveillance off of Molly Avenue and block the exit they assumed Weber would use to escape, since he was drawing JR into the compound from the north.

After parking the SUV across the main entrance at its narrowest point, the exit was effectively blocked. Any vehicle attempting to exit would have no way around the big truck, given the large trees surrounding the entrance. Placing the ear bud of one of Knoll's com-systems in his left ear, Kruger requested a radio check. Two quick clicks were his response. The second ear bud was placed in his right ear to listen to JR's cell phone. JR was to call just before exiting his car and leave the phone on.

Satisfied, he exited the vehicle and walked north up the steep road until it made a sharp turn to the east. A hundred feet past the turn, it took another turn to the north and continued up toward the compound. He found a spot just inside the tree line on the east side of the road with a good visual of any car or truck trying to exit the area. Finally he pulled his Glock, made sure there was one in the chamber, and patted his vest to double-check the location of his extra magazines. Leaning against a tree, Kruger relaxed and waited.

A minute later, JR called. "I'm at the end of a gravel road, the trees have been cleared to my south. I'm getting out."

Kruger heard two clicks in his left ear and said quietly into his cell phone, "Everyone is in place—go."

Five minutes passed, during which time all Kruger heard was a combination of wind rustling leaves, birds chirping, and the occasional small creature scurrying through the dense underbrush. The place smelled of cedar and rotting leaves. His thoughts drifted from the task at hand to Stephanie. He smiled, wondering where she was and what she was doing. In his left ear he heard a quiet voice say, "Stand by. We have something." The smile disappeared and he brought his attention back to the present.

Kruger hit the transmit button twice and waited.

Then he heard Sandy Knoll say, "We've found Mia's car. She's tied up in the back seat and appears to be unconscious. The doors are locked and the engine is idling."

Kruger's eyes widened. He straightened and yelled, "Break a window. Get her out of there."

"Roger. Wait one—"

CHAPTER 29

New York City

Abel Plymel's eyes snapped open at the sound. Where was he? He couldn't remember. Wherever it was, it was pitch black. All he could see was a sliver of light outlining what he assumed was a window on a far wall. Disorientation and confusion swept over him, and then the sound shrieked again. What was it?

He glanced toward the sound and saw the digital clock on the nightstand next to him. Realization of being in his hotel room suddenly flooded back to him. Dizziness and a slight sense of nausea accompanied his reaching for the shrilling phone next to his bed. The effects of too many single-malt scotches consumed during the previous evening remained. He moaned and mumbled, "Who the hell is calling me at eight in the morning?" He sat up and lifted the handset. "Yes?"

The voice on the other end said, "Mr. Plymel, this is Robert at the front desk. There appears to be a problem with the method you gave us for settling your account."

Plymel leaned forward and supported his head with the palm of his hand, elbow on his knee. "There shouldn't be any problems. Check with American Express."

"Uhhh… Sir, unfortunately, you personally will have to do the checking. We would not have the ability or authority to contact American Express for you. Perhaps a quick phone call will straighten everything out."

Plymel was silent for a few moments. He sighed. "Very well, I'll give them a call."

He slammed the handset back onto the phone base and lay back down. The disorientation was fading, but the nausea remained. After lying there for several minutes, he got up and went into the restroom. He stared at his image in the bathroom mirror. His thinning hair was disheveled. The dark half-moon circles under his eyes were more pronounced, and his face was gaunt. Splashing cold water on his face didn't help. He barely recognized the person staring back at him in the mirror.

Returning to the bedroom, he sat back on the bed, took the American Express Black Card from his wallet and called the number on the back. After several unsuccessful attempts to talk to a real person, a woman calling herself Joan said in a heavily accented voice, "How may I help you today, sir."

"I need someone to find out why my card has suddenly been rejected."

"I would be most happy to check that for you, sir. Can you give me the number?" After giving her the number, there was silence on the line for what seemed liked minutes. When she spoke again, her cheeriness was gone, she said, "This card was reported stolen."

Plymel was quiet, his anger starting to surface. "That's incorrect. I'm holding the card in my hands right now."

"I'm sorry, sir, you will have to speak to our card security department."

The call was transferred and answered by a live person with a Texas drawl. "Card services, this is William, how may I help you today?"

Plymel took a deep breath. "There seems to be a mistake. My card has been reported stolen, but it wasn't."

"If you will read the card number, sir, I will be glad to help you."

Once again, Plymel read the number and was told to hold for a minute. One minute later, William returned. "Sir, can you give me your authorization code and pin number?"

Plymel knew the numbers and recited them to the voice on the phone. There was more silence. "I'm afraid those numbers don't match our records, sir. There's nothing I can do at this point. Thank you for calling." The call ended abruptly.

He stared at the now silent handset. The nausea he had experienced earlier intensified as he rushed into the restroom to bend over the toilet. When he was finished heaving, he stood once again over the sink and used a washcloth soaked in cold water to wipe his face and mouth. As he stood there, a horrifying thought occurred to him. He hurried to the room's computer and accessed one of his remaining bank accounts. The balance was two cents. Wide-eyed and sweating, he accessed the second of his two accounts. The balance was also two cents.

The sound he emitted was not quite human.

***

Alton Crigler sat at his desk studying his computer screen. His assistant opened his office door half way and leaned in. "Abel Plymel's on three, says it's an emergency. He demanded to talk to you and you only."

Crigler frowned; talking to Abel Plymel was not a task he needed at the moment. He picked up the phone. "How can I help you, Abel?"

"That son of a bitch computer hacker stole more money from me! What the hell are you doing about it, Crigler?"

"I'm personally not doing a damn thing about it. He stole the money from you, not me. You're the one who should be doing something about it."

Silence was his response. Finally Plymel said, "I have no

access to funds. He's even stolen my Amex Black Card."

"I'm not sure what you want from me, Abel. You're no longer associated with this firm. Now if you need a personal loan—"

"Absolutely not." Plymel was silent for a few moments. "Sell some of my shares in the company and transfer the settlement."

"May I suggest you sell all of them. The board will request it eventually. They want nothing to do with you, Abel. You embarrassed them."

There was silence again on the call. "Fine, sell all of them. I'll email you the account number. Thanks for the support, Crigler. Just remember who nominated you for your position with the company." With that comment, Plymel ended the call.

Crigler smiled. With his stock sold, Abel Plymel would have no further ties to P&G Global. Finally, after being passed over for the top spot all these years, Crigler would take his rightful place as the head of an organization.

***

Abel Plymel stared at the wireless handset. He started shaking uncontrollably and threw the phone at a wall. It hit, dented the drywall, flew apart, and fell in pieces on the carpet.

Breathing hard, he could feel his heart pounding. He stood, walked to the window, and then back to the bed. He did this for five minutes until he sat on the corner of the bed, put his elbows on his knees, and buried his face in his hands. He stayed like that for fifteen minutes.

Finally, he got his breathing under control and sat up. He stood, walked into the living area of the suite, and turned on the laptop. After emailing the account number to Crigler, he showered, dressed, and checked to see how much cash he had. Two-hundred dollars remained in his billfold—enough for taxi fare.

By noon, everything was arranged at the bank. While

funds were not available yet from his stock transaction, the bank issued a Gold Visa Card tied to the account and would cover any transactions until the funds arrived. He took another taxi back to the hotel, paid for the damaged wall in his room and the destroyed phone. After packing his new clothes purchased the day he checked in, he went back to the front desk and checked out.

It had been a week since he'd set foot in his apartment. Numerous police searches had left the space cluttered and disheveled. He didn't care. The reason for returning to the apartment was hidden in the master suite closet. If the police had not discovered the contents of the safe, he would be out of the apartment within the hour, never to return.

In a corner of the master bedroom closet, the carpet was not tacked down. Kneeling on the closet floor, he pulled at the loose section, revealing a panel cut into the floor. As he slid the panel aside, a hidden safe was exposed, its door facing up. He dialed the combination and opened the door. The contents of the safe were still there. Smiling, he took a deep breath and extracted three items.

He stood and carried two cigar boxes and a nine-by-six envelope from the safe to his bed, laying them down with reverence. One of the cigar boxes contained twenty thousand US dollars and twenty thousand Euro notes. Tipping the envelope up, a Czech Republic driver's license, a Czech passport, and several credit cards slid out onto the bedspread. The passport and driver's license had been kept current by traveling back and forth to Europe over the years. Toronto, Canada, was his normal starting point.

Opening the passport, he smiled and stared at the picture, it was a younger version of the man who held the passport; the man in the picture was identified as Alexei Kozlov, his real name. As of this moment, the man known as Abel Plymel ceased to exist. Finally he opened the second cigar box and took out the Makarov nine-millimeter automatic pistol and five magazines of ammunition.

Alexie Kozlov had been sent to the United States in

1980 with the intent of being heavily involved in the financial markets. His assignment was to learn about, understand, and report back to his KGB handlers on methods to undermine the economy of America. He had a natural talent for stock trading and started building a reputation within the industry. The semi-annual trips back and forth from Europe to pass information to his handler became a ritual. The trips were made under his old name, thus diverting unnecessary attention away from Abel Plymel.

After the Soviet Union collapsed in 1991 and the KGB ceased to exist in its pre-1991 format, Kozlov learned his handler had died of a sudden heart attack. No records of his mission had ever been committed to paper; they were only in his handler's head. With the news of the man's death, Kozlov realized he was a free man and could pursue whatever he wanted to in the US. Twenty years later, he had made a small fortune and was planning a clean exit. But now, his fortune had been ripped away. It was time for retribution.

He pulled out a fresh dark gray suit, white silk shirt, and a red-striped tie from his closet and changed. The Makarov, the old passport, and money were placed in a leather briefcase. As he glanced around the apartment, a thin smile came to his lips. He stood straight, walked to the front door, and left the apartment.

A taxi ride and an hour later found him in the Starbucks across from the P&G Global building. It was a little after five in the afternoon, and he watched as the building disgorged its workers. He sipped his coffee and waited. He had at least another hour to wait.

At ten minutes of six, he discretely opened the briefcase and slipped the Makarov out and into his side suit coat pocket. He then threw a twenty-dollar bill on the table, left the Starbucks, and walked back across the street to the front entrance of the building. At five minutes after six, a black Mercedes sedan pulled up to the curb in front of the building and sat with the engine idling. Ten seconds after the car stopped, Alton Crigler walked out of the building heading directly toward the car. Plymel reached into his suit coat pocket, pulled the Makarov out, and caught up with Crigler as he opened the back passenger door of the Mercedes.

He placed the barrel in the small of Crigler's back. "Get in."

Crigler stopped, looked around, frowned, and did what he was told.

Once inside the car, Crigler said, "Are you crazy? Aren't you in enough trouble without creating more for yourself?"

"Shut up and tell him to drive." Plymel pointed the gun at Crigler and nodded at the driver.

"Where should I tell him to go?"

"Your place."

The driver looked nervously at the rearview mirror, his eyes staring at the gun and then at his boss. Crigler said, "Bob, please take us to my apartment."

The driver nodded and accelerated away from the curb. Once they were in traffic, Crigler turned to Plymel. "Would you like to explain yourself, Abel?"

Plymel smiled. "How long have you been planning this, Alton?" He paused and stared at the man. After several moments without a response from Crigler, he said, "You're not smart enough to plan this step by step. You just took advantage of the situation, didn't you?"

"One has to be ready to act when opportunity arises. You gave me the opportunity." He shrugged. "I took it."

Plymel nodded. "As would I. But I can't let you get away with it."

"I'm sorry. Just exactly how are you going to change anything? You're the one out on bail. You're the one facing prison."

Plymel shrugged. "We'll see."

The car entered the underground parking facility for Crigler's apartment building. Bob drove the Mercedes to its designated slot, put the car in park, and shut off the engine. He sat and stared at the rearview mirror. Plymel shook his head, pointed the Makarov at Bob's head, and pulled the trigger. The noise was deafening. The force of the bullet slammed Bob's head into the driver's-side window, coating it in gray brain matter and blood. The lifeless body slumped forward, restrained only by the seatbelt.

His calm demeanor gone, Crigler stared at Plymel, who was once again pointing the gun at him. He shrieked, "Why the hell did you do that?"

Plymel shrugged. "No witnesses."

"I found the hacker!"

Plymel was quiet for a few moments. "If you want to live, tell me."

"Not till I'm out of this car. Alive."

Plymel shook his head. "Not going to happen." He raised the Makarov, pointed it at Crigler's forehead and pulled the trigger. The man's head snapped back against the C-pillar. His eyes remained open and his body twitched. Plymel reached inside Crigler's suit coat and found his wallet and cell phone. As he opened the car door, he noted the look on Crigler's face: surprise and disbelief.

Grabbing his briefcase, he exited the car and discreetly looked around for witnesses. Seeing no one, he slipped the Makarov back into his suit coat pocket. Just as quickly, he placed the cell phone and wallet, liberated from Crigler, inside the briefcase. With this accomplished, he calmly walked to the elevators and pressed the up button. Ten seconds later, it opened and an elderly man exited. Plymel, keeping his head down, quickly stepped in and pressed the button for the lobby. Once on the street, he hailed a cab and said to the driver, "JFK."

CHAPTER 30

Southwestern Missouri

"Roger," said Knoll. "Wait one—"

JR gripped the steering wheel of his Camry so tight his knuckles turned white listening to the exchange between Knoll and Kruger. His heart was beating so rapidly, it felt like it would jump out of his chest. "What's going on? Is she okay?" The answer to his question seemed to take an eternity.

Finally Knoll said, "She's alive."

JR bowed his head, took a deep breath, and let it out slowly as relief swept over him. She was no longer a hostage. The options of how to handle the next few minutes increased exponentially. As he looked up, a figure emerged from the trees on the dirt road two hundred yards south. Unconsciously he touched the Glock resting in the holster on his right hip. He slowly opened the car's door and stood using it as a shield. A light jacket covered the weapon perfectly. The figure gestured for him to walk forward.

As JR decided what to say, he was silent, noticing the stillness of the afternoon, the slight breeze, the sun midway to the western horizon, and the sound of birds chattering in the background. The air held the scent of cedar trees and dust.

He yelled, "Not until you tell me where she is."

The man responded, "Then I guess we're going to stand here all day staring at each other. Give me the location of the money and I'll tell you where she's located."

"It's not here, I will tell you that."

"Account numbers, password, and location will work nicely. Once I confirm the money's there, I'll tell you where she is."

JR thought about telling the man Mia had been found, but he dismissed the idea immediately. His next thought was to get back in the car and leave. But, until he knew Mia was out of the area, this was not an option. Finally, he started walking south down the gravel and dirt lane toward the man. Keeping to the right side of the road, he stayed as close to the tree line as possible. He was good with an automatic pistol, but no one was good at over six hundred feet. When he was within thirty yards, the man pulled a pistol from a shoulder holster and pointed it at him.

The man said, "That's close enough."

JR stopped. "Who are you?"

Smiling, the man shook his head. "Who I am isn't important. But returning the money you stole is very important."

Smiling, JR said, "Can't do that."

"Then your girlfriend will die."

"I can't give it back because I don't have it anymore."

Weber was silent, caught off guard by the comment. "What do you mean you don't have it anymore?"

"I never did. I transferred it to a bunch of charities. It's gone. Spent. Plymel stole it and I gave it away."

"That wasn't very smart."

JR shrugged. "Maybe not. But it's what I did."

Surprised by the turn of events, Weber stared at JR, trying to determine if he was telling the truth or not. Finally, after almost a minute, he said, "Those funds belonged to the investors. They weren't Plymel's."

JR shook his head. "Your information's faulty. P&G

Global was a scam from the start. Both Plymel and Crigler were lining their pockets every time they bought and sold a business. How many lives were screwed up because of their greed? They've been doing it for years." He paused and let the man digest this revelation.

Weber was silent and just stared at JR.

JR continued, "Plymel wasn't even the biggest thief. Alton Crigler stole more than Plymel. As managing partner, he had more access to funds. Who hired you?" He paused for effect. "I bet it was Crigler. He's probably paying you a trivial amount to find me, locate the funds, and make me disappear. How much is he offering you to find me?"

Weber remained silent, although the pistol wavered, its barrel pointing more toward the ground than at JR. The man continued to stare. Finally he said, "Nice story. Imaginative, but nothing more than BS."

JR shrugged. "You can choose to believe what you want. But, you were instructed to kill me. Correct?"

"That part is correct." Weber started to bring up a Sig Saur nine-millimeter. But JR was ahead of him and made a quick dash to his right through a thick patch of cedar trees. The Sig Saur discharged twice and he felt chips of bark bounce off his face as the bullets struck a tree to his left. He turned back north, found a large oak tree, and stood behind it.

He pulled his Glock from his holster and listened. The background noise of birds, insects, and small creatures was gone. In the eerie silence, JR could hear Weber's steps crunching on the gravel road as he walked north, searching for any sign of his quarry.

As the sound moved north of his position, JR moved as quietly as possible through the underbrush to the south. When he had estimated moving twenty yards, he moved back toward the gravel road. The cover thinned as he moved closer to the road. Now he could barely make out the shape of the man, who was now forty or fifty yards north of his position.

He burst from his cover, pointed his Glock toward

Weber, and fired two shots. He then ran south toward the center of the complex, where Knoll and his team would be heading. As he reached a series of earthen berms used to separate firing lanes, he stopped and listened. Standing with his back to the northern-most berm, he heard the crunching of gravel as the man ran toward him. The sound stopped and Weber said, "The girl's dead by now, Diminski. You lost."

Checking his Glock, JR stepped out from behind the berm and fired two quick shots. Keeping low and using a series of berms as cover, he ran south for another fifty yards. He ducked behind a wooden structure used for storage. Looking for additional cover, he spotted a row of steel barrels a hundred feet further south. He sprinted toward the barrels and got behind them. Filled with sand, they were being used to separate two pistol stations. The barrels were aligned east to west, were waist high, and provided excellent cover. Their position also provided a clear view of the path Weber would have to take to follow him. All he had to do was crouch down and wait.

During the chase, the earpiece for his cell phone had fallen out of his ear. He noticed it dangling from its clip attached to his shirt. He quickly fitted the piece back into his ear and heard Kruger in the middle of a sentence, "Gunshots. JR, what is your status?"

As quiet as possible, he spoke into the microphone, "Weber's north of the pistol ranges. He's coming south down the gravel service road toward my location. I'm in the middle of the compound behind a steel drum barrier."

"Ok, Knoll and two others are heading your way. Mia's alive, but we can't waste any time getting her to a hospital, we've called for an air ambulance."

***

Weber saw his quarry dash out of the trees fifty yards south of his location. The man was quick and got off two shots before he ran behind more trees on the opposite side of the road. Raising his Sig Saur to return fire, he stopped, realizing he was too far out of range. He started to pursue, but paused just before making the small turn leading to the center of the compound. It suddenly dawned on him that he was an easy target standing in the middle of the gravel road. Entering the tree line on the west side of the gravel road, he moved as quietly as possible south, past the cleared areas containing two large pistol ranges. Ten-foot earthen berms surrounded the ranges and provided cover as he moved toward the center of the compound. Once past the pistol ranges, he found a path that led downhill toward more training locations. The path was narrow and surrounded by head-high weeds and scrub brush. He bent low and ascended the path toward the center of the compound.

Just before emerging into a clearing, he heard voices to his left. Stopping at the edge of the woodland, he observed three men dressed in camouflaged clothing talking to Diminski. One of the men was the big guy he'd seen at the fugitive's apartment. His suspicions that the man was military were confirmed. The other two men dressed in camouflage kept calling him major. The high-powered sniper rifle slung over the big man's shoulder helped Weber determine his next move. He quietly backed deeper into the brush. The arrival of reinforcements had been anticipated, so he turned around and headed west, farther into the brush. He worked his way south through the oaks and cedars, toward a small clearing close to the compound's southern entrance. His progress was slow, and he was careful to make as little sound as possible. Halfway to the clearing, he heard a helicopter southeast of his location. His first thoughts were they had brought in a sheriff's department to start a more thorough search. Picking up his pace, he moved quickly to the clearing.

The clearing was at the end of a rutted one-lane dirt road. Weber wasn't sure of the road's purpose, but he had found it when studying the compound on Google Earth. As part of his escape plan, Weber had hidden an old Jeep Wrangler in the clearing the previous day. Just as he was climbing into the driver's seat of the Jeep, he heard the helicopter taking off and realized what it was. They had found the girl and were airlifting her to a hospital.

He hit the Jeep's steering wheel with his hand. Staring out the window, he realized he had been out-maneuvered at every step of the operation. He pulled his cell phone out and dialed Crigler's cell phone. The call went straight to voicemail. He thumbed a quick text message and hit the send icon. He then started the Jeep and drove up the steep bumpy dirt path toward the main service road.

***

Kruger watched as the air ambulance settled onto the highway. After being extracted from the car, Mia was unresponsive with shallow breathing. One member of Knoll's team was a medic named Stan. He immediately started CPR and kept it going until the air ambulance arrived.

A female EMT emerged from the helicopter and rushed toward Mia's position. As she was getting her equipment set up, she said, "What's the situation?"

Stan said, "Carbon monoxide poisoning. Female, mid-thirties, weight fifty-two kilo's..."

The EMT said, "You military?" Stan nodded. She said, "Pounds, what's her weight in pounds?"

"Approximately one fifteen."

"Got it. What else?"

"Pulse Ox was eighty when we found her. CPR was applied and as you arrived, we'd just gotten it to ninety."

"How long?" The EMT's pleasant demeanor changed to one of concern as she applied an oxygen mask to Mia.

He shook his head. "We don't know. She was tied up in a car with the engine running. The exhaust had been funneled into the passenger compartment."

"Shit..."

A second EMT appeared with a gurney, and they immediately lifted Mia onto it. Once she was properly secured, they rushed her to the waiting helicopter.

Kruger watched as Stan followed the EMTs to the air ambulance, said something to the female. She nodded and he climbed into the back of the helicopter. As the rotors on the helicopter spooled up, he started walking back to the compound's entrance. By the time he arrived, the air ambulance disappeared as it turned north toward Springfield.

He stood behind the Denali, which still blocked the compound exit. The view up Molly Avenue stretched north uphill into the compound for three hundred feet before it made a sharp right turn. Kruger could not see around the corner from his location, but he could hear a vehicle approaching on the gravel road.

He drew his Glock out of its holster, pointed it up the path, and stood behind the hood of the big SUV. His position placed the engine block between him and anyone coming down the road. He said into his com-set, "I have a vehicle approaching my location, please acknowledge."

"It's not us Sean. Weber disappeared. It's probably him. Can you see him?"

"No. Wait a second. A vehicle just cleared the curve. It's a dark-brown Jeep. If it's Weber, he's stopped." Kruger smiled grimly. The headlights and grill of the Jeep were visible, but the windshield was still in the shadows.

Kruger heard in his ear bud, "We're heading your way. We'll be on foot."

"Got it. The Jeep is still stopped at the curve. The driver is probably deciding what to do. I doubt he expected his exit to be blocked."

The Jeep did not move for several minutes. Then Kruger heard the engine whine as the driver accelerated the vehicle toward the blocked exit.

The compound entrance was narrow, slightly larger than the length of the Denali. This allowed a steel-pipe gate to block the entrance when the compound was not in use. Kruger had parked the SUV just outside the gate and left it closed. As the Jeep accelerated, he backed away from the

Denali and moved east to keep an eye on the driver's side of the Jeep as it approached.

Dust billowed around the approaching Jeep as it gained speed. The combination of flying dirt and shadows from the surrounding trees obscured Kruger's view of the driver. The Jeep was traveling at over thirty miles an hour when it struck the gate and the Denali. The screech of metal on metal and swirling dust caused Kruger to shield his eyes for just a few seconds. But when he brought his Glock up to cover the driver, the Jeep was unoccupied.

The tree next to Kruger took the bullets aimed at him. The two shots had been fired from north and slightly west of where he stood. He quickly ducked behind a large tree and said into his com-set, "Shots fired. He's in the trees north of the gate on foot."

"Roger, we copy. We're at least five minutes from your location."

Kruger took a deep breath, quickly reviewed his options, and realized there were not many. Five minutes was an eternity in a gunfight. He yelled, "FBI, Weber, give it up."

Two more shots were his answer. The bullets struck the opposite side of the tree he was hiding behind. He lowered himself to a crouch. Realizing those two shots were fired from a location east of the first two shots, Kruger knew Weber was moving. "We found the girl, she's alive. Your plan didn't work."

There was a long pause before he heard his answer. "Doesn't matter. I got the information I needed."

The direction of the voice was even farther east, Kruger knew he had to move or become a sitting duck. He bent over and made a quick dash to a larger tree to his left. Another shot was fired, and the bullet passed between the smaller and larger tree, ricocheting off the highway fifty feet to his south.

Crouching again, he stepped out from behind the tree and fired his Glock in the general direction of the previous shot four times, moving the barrel an inch to the right each time. He quickly ducked back behind the tree as three more shots were fired in his direction.

Picking up a hand-sized rock lying a foot in front of him, he tossed it to his left. The rock struck a tree and more shots were fired at the sound. Kruger stepped to his right and repeated the four-shot pattern in the direction of the gunshot. Two more shots were fired, this time hitting the front of the tree where he was hiding.

His radio crackled, "Sean, we're at the curve. Cease your fire and get behind something solid. We're going to flush him out."

"I copy, making myself small." He sat down behind the tree and waited. Five seconds later, the sound of automatic weapons firing was deafening.

CHAPTER 31

New York City

The name Abel Plymel was given to him by his handlers; there had been no debate in the matter. To him, it was a distasteful name, one he had never really embraced. Now free of the pretense, he relished the thought of once again using his real name.

His appearance needed to change. The passport picture of Kozlov showed a man without glasses. The other difference was shorter hair. On the way to JFK, he had requested the cab driver stop at a Walgreens. Once inside the store, he purchased an electric beard-trimmer, shaving cream, and disposable razors. Now in a men's room at the airport, he used the trimmer and razor to remove his thinning hair. Contacts from his apartment were used to complete the transformation of Abel Plymel to Alexei Kozlov. He smiled as he stared into the mirror.

He had tossed the Makarov and extra magazines into a trash bin outside the airport, concealed in the Walgreens bag. Now he sat in front of the ticket counters trying to determine where Alexei should go.

He heard Crigler's cell phone ringing inside his briefcase.

By the time he opened the case the call was gone. He looked at the missed call file and noticed there were three from the same number. The number meant nothing to him. A minute later, a text message arrived from the same phone.

Kozlov read the message, smiled, and walked to the ticket counter of American Airlines. A middle-aged female ticket agent smiled. "May I help you?"

He returned the smile, handed her his Kozlov passport, and in the accent of his native land said, "Yes, I need to go to Springfield, Missouri."

***

The lower-level parking garage was illuminated by the rotating lights from at least ten patrol cars. The effect was both hypnotic and annoying. Detective Preston Alvarez drove his unmarked car down the ramp and steered it toward the concentration of lights. He noted the crime-scene tape at the back wall and drove the car to a position fifty feet from the center of activity. After shutting the engine off, he exited the car and walked toward the cluster of uniformed officers. His first thought, when he received the call, was it would be just another gang murder or drug deal gone badly. But the number of officers involved indicated otherwise. He ducked under the crime-scene tape, found the precinct watch sergeant giving instructions to two officers, waited until he was done and said, "What've ya got, sarge?"

The sergeant smiled. "I think you're going to find this one interesting."

Alvarez raised his eyebrows. "How so?"

They stepped over to the dark Mercedes sedan. Sergeant Arlen Hildreth pointed toward the back seat. "Look inside. You'll recognize the one in back. It looks like he pissed off the wrong person."

Alvarez walked over and peered into the Mercedes. Alton Crigler's body was slumped against the passenger door on the opposite side from where he stood. The man's eyes

231

were open and he had a look of utter surprise on his face. Glancing to his right, he saw the body of the driver slumped forward against the seat belt. A pattern of blood and gray matter were splattered on the side and front glass. Alvarez backed out of the car and turned to Hildreth. "How long?"

"We won't know for sure until someone from the coroner's office gets here. But it hasn't been that long."

"Shit," said Alvarez. "Who reported it?"

Hildreth nodded toward an elderly man surrounded by several uniformed officers. Alvarez thanked the sergeant and walked toward the group. When he approached, one of the uniforms said, "Lieutenant, this is the gentleman who found the bodies, Aaron Schwartz." He turned to the elderly man. "Sir, this is Detective Alvarez. He's a homicide detective."

Alvarez stared at the man. "Tell me what happened."

"As I told these officers, when I got out of the elevator, there was a man waiting to get on. He had his head down and didn't say a word. You know, just like everyone else in this city. I was halfway to my car and realized I had left my car keys in the apartment. So I went back up. Once I had my keys, I returned to the parking garage. My car is parked next to the Mercedes." The man paused, took a deep breath, and slowly let it out.

Alvarez frowned. "Go on, sir. You said your car was parked next to the Mercedes.

The older man nodded and took another deep breath. "I noticed liquid running down the driver's-side window. When I looked in…" He paused again. "Well, I kind of got sick to my stomach."

Nodding, Alvarez said, "I understand, sir. What did you do then?"

"I called 911. I've been here ever since."

Alvarez looked at the elder man. "The man you saw getting on the elevator, was he your height? What is that, five foot eight or so?"

Schwartz nodded. "Five foot seven and a half. I've shrunk over the past few years."

"How was he dressed?"

"Very expensive suit, hand tailored. I used to be in the garment industry before I retired. The cut looked British."

"What else can you tell me about him?"

"Well—let me see, I just saw him for a second." The man stared out into the parking garage. After several moments he said, "He wore glasses, gold-rimmed ones. His hair, it was combed straight back, kind of thin on top. The hair was brown, I think. Yes—yes, his hair was dark brown." He tapped his finger on his lips for a few seconds and frowned. "That's really all I remember, sorry."

"No problem, sir, you did fine." Alvarez turned to the watch sergeant. "Put a BOLO order out on Abel Plymel. There will be a current mug shot on file. I'll head over to his apartment and see if he's there. Give me two of your guys as backup."

He headed back to his ancient unmarked Ford Crown Vic, got behind the wheel, and closed the door. He pulled out his cell phone and dialed a number. It went straight to voicemail. He said, "Sean—it's Preston. We just found Crigler and his driver dead. They were both shot at what looks like close range. Eyewitness described a man resembling Plymel leaving the scene. We're trying to find him. Call me when you can."

He ended the call, started the car, drove out of the parking garage, and headed toward Plymel's apartment. He turned on his emergency lights and followed a patrol car containing his two backup officers. They were also running with sirens and light bar rotating. Fifteen minutes later, another patrol car with two additional uniformed officers met them at Plymel's apartment building.

Alvarez decided to leave two officers in the front lobby and take the two he had followed from the parking garage up to Plymel's apartment with him. The building manager, an overweight balding man, in his mid-fifties, escorted them to the apartment on the tenth floor and used his passkey to open the door. Before pushing the unlocked door open,

Alvarez told the building manager to stand back. The two uniformed officers stood on the right side of the door; Alvarez stood on the left. All three men had their service weapons out and ready. "Okay guys, let's see if Plymel's here. Be ready for anything."

Alvarez pushed the door open and yelled, "Police. Let me see your hands Plymel." There was no response.

One of the uniformed officers took a quick look inside the open apartment and quickly shook his head. "I don't see anyone."

Nodding, Alvarez said, "We're coming in, Plymel. Don't do anything stupid." He turned to the other officers. "Let's clear the rooms." He rushed in with his gun ready. Five minutes later, Alvarez was in what appeared to be the master bedroom, staring at two cigar boxes and a flat envelope on the bed. He bent over and sniffed each box. One had a distinct odor. He stood up and frowned. "Hey Bob tell me what you smell in that box." He pointed to the open box on the left.

Officer Robert Torres walked over to the bed, bent over, and sniffed. "Hoppe's number nine."

Alvarez nodded. "That's what I thought, he had a gun hidden."

The other uniformed officer, Leland Page, said, "Lieutenant, you need to see this." Page was standing just inside the bedroom closet. Alvarez walked over and stood next to the officer and glanced in the direction Page was pointing. The carpet was pulled back from one of the corners and Alvarez could see the open safe door.

"Damn. Okay, seal the place and I'll get the crime lab headed this way."

He walked back out to the spacious living area and used his cell phone to call the precinct house. The call was answered and he asked to be connected to his boss, Bill Mathews, chief of detectives. When Mathews answered, Alvarez said, "Alton Crigler and his driver were just murdered."

"Yeah, I just heard. What've you got?"

"We're at Plymel's apartment. We found a hidden safe and two empty cigar boxes. One smells like gun-cleaning solvent. No Plymel and no gun."

"Great. What now?"

"I'm calling in the crime lab. Get his picture out to the TSA offices at all the major airports. He's got a two hour head start, he may already be in the wind."

"Got it. Keep me posted."

The call ended and Alvarez dialed Kruger's phone. Again, it went immediately to voicemail. He said, "Sean, it's Preston. We've got an urgent situation here. You need to call me immediately." Ending the call, he looked around the room. His instincts told him he was missing something, but what, he didn't know.

***

Kozlov sat in first class, sipping a glass of Cabernet, waiting for the plane door to close. His flight would take him to Los Angles and then to Dallas on an overnight flight. He was booked on a regional jet that would get him into Springfield by midmorning. He doubted anyone would be looking for him yet. Connecting Abel Plymel and Alexei Kozlov would be problematic at best. Nowhere in his apartment or office was any reference to his former identity. As far as he knew, the only known reference might be in a filing cabinet deep in the bowels of some obscure building in Moscow. Suddenly, he frowned and closed his eyes. He had made a mistake and forgotten something in his apartment.

He glanced at his watch; three hours had passed since he'd followed Crigler into the Mercedes. As the plane lifted off the runway, he eased his seat back. After a few minutes of mulling over his mistake, he shrugged and closed his eyes to get some sleep.

CHAPTER 32

Stone County, MO

Whether you call it luck, fate, chance, a fluke, or being in the right place at the right time, it doesn't matter. Adam Weber's position and the girth of a thirty-year-old white oak tree saved his life. He was standing slightly crouched, with his Sig Saur pointed in the direction of Sean Kruger's voice, when the onslaught of two MP5s, on full automatic, shattered the quiet of the afternoon.

His pistol was ripped from his grip, as a bullet struck its barrel. Another ripped through his jacket sleeve halfway to his elbow, leaving exposed flesh and a bleeding gash in his arm. The next three bullets would have punctured his right lung, severed his aorta, and shattered his left shoulder if he had not been standing behind the large oak tree.

Immediately falling to the ground saved further injury as bullets tore through foliage and tree limbs around him. He stayed motionless until the MP5s grew silent. Then as quietly as possible, he crawled east through the underbrush and rotting leaves of the woodland floor.

Fifty yards from his previous position, he stopped crawling and listened. Voices from behind could be heard, as men started a careful but noisy search for him. With the realization he was outnumbered and outgunned, different escape scenarios ran through his mind. After several minutes, he smiled and started making his way east through the underbrush.

***

Although it seemed longer, the automatic gunfire lasted less than ten seconds. But the amount of ordinance thrown out by the two MP5s was incredible. The giant pin oak tree Kruger was sitting under was at least fifty years old and provided a perfect shelter from the onslaught. His radio crackled and he heard Knoll say, "We're spreading out, Sean. What's your twenty?"

Standing, Kruger replied, "Behind a very large oak tree thirty feet east of the entrance."

Knoll chuckled, "Circle back to the entrance road. We're heading your way."

Less than a minute later, Kruger watched as Knoll and his two team members headed into the trees and brush to search for Weber. JR was standing next to him and said, "Do you think they got him?"

Kruger shook his head. "I doubt it. Too many trees to hide behind. But, they probably pushed him toward the east."

JR stared in the direction Knoll and his men had headed. "Will she be okay, Sean?"

Kruger placed his hand on JR's shoulder. "Yeah, she'll be fine JR. They found her in time." He wasn't sure if he believed his own words, but saying otherwise just wasn't productive.

Knoll and his men were communicating over the com-system, and from what Kruger could tell, not finding anyone. As he was listening, his cell phone vibrated. Glancing at the caller ID, he quickly accepted the call. "Kruger."

"Sean, where the hell've you been?" asked Preston Alvarez.

"I've been a little busy. What's going on?"

"Crigler was found shot to death in the parking garage of his apartment building tonight."

Kruger was silent. He glanced at his watch. It was seven and the sun was low in the sky. Finally after several moments he said, "Where's Plymel?"

"He's in the wind. I'm at his apartment right now. Clothes are missing and he had a hidden safe."

"Wonderful. Any idea of what was in it?"

"Not at the moment, but there's evidence of a gun.

Kruger lowered the phone from his ear and stared toward the east. A few seconds later, he raised the phone and said, "I need to bring you up to speed on developments here, but I'm a little tied up right now. Where will you be in two hours?"

"I'll probably still be here. This case is killing my sex life."

Kruger chuckled and said, "Amen. I'll call you around ten your time." He ended the call and looked at JR.

"I take something's happened in New York," said JR, his voice flat as he stared out at the wooded land east of their location.

"Crigler was shot and killed earlier today."

JR slowly turned toward Kruger and half smiled. "Plymel?"

Kruger nodded. "Probably. They found a hidden safe in his apartment. Not sure what was in it, but Alvarez said there was evidence of a gun."

JR nodded and returned his attention back toward the east. "A nine-millimeter Makarov. It's referenced in some old files I found on his computer."

Kruger stared at JR. "Were you going to share that information? Or just keep it to yourself?" His tone was sharp and louder than normal.

JR shrugged. "At the time, I didn't think it was relevant. Have them check the ballistics on the bullet that killed Crigler. Makarovs use a larger-diameter bullet than standard

NATO nine-millimeter ammunition."

Despite his irritation, Kruger nodded and called Alvarez. His call was answered on the first ring. "Preston, have they done any ballistic work on Crigler yet?"

Alvarez said, "I doubt it. Too early. Why?"

"We have information Plymel owned a Makarov. The bullet will be slightly larger than a standard nine-millimeter."

"Shit, okay. I'll have them get right on it."

The call ended and Kruger took a deep breath. "Anything else I need to know at this point you haven't told me?"

JR turned and stared at Kruger, his eyes cold and his face flush. He said through clinched teeth, "I found a lot of shit on his computer—the important stuff, you know. I didn't think the Makarov was a big deal or even remotely important. Besides, it was just a reference, nothing more. Okay?"

Kruger nodded. "Yeah, sorry."

JR turned his attention back to the woods. "We're all on edge. Don't worry about it."

Neither man spoke as they watched Knoll and his men returning to their location. Before they arrived, Kruger's phone vibrated again. He accepted the call. "Yeah, Preston. Did they find something?"

"An ejected shell casing in the Mercedes front floorboard. It was a Makarov. I called the ballistics expert on the scene and he asked how I knew. I chuckled and said, 'Superior police work.' I won't tell you what he said in return."

Kruger was silent. After a few seconds he said, "It's circumstantial, but points toward Plymel as the shooter."

"Yes, it does."

"Okay, Preston. I'll call you later." The call ended and Kruger turned to JR. "You were right."

JR nodded, but said nothing.

***

The small clearing was empty, except for Mia's Ford Fusion. Weber could still hear voices west of his location, but they were farther away now. He stood in the shadows of the trees for several minutes. As far as he could tell, no one was guarding the car. Crouching low, he duck-walked to the driver's side, peered into the car, and checked for the keys. They were still in the ignition. The rear passenger door was open, its window missing, and shattered glass was on the rear seat. Staying low and keeping the bulk of the car between him and the direction of the search team, he quickly went around and closed the open door.

The small plastic hose used to pass exhaust fumes into the car was lying on the ground next to the car. He smiled grimly and returned to the driver's side of the car. As quickly as possible, he opened the front door and slid in behind the wheel. The interior still smelled of exhaust fumes, so he kept the door open. He turned the key to check on the fuel level. Quarter of a tank; it was enough to get him out of here.

He unconsciously took a deep breath as he turned the key farther. The car started without hesitation. He closed the door and placed the transmission into reverse. The smell of exhaust fumes was overpowering. After all the remaining windows were powered down, he breathed easier.

The dirt path leading to the clearing was rutted and rarely used. When he originally drove the car to this spot, he gave little thought to backing it out again. The path was narrow and severely overgrown. But because the slope of the land was not severe, the car managed the climb with only slight difficulty. Halfway to the main service road was a wide section of open land. The clearing allowed him to do a K turn. Now driving forward, he headed toward Molly Avenue. At the intersection, Weber turned the car right toward the center of the compound and the northern exit.

As soon as he was on Molly Avenue, he glanced in the rearview mirror and to his surprise saw two men running toward him. As they raised their MP5s to fire, he sped north through the main center of the compound. He ducked down just as the rear window of the car was blown out. Weber accelerated the Ford, as the road curved to the left and out of their field of vision.

Diminski's gray Camry was still parked at the north end of the compound. As Weber passed the car, he double-checked to make sure no one had returned to ambush his exit. Driving east, the car moved down the gravel road until it intersected with Stoops Lane Road. Weber briefly stopped the car as he determined the best route to take. Turning right would take him back toward the south. Without knowing exactly how many men were at the compound trying to catch him, turning left was his only option.

***

Knoll emerged from the woods first. "We didn't find him. Too much brush and too many places to hide. Joseph's heading this way with the Stone County sheriff, six deputies, and a search dog."

Kruger shook his head. "He's pretty resourceful and it's going to be dark soon. If we don't find him in the next fifteen minutes, he'll be gone."

Just as Kruger finished his statement, they heard the faint sound of a car starting. With all the trees in the surrounding area, the direction of the sound was hard to pinpoint. Knoll said, "Shit, he's using Mia's car." He turned to his men, pointed to the north. "The path the car's on will intersects this road about a quarter of a mile north of here. See if you can cut him off."

Both men nodded and started running toward the top of Molly Avenue.

Kruger looked to the east and shook his head. "Damn, we've lost him."

***

The road was paved but crooked. As the miles clicked by, Weber started breathing easier. It was dusk and so far no headlights appeared in his rearview mirror. With no idea of where he was or where the road would take him, he kept driving. Fifteen minutes after leaving the compound, Weber stopped when the road intersected Highway 60. Checking the rearview mirror one more time, he confirmed no one was following him. Turning north would take him back to Springfield. South would take him toward the Branson, Missouri, area. The area was thick with cheap hotels off the beaten path and lots of tourists. He smiled; it would be the perfect place to hide until he could contact Crigler. Turning the steering wheel to the right, he accelerated the car southward.

***

The drive back to Springfield in JR's Camry was quiet and uneventful. Kruger drove and JR sat in the passenger seat, staring out into the dark of night. Neither man had spoken since leaving the compound. As they passed a Springfield city limits sign, JR said, "It's not over yet, is it?"

Kruger shook his head. "No."

JR nodded and returned to staring out the passenger-door window. He remained quiet until they pulled into the Mercy Hospital parking lot. Kruger parked the car in a lot next to the emergency room. JR stepped out and said, more to himself than anyone, "God, please let her be alive."

Kruger showed his FBI credentials at the admittance desk, and they were quickly told where Mia was located. When they arrived, Stan was standing outside the curtain.

JR stared at the curtain, his eyes wide, and then at Stan. "How's she doing?"

Stan smiled. "She's doing better. A doctor and nurse are in there right now. She's breathing on her own and her vitals are stable."

JR smiled slightly and leaned against the wall next to the doorframe. Closing his eyes, he lowered his head and took a deep breath. Kruger could barely hear it, but JR said, "Thank you, Father," as he made the sign of the cross.

The curtain was drawn back, and a tall woman dressed in scrubs emerged. She had black hair pulled back in a ponytail, a thin face, and fashionable glasses in front of dark-brown eyes. She looked at JR, then at Kruger. She smiled and returned her attention to JR. "Are you the fiancé?" JR nodded. The woman held her hand out and JR automatically shook it. "I'm Doctor Morrison. Mia is going to be fine. She's asleep again, but she's been asking for you."

JR just stared at the doctor. Finally after a few brief moments, he said, "Was there any…"

She shook her head. "No, we don't think there was any brain damage. Her vitals are stable and her reflexes are normal." She nodded toward the now open curtain. "You can go in now if you want to. We'll be transferring her to a room shortly."

JR said, "Thank you, doctor."

She smiled, nodding at Kruger and Stan as she walked off.

***

It was 2:40 a.m. JR was sitting in a recliner next to Mia's hospital bed holding her hand. He had dozed several times, but was currently awake watching her sleep. At the insistence of Kruger, she had been placed in a private room. Two of Knoll's men were standing in the hall outside the door. No one was allowed in except hospital personnel. JR watched as she blinked several times and her hand twitched. Eventually, her eyes opened and she turned her head toward JR. In a croaky whisper, she said, "How long?"

He smiled. "Not long. Just a couple of hours."

"Liar."

He was silent waiting for her to be more alert.

"Did you get him?"

JR shook his head. "No."

She closed her eyes again and was silent for a minute. "This isn't going to be over until you kill him, JR."

JR frowned. "What do you mean?"

"JR—listen to me. He's not going to give up. He told me everything. He wouldn't stop talking. That's when I knew I was in trouble. Once he forces you to tell him where the money is, he'll kill you."

JR nodded. "Are you going to be okay?"

She smiled weakly. "As long as you're with me, I will be." Her eye's closed again and within thirty seconds her breathing became soft and rhythmic.

JR held her hand for a few more minutes. He stared at her, released her hand, and stood. "I'll never leave you, Mia." He got up and walked out of the room to find Kruger.

He was asleep in the waiting area down the hall from Mia's room. JR sat down beside him and waited. Several moments later, Kruger opened an eye. "Well, how is she?"

"She'll make it."

Kruger nodded and sat up straighter in the lounge chair. "Weber may not know Crigler's dead. I'm betting Plymel will try to find you through Weber."

JR nodded.

"You need to get on the computer and use your skills to find him."

JR didn't say anything and just stared at Kruger. Finally he said, "Yeah… You're right. Will you give me a ride?"

***

It was nine in the morning when JR said, "Sean, I think I've found him."

Kruger had been dozing on a sofa in JR's computer room. He hurried over to the computer JR was staring at. "What've you got?"

JR pointed to the computer screen. It showed a security

camera shot of a man at a ticket counter. "He's shaved his hair and the glasses are gone, but it's him."

"Where is this?"

"JFK International, American Airlines ticket counter." JR looked at the time stamp on the video. "Seven fifty-three last night."

Kruger stared at the picture and was silent for a moment. Finally he said, "Can you tell where he went?"

JR shook his head. "This is the only shot the TSI system has of him. I've checked. He must not be flying under his real name." JR looked up at Kruger. "Weber didn't know Crigler was dead when I spoke to him yesterday. Do you think Plymel will try to contact Weber?"

Kruger shook his head. "Don't know. Unless..." He stopped in mid-sentence, took his cell phone, and made a call. It was answered on the third ring.

"Alvarez."

"Preston, it's Kruger. Did Crigler have a cell phone on him when he was found?"

"Good question. Let me check."

Kruger held the phone to his ear as he waited. Two minutes later, Alvarez said, "Nope. His wallet was missing too. We think Plymel was trying to make it look like a robbery. Do you know something I don't?"

"Not yet. Thanks for the info. I'll call you later." Kruger ended the call and turned to JR. "We have to assume Plymel has Crigler's cell phone." Walking to a window in the computer room, Kruger stared out. He was quiet for several minutes, his finger tapping his lips. Finally he said, "American Airlines planes landing at Springfield originate from either Dallas or Chicago. Can you check to see if any recent passengers connected from JFK through either city?"

JR smiled and nodded. "I should have thought of that."

Even though JR was already in the American Airlines system, it took over an hour to compare the passenger manifests for flights the prior evening. Finally, he said, "We have five names; two are female, one is under ten years old, and two adult males."

Kruger had walked back into the computer room with a cup of coffee. "What about the males?"

Looking up from the computer with a smile, JR said, "Brian Griggs, age twenty-four." He paused, his grin growing larger. "And Alexei Kozlov, age fifty-eight, JFK to LA International, connected with a red-eye flight into Dallas. Kozlov was on a nine a.m. flight from Dallas to Springfield. It landed about twenty minutes ago."

"That's him."

Nodding, JR's fingers danced on the keyboard. Five minutes later, they heard a ping as JR's facial recognition software found a match for the picture taken at JFK. Staring at the screen, he pointed at an older man walking through the security exit. "Bingo, there he is."

Kruger bent over and stared at the picture on the laptop. "Welcome to Springfield, Mr. Alexei Kozlov."

CHAPTER 33

Branson, MO

Adam Weber sat inside Waxy O'Shea's Irish Pub, just off the Main Street entrance to the Branson Landing. The small two-person table had a clear view of both the breezeway leading into the outdoor mall and the intersection of Main Street and Branson Landing Boulevard.

The Branson Scenic Railway station could also be observed across the street. The Hilton Convention Center was partially hidden west of the train station, but from Weber's viewpoint, he could see cars entering the circle drive of the hotel. The last message from Crigler had instructed him to wait in the breezeway for a black Ford Explorer to pick him up.

He trusted Alton Crigler, to a point, but alarm bells were ringing concerning the method he was using to communicate. Text messages only, no conversation over the phone. When asked why, Crigler had simply sent a message explaining text messages were harder to trace and voiceprints could not be used to identify the callers. While it made sense, it also raised a few questions about who was actually communicating with him. The other question he needed answered was why Crigler was in Missouri. There had never been a discussion about his joining Weber. The only explanation he had been given was vague at best—something about wanting to assist with finding the fugitive. Another reason Weber was being overly cautious.

He had arrived an hour before the rendezvous, and it was now an hour after the appointed time. During the entire two hours, not one black Ford Explorer had passed through the intersection, nor had he seen anyone remotely resembling Crigler. He paid for his beer and sandwich, glanced around the pub to see if anyone was paying too much attention. Seeing no one with an elevated interest, he exited the pub. Outside, Weber turned right and walked east on the breezeway to the main avenue of the outdoor mall. While the peak tourist season was almost over, the mall was still crowded with shoppers and sightseers.

He had abandoned the Fusion in a Walmart parking lot in Branson West the night before. He'd walked to a Walgreens across the street and called a taxi, which had taken him to the Branson Landing area. Last night had been spent at the Hilton, directly across the street. Now it was midafternoon the following day and the tourist traffic was heavy. At the intersection of the breezeway and the main thoroughfare of the mall, Weber stood and watched the crowd. Just as he decided to return to his hotel room, he sensed someone behind him. He started to turn his head when a voice behind him said, "Don't turn around. There's a black Explorer parked in the Hilton's circle drive. Turn around slowly and let's start walking that way."

"What if I don't?"

"You'll get a hollow point twenty-two slug in your spine."

Weber nodded, turned around, and started walking back toward the crosswalk at the mall entrance. "Where's Crigler?"

"I'm afraid Alton will not be joining us today."

"He's dead, isn't he?"

"Very."

Weber nodded and stopped at the crosswalk to wait for the light to turn green. "Nice explanation about the text messages. I actually bought it. Once we get to the car, what's your plan, Plymel?"

"Alas, Abel Plymel doesn't exist anymore; he's as dead as Alton Crigler."

The walk across Branson Landing Boulevard and up Main Street to the Hilton circle drive only took three minutes. Weber's eyes darted from left to right, searching for an escape opportunity, but nothing he saw offered much of an opening. When they arrived at the Explorer, Kozlov said, "The vehicle is unlocked. Get in the driver's seat." Weber did as he was told, while the other man slipped into the rear passenger compartment. The gun was still pointed at Weber when he looked in the rearview mirror. This was his first opportunity to see his captor. Kozlov's face was gaunt, the combed-back hair gone, as were the glasses. But the eyes were the same: crystal blue and cold.

Weber was silent, thinking through his odds. After a few moments, he said, "I know where the man you're looking for is located."

"You mentioned that in your messages. Where is he?"

"If I tell you, what's in it for me?"

"You know, that's what I love about this country, everything's for sale. Take for instance this Ruger twenty-two. I bought it this morning at a pawnshop. At first he wouldn't sell it to me, but when I offered him two-thousand dollars, he threw in a suppressor, subsonic ammunition, and didn't even ask my name."

Weber adjusted the rearview mirror so that he could see the man in back better. The gun was pointing directly at his head. "You don't have to point that at me, you know."

"For the moment, I do. Start the car and drive toward Springfield. I assume that's where the man with my money is located?"

Weber started the Ford SUV and backed out of the angled parking slot. He turned right onto Main Street and drove the short distance to the stoplight. When the light turned green, he turned left on Branson Landing Boulevard and accelerated toward the north. "Crigler was paying me to find the fugitive, learn the location of the money, and then kill him."

Kozlov stared at Weber, but remained quiet.

With a faint smile, Weber said, "He didn't want you to find the guy and get your money back."

Kozlov remained quiet for several more moments. Finally he said, "That didn't work out so well for Crigler, did it?"

Weber shook his head. "Guess not. I know the name of the man who took your money. I also know where he lives. How much is that worth to you?"

"You're in no position to bargain?"

Weber shrugged. "You kill me and you'll never find him. He hid his trail perfectly. I know how to find missing people and I only found him by accident."

Weber accelerated the Explorer as he merged onto North Highway 65. Ten seconds later, he saw a sign on the shoulder of the highway. Springfield was thirty-five miles ahead. He put the Ford on cruise control. "Even if you find him, he has five military types guarding him. I had to kidnap his girlfriend to get close to him."

Kozlov remained quiet.

"We're in a position to help each other, you know. By the way, you said Abel Plymel is dead. What are you calling yourself now?"

"It's not important." Kozlov briefly stared ahead at the highway. He was silent for awhile. "Tell me, how do you think we can help each other?"

"You need to find this guy and I need money to get out of here. It's simple. You pay me, I give you the information, and then I disappear."

"So, how much do you think this information is worth?"

"Oh, let's say a million dollars—give or take a few hundred thousand."

Kozlov laughed. "You're not in a position to demand a sum that large."

"Okay, I had to give it a shot. Crigler was going to pay me a hundred thousand."

"I'll give you fifty thousand—no more."

Weber knew he would be lucky to get out of this alive, let alone get paid. He just needed some time to think of an escape plan. "How do I know when I tell you the information you won't shoot me?"

"You don't—you'll have to trust me."

Weber shook his head. "That's not in my best interest. We're going to have to work this out before I tell you anything."

"There's nothing to work out. You tell me and I don't shoot you."

Weber laughed. "Do you plan to shoot me while we're driving sixty-five miles an hour?"

His answer was silence.

***

Kruger waited for Preston Alvarez to come to the phone. Finally, after being transferred six times, he heard, "Alvarez."

"I thought you had a cell phone?"

"I do, but unlike you, I have to work in a concrete jungle. The cell phone reception sucks in this building."

Kruger chuckled. "I got your message. What's up?"

"We found something very interesting in Plymel's apartment."

Kruger was silent for a moment. Then he said, "Yeah, what did you find?"

"Airline ticket stubs to Russia, originating in New York and Toronto. Not one or two, but dozens, dating back to the early eighties. They were hidden in a floor safe, along with several empty fireproof boxes."

"Let me guess, the name on the tickets is Alexei

Kozlov."

Now it was Alvarez's turn to be silent. Finally he said, "What do you know that I don't?"

"One of my associates just identified Plymel arriving here in Springfield last night. He was flying under the name Alexei Kozlov. Apparently, it's an old alias. We also found out there's a problem with his resume prior to 1981."

"What problems?"

"Well for one, the college he claims his degree is from has no record of his attendance. There are no contributions to Social Security prior to 1981, and now we find out he's been traveling to Russia as Alexei Kozlov."

"Oh boy. What have we got here, Sean?"

"Well, if he was a Muslim, I'd say we have a terrorist on our hands. But that far back, he just might have been a sleeper agent for the Soviet Union. An agent who decided to stay here and earn a small fortune after the wall fell down."

"Why weren't we notified about this guy?"

"I had the same question, but it was a long time ago. Computers were in their infancy and records were probably misplaced on purpose. A lot of those guys probably just slipped through the cracks. But, if that's who he is, we have a bigger problem than we originally thought."

***

"What did you find out about our mystery man, Mary?" Joseph said as he stepped into an empty bedroom of JR's apartment after taking the phone call.

"My dear Joseph, have I ever disappointed you?"

"No, my love. You never have."

"It seems our Mr. Plymel had a deal worked out with the CIA. He could stay here and make as much money as he wanted." She paused for a few moments. When Joseph didn't say anything, she continued, "He was allowed to stay as long as he passed bogus information to his Russian handlers. He was protected, Joseph—nothing more and nothing less."

Joseph stared out one of the bedroom windows, saying nothing.

"Alexi Kozlov is his real name. The agency allowed him to freely travel back and forth to Europe using his Russian-issued passport. The only stipulation was he had to report trips three weeks in advance.

Joseph closed his eyes; he backed up and sat down on the bed in the room. "Go on."

"His official file calls him, and I quote, 'Narcissistic, extremely volatile, and possibly dangerous to those he encounters. He is to be watched and monitored. Personal contact is to be handled with care and extreme caution.' This is a notation in his official file after the fall of the Soviet Union." She was quiet for a second. "Let's see, the notation is dated November 14, 1992."

Joseph sighed. "Does it say who his case officer was?"

"Yes, it does. Is it important?"

"Yes, it is. Tell me."

"I know most of these guys had pseudonyms. Let me see. Okay here it is. The name is Charlie Rose. Do you know him?"

Joseph was silent. He leaned over and supported his head with the palm of his hand, his elbow on his knee.

"Joseph, are you there? Are you okay?"

"Yes, I'm here."

"Do you know who Charlie Rose was?"

"Yes, I know who Charlie Rose was. I was Charlie Rose."

CHAPTER 34

Springfield, MO

"You don't remember him?" Kruger said sarcastically. "Really?"

"No, I don't remember him," Joseph's irritation grew as Kruger continued his rant.

"How can you not remember someone you described as, and I quote, 'Narcissistic and dangerous'? Please explain."

"It's simple, I don't remember him. Do you remember everyone you dealt with thirty or more years ago?"

Kruger shook his head. "No."

"I didn't think so. I was the managing case officer for every sleeper agent we turned during those years. There were a dozen of us on the team. We were trying to locate them and turn them. A lot of them were under so much stress it caused them to flip out when we confronted them. I only remember the ones we had to institutionalize, or the ones we had to retire."

JR sat on a kitchen barstool as Kruger and Joseph argued. He frowned and said loudly, "*Enough*, he's here now. What's our next step?"

They both looked at JR. Joseph blinked several times.

"You're right, arguing won't help."

"By the way, how did Mary get her hands on his file?" said Kruger.

Joseph shrugged. "Mary can be very resourceful."

"She may be, but those files are top secret. How would she know where to find them?"

Joseph was quiet as he stared at a point on the kitchen floor. After a few moments, he smiled. "That's about the time I met Mary. She—uh—she and I worked together for awhile during those years."

JR and Kruger watched Joseph as he remained quiet, still staring at a spot on the floor. Joseph sighed. "They were all alike. Arrogant, self-absorbed, well trained, intelligent, and most of all adaptive. They might have looked different, but the Soviets picked only the ones with similar personalities." He raised his head. His eyes focused. "All of this is the past. We have to deal with Kozlov in the present. The fact is all of the individuals the Soviets sent over were highly resourceful and capable of brutal behavior. He will be dangerous."

Kruger remained silent. Finally he said, "I agree. I'm going to assume he's contacted Weber with Crigler's cell phone. If he has, they've either teamed up or Plymel's extracted the information he needed and killed him."

"Regardless, we have to assume he knows about JR. Mia's safe at the hospital. Sandy will need to pull a couple of guys to monitor this apartment."

JR slapped the kitchen table. He shook his head and said loudly, "*No!* Dammit, this is my fight. I'm responsible for Mia being in the hospital. I'm responsible for Kozlov being here, and I need to take care of this myself. I'm not helpless."

Kruger smiled. "Nobody said you were helpless. This guy's dangerous. I don't want to take any chances."

JR stood. "I don't want to take chances either. But, his training was over thirty years ago. He may still be dangerous, but at one time so was I."

***

The black Ford Explorer exited Highway 65 at the Sunshine Street exit. The light at the intersection was green, so Weber drove under the highway without having to stop. His plan to get out of the SUV without getting shot would need perfect timing. Now moving west into the central section of town, the street he was looking for would be on his right.

"I'm going to show you where he lives and then I'm going to park and walk away." They passed a large hospital at the intersection of National Avenue and Sunshine. Weber's destination was two blocks west. Turning right onto Hampton Ave, he accelerated. The first street to the north was University and on the northwest corner of the intersection was a utility pole with a large tree ten feet behind it.

Weber kept his foot on the accelerator as they approached the intersection. From the back seat, Kozlov said, "Slow down, you idiot."

As the Ford entered the intersection, Weber turned the steering wheel hard to the left and hit the brakes. The result was a high-speed skid into the utility pole with the impact on the passenger-side rear door, exactly where Kozlov was sitting. The resulting crash jarred the Ruger out of Kozlov's hand, and his head impacted the C pillar of the SUV. Weber quickly unbuckled his seatbelt, opened the door, and ran southeast into the neighborhood.

Kozlov recovered quickly, determined he wasn't hurt, searched for and found the pistol. He secured it in his belt and exited the vehicle on the undamaged side. Residents of the neighborhood were now looking out their windows and doors to see what all the noise was about.

Kozlov glanced around searching for Weber, but he had disappeared into the densely populated neighborhood. Attention to the crashed SUV from surrounding neighbors was increasing. Without thinking, Kozlov ran north on

Hampton Street away from the accident.

Weber ran east and then north, cutting through the yard of a house with a for-sale sign in front. He stopped in the back yard, peered into a window, and saw the house was empty. The back yard was heavily landscaped, and the view from the house behind was obscured by dense bushes and trees. Sitting down on the back porch, he pulled Mia's cell phone from his pocket and turned it on. Checking the recent call listings, he selected a number and hit the send button.

***

JR's cell phone rang. He looked at the caller ID. "Got a call coming in from Weber." Both Kruger and Joseph stopped their conversation as JR accepted the call. "Yes."

"Congratulations. You outsmarted me in the woods. Well played."

"What do you want, Weber?"

"Tell your FBI friend I have some information for him."

"Tell him yourself. He's right here."

JR handed the phone to Kruger. "This is Agent Kruger." Kruger pointed to JR's laptop and mouthed, "Find him" as he listened.

"Agent, you might be interested in a car accident that just occurred on the corner of Hampton and University. A person of interest was in the rear passenger seat. He may be injured."

"Who's the person…" But the call had ended. He looked at JR. "Any luck?"

JR shook his head. "Didn't have time. What did he say?"

Kruger walked toward the door. "He told me there was a car accident and someone was injured. I assume he meant Kozlov. I'll call you when I know more. How do I get to Hampton and University?"

As soon as the Mustang was out of the parking lot, Kruger flipped the switch that activated the car's siren and flashing headlights. Eight minutes later, he turned left off of

Kimbrough Street onto University. Four blocks ahead, he saw flashing lights from two fire trucks, three police cars, and an ambulance.

He pulled in behind one of the police cars, got out, and clipped his badge to his belt. Opening the Mustang's trunk, he retrieved his FBI windbreaker, slipped it on, and walked toward a police officer talking to several elderly women. Over the police officer's right shoulder, he saw a black Ford Explorer smashed against a leaning utility pole.

As he walked closer, the police officer looked up and said to the women, "Excuse me ladies." To Kruger he said, "Who are you?"

Kruger showed his ID and noticed the officer's name badge. "Officer Bradford. I'm Agent Sean Kruger, FBI. Where are the passengers?"

"FBI? Why's the FBI interested in a car accident?"

"Officer Bradford, just answer my question. Where are the passengers?"

"Not until you tell me why the FBI is interested."

"I have information that a fugitive may have been in the SUV. Now once again, where are the passengers?" Kruger stared intently into the young officer's eyes.

The policeman stared back at Kruger and shook his head. "No one saw the driver leave the scene. But several witnesses saw a man get out of the back seat, look around, and start running in that direction." Bradford pointed north. "They describe him as being somewhere between five foot six and five foot ten, bald, clean shaven, and wearing a dark suit with no tie. One lady said she saw blood on his forehead, and we have a few drops on the back seat. Do you know who this guy is?"

Kruger nodded. "Yes, his name is Alexei Kozlov. He's wanted for a double murder in New York City. He's armed and extremely dangerous. My suggestion would be to lock this neighborhood down and get the word out immediately. If someone tries to stop him without backup, you'll lose a fellow officer."

Officer Bradford stared at Kruger without saying a word. He blinked several times then stepped away and started talking into his shoulder microphone. Kruger walked closer to the wrecked vehicle and peered inside. He noticed a smear of blood on the damaged side of the vehicle and drops extending across the seat. He turned to Officer Bradford, who had finished talking to his dispatcher. "Do you have a crime lab here in town?"

Bradford nodded.

"Seal the vehicle and get someone to get samples of the blood. I have access to information that will help you confirm his identity."

Nodding again, Bradford said, "Are you taking over the scene, agent?"

Kruger smiled. "No officer, this is your crime scene. I'm just here to offer assistance, if needed."

The policeman gave Kruger a slight grin. "My chief will appreciate that. Excuse me while I get the lab headed this way."

Kruger walked back to his car, retrieved his cell phone, and called Alvarez to get the information sent to the local lab.

After the call, Kruger stared at the Ford Explorer and then glanced up and down the neighborhood. It would be dark in less than an hour. Kozlov would be looking for somewhere to hide for the night. He shook his head. Someone was going to get hurt.

***

The large spruce was located on the southwest corner of the house where Alexei Kozlov now stood. The home was two houses west of the accident site. After running north, he had doubled back to determine who might be in Springfield looking for him. His efforts were rewarded as he watched FBI agent Sean Kruger talk on a cell phone. Smiling, he pulled the Ruger out of his waistband, leaned against the corner of the house, and aimed at the FBI agent. He judged the distance to his target at two hundred feet or more. The little Ruger would be completely ineffective at this range. He lowered the gun, put it back in his waistband, and relaxed. There would be another time and place for putting a bullet into Kruger.

The sun was low on the western horizon, and due to all the mature trees in the neighborhood, light was fading quickly. Kozlov checked the time on Crigler's cell phone; he only had a few more minutes before it would be dark enough to leave his hiding place. He needed to find a house to stay in for the night. Locating the hacker would be tomorrow's business.

As twilight descended on the neighborhood, he turned back to the north and started walking. Five blocks later, the sound of sirens could be heard in all directions. Kozlov stood, still listening. The search for him would only intensify as it got darker. Soon, they would be going house by house. After checking several homes, he picked a small bungalow, two houses west of the intersection of Kings Avenue and Kingsbury Street. Curtains were drawn across the front room picture window, but Kozlov could see the glow of a lamp behind the curtain. He walked to the door and pushed the doorbell. The door was opened twenty seconds later by an elderly woman. Her eyes grew wide as he pushed the door open wider and pointed the Ruger directly at her head.

"Don't say a word and you won't get hurt."

She backed into the room as Kozlov followed. The woman opened her mouth to scream just as he shot her in the forehead, point-blank. She collapsed onto the living room floor, which made more noise than the sound of the suppressed Ruger.

A voice from further back in the house said, "Who is it, Cindy?"

Kozlov followed the sound of the voice and found a wheelchair-bound man watching television in a back bedroom. As Kozlov walked through the bedroom door, the man turned to say something and was shot in the temple. His now limp body slumped forward and tumbled to the floor out of the wheelchair.

Kozlov walked over to the television and turned it off. The house was quiet. In the distance, more sirens could be heard converging on the neighborhood.

CHAPTER 35

Springfield, MO

The restaurant was located at the corner of National and Bennett, less than a mile from the accident site. Four police cars, their light bars flashing, were in the parking lot. Each of the restaurant's two exits had a uniformed officer standing watch, preventing anyone from entering or leaving. Kruger was escorted into the building through the front door. As he entered, he saw Adam Weber sitting in a corner booth drinking a glass of ice tea. The place smelled of onions and cumin. A tall police officer with sergeant's stripes stood five feet away. Kruger walked over to the booth and sat down.

Weber said, "Want some ice tea? It's really good."

Kruger stared at Weber. "Where's Plymel?"

Weber shrugged. "No idea. I slid the Explorer into the pole and bailed out. I didn't even look to see if he was hurt. I just ran." A crooked grin appeared. "You might want to know he's going by the name Alexei Kozlov now."

Kruger nodded. "Yes, we already knew that." He paused for a few moments, then leaned slightly forward. "You almost killed the girl."

Again Weber shrugged. "If I'd known Crigler was dead, I

might have played it different. But I didn't know. My job was to kill Diminski." He sat back in the seat and smiled. "The only way I could get him away from his babysitters was the girl. You understand, Agent Kruger, don't you? I couldn't have witnesses."

Kruger was silent for a few moments. "You told the police you had information for me. What is it?"

"When I heard all the sirens, I figured they'd find me eventually, so I walked in here, ordered an ice tea, and a couple of tacos. Then I just waited. After a while, I thought I was home free until a couple of cops came in and asked what car I was driving. I told them to call you." He smiled. "I had information you need."

Kruger started to stand. "I don't have time for this." He glanced toward the uniformed policeman. "Sergeant, get this man out of here."

Weber's eyes grew wide. He looked at the police officer and then back at Kruger. "Wait."

Kruger turned back toward Weber. "What?"

"My information is critical. Let's deal."

Kruger chuckled, "I don't think you understand the situation, Weber. We have evidence you killed Sharon Crawford. DNA evidence—fairly ironclad, in my opinion. That's enough to put you away for life. Then we have the attempted murder of Mia Ling. You really don't have a lot of bargaining chips."

Weber stared at Kruger. Beads of sweat formed on his forehead, but he kept his expression blank. Finally he shrugged. "He's got a suppressed Ruger .22 with subsonic hollow points. He also has a serious chip on his shoulder for Diminski." He nodded in Kruger's direction. "And for you. Lucky for me he babbled all way from Branson. It gave me time to figure out my escape plan. If you ask me, the guy's over the top. He's crazy."

"Where did he get the twenty-two?"

"He said he paid a guy two-thousand dollars for it. Some pawnshop here in Springfield."

Kruger looked up at the officer, who frowned and walked out of the building. Another officer came in immediately and took his place.

"Okay, so he's got a gun?

"He knows where Diminski lives."

Kruger was silent and just stared at Weber.

"I needed a bargaining chip to keep him from shooting me. He's going to outwait this manhunt, show up at Diminski's and shoot him. He doesn't care about the money anymore. It's all about revenge. I told you he's crazy."

Kruger stood up and turned toward the door but stopped and turned back around. "You don't know how crazy." He walked through the exit door, turned to several of the cops getting ready to go in. "Throw his ass into the dirtiest cell you have." They all smiled as they entered the building.

***

Kozlov dragged the bodies of the elderly couple to the garage of the small home and placed them in a ten-year-old Honda Accord. To his dismay, the couple only had one car. But he needed them out of the house and sealed away. He now had an extra day or so before the stench of decomposition forced him to abandon the house. Searching the bedroom where he'd shot the old man, he found what he had expected. Two shotguns, an AR-15 and two S&W 1911s. One was a forty-five caliber and the other a nine-millimeter. Kozlov smiled, the NRA decal on the front door had not lied; the old man liked his guns.

The refrigerator was neat and full of juices, vegetables, fruits, and beer. The freezer was half full and there were plenty of canned goods in the pantry. If no one tried to contact the couple in the next few days, he would be able to stay here, eat, and hide while the door-to-door search was conducted. A black leather recliner was in the front bedroom. He moved it so he could see out, but no one looking in could see him. He turned out the lights, held the Ruger in his left hand, and waited.

The first visit came at 11:00 p.m. Two police officers were going door to door, with two other officers in a patrol car on the street backing them up. The doorbell rang three times and they knocked twice. After several minutes, one of the officers wrote something in a notebook and both walked to the next house. A half-hour later, a patrol car drove by slowly with its search light moving across the houses in the neighborhood. As it shined on the window he was behind, it paused briefly but then moved on. At 3:15 a.m., he heard voices and watched four men dressed in desert combat uniforms walk down the street. Each was armed with an M-16, held at ready.

Kozlov frowned. The National Guard complicated his situation. Somewhere around five in the morning, fatigue took him and he dozed in the recliner. The sound of a key in the front door and it opening woke him from his restless sleep. Slightly confused, he quickly regained awareness of his situation when he heard a female voice call out, "Cindy, it's Brenda. Are you two okay? Lot's happening in your neighborhood this morning."

He glanced at the digital clock next to the bed and saw it was five minutes after eight. Standing, he quietly walked to the bedroom door as the woman walked past. She was dressed in blue scrubs and headed toward the back bedroom. She opened the bedroom door. "Hey guys, where are you?"

Kozlov walked up behind her, pointed the Ruger at the back of her head, and pulled the trigger.

***

Kruger parked the Mustang behind an unmarked police car and got out. Joseph exited the vehicle on the other side, both of their faces grim. They ducked under the yellow crime-scene tape and showed their IDs. Joseph produced an ID from the CIA, which Kruger frowned at but didn't question. They were escorted into the residence as crime-scene investigators scurried from one room to the other. A plainclothes detective walked up to them, offered his hand, and introduced himself. "I'm Lieutenant Dick Childress. I was told you two were coming."

"Sean Kruger, FBI," he said, shaking his hand. "This is Charlie Rose, CIA."

Detective Childress stared at Joseph. "I didn't think the CIA could operate inside the US."

Before Joseph could comment, Kruger said, "Mr. Rose is here as an advisor. He's dealt with the suspect before and has certain insights." Joseph smiled and Kruger continued, "Can you tell us what happened?"

Childress nodded and started walking toward hall. He said, "Early this morning the Brewers' nurse arrived for her weekly visit." He pointed to a body lying in the doorway of a bedroom in the back of the house. "My guess is she never knew what happened. She was shot from behind with what looks like a twenty-two."

Walking back up the hall toward the front of the house, Childress opened the door to another bedroom and pointed at a recliner next to the window. "We think he sat in the chair and watched the police go door to door last night. If the nurse went straight to the back bedroom, she probably didn't realize he was here."

Kruger nodded. "Where are the Brewers?"

Childress frowned and motioned for them to follow him. He opened the door to the garage and pointed at the car. Several men dressed in white lab suits were preparing to extract two bodies. Kruger breathed through his mouth; the stench of death overpowering in the small garage. He looked at Joseph, who just stood there, breathing normally.

Childress said, "Cindy Brewer was shot in the forehead from close range, powder burns next to the bullet's entrance. We found stains on the front room carpet; she was probably shot as she opened the front door. Her husband was shot in the back bedroom. We think he was turning toward the door when he was shot by the intruder."

Joseph said, "How long was Kozlov here?"

"The ME puts the time of death at about an hour to an hour and a half after the accident on University. He was here overnight. The nurse wasn't scheduled to be here until eight this morning. Her car's missing."

Kruger turned and walked back to the living room. He looked around the room, took a deep breath, and said to Childress, "Please tell me Mr. Brewer didn't own any guns."

Childress's lips pressed together and he looked toward the bedroom. "Wish I could. Mr. Brewer registered two shotguns: two AR fifteens and two nineteen elevens. We found the shotguns. The others are missing and we have no idea how much ammunition was taken."

Kruger nodded. "Walk with us, lieutenant." They walked out of the house and into the tree-shaded yard. Kruger turned to Childress. "Do you want me to bring in the bureau on this?"

Childress stared at Kruger, nodded. "The chief of police called me just before you arrived. He would prefer a joint task force, if possible."

Kruger smiled. "The SAC in Kansas City is an old friend of mine. He's a good man and won't step on anybody's toes. Tell your chief you'll get help."

The radio attached to Childress's belt came to life as a female voice said, "Multiple shots fired at five one six south Jefferson. Code three. SWAT has been alerted."

Childress grabbed his radio. "Repeat address." The dispatcher repeated it. "Damn, this town's going crazy. I'll talk to you two later." He walked off and started pulling officers aside and sending them to their patrol cars.

Joseph grabbed Kruger by the arm and pulled him toward the Mustang. As they walked, he said, "Five one six south Jefferson is JR's address."

Kruger looked at Joseph, his eyebrows raised in understanding. They both started running toward the Mustang.

***

Kozlov stood behind a multicar garage thirty yards southeast of the parking-lot entrance to JR's apartment. He was dressed in scuffed work boots, baggy khaki Dockers, an old plaid shirt, a faded brown boonie hat, and large sunglasses from the old man's closet. The boots were a little big, but that didn't matter. He wore the shirt outside the pants, which hid the S&W 1911 tucked inside his pants next to his back. The suppressed Ruger was in his right front pocket.

A large man with tightly cropped hair stood by the door to the apartment building making no pretense he was anything but a guard. His camouflaged desert BDU dress was devoid of rank and unit insignias, but the holstered Beretta M9 on his right hip told the story.

Kozlov emerged from behind the garage and started shuffling slowly through the parking lot. His head was down and he was muttering.

Sandy Knoll stood in JR's apartment watching the parking lot. When he saw the man emerge from behind the garage, instinct told him something wasn't right. The clothes were too baggy and looked recently laundered. Plus, the man's stride had purpose, not the aimless easy shuffle of a man with nowhere to go. He decided to go downstairs and watch closer from the door leading to the parking lot.

He hurried down the stairs two at a time until he was on the ground floor. When he got to the door, the man was just passing Mike. Suddenly the old man straightened, pulled a small pistol from his pocket, and fired in Mike's direction. Knoll pulled his Beretta as he charged out the door.

CHAPTER 36

Springfield, MO

The GT Mustang engine's growl could be heard above the siren as Kruger accelerated toward the downtown area. Five minutes after Kruger and Joseph heard the broadcast over Childress's radio, the car skidded to a stop in the parking lot of JR's apartment. A patrol car arrived at the same time, and two officers got out. In the distance, Kruger could hear more sirens approaching. He saw two men in BDUs lying on the ground next to the apartment building entry door. Joseph jumped out and ran toward the two men. One of the police officers demanded that he halt, but Kruger yelled, "FBI, officer. FBI." He held his badge up and rushed toward Joseph who was already kneeling next to the large sandy-haired man closest to the door.

Joseph yelled, "I need an ambulance, *now!*"

Kruger walked up to the other man on the ground and noticed a small hole just above his left eye; he knelt and closed the man's eyes. He looked toward Joseph. "Is Sandy alive?"

Joseph nodded as he put pressure on the wound in the upper area of Sandy's chest. "He won't be if we don't get an ambulance soon." As he said that, an EMT vehicle and crew pulled into the parking lot, lights flashing and siren winding down. One of the technicians jumped out of the still-moving truck and ran to where Joseph was kneeling.

The EMT looked at Mike, then at Kruger, who shook his head.

Joseph stood and said to the EMT, "He took one in the chest. He's alive." As the emergency responder took over, Joseph backed up and got out of the woman's way.

Joseph stared at Mike's body and shook his head. Kruger walked over to him and placed his hand on his shoulder. He said nothing.

Joseph looked at Kruger. "Where's JR?"

"He's at the hospital with Mia. He's been there most of the day."

Joseph nodded and returned to staring at Mike.

As Kruger glanced around the area, he noticed something. Walking a few steps to the north, he knelt down and pointed to a small pool of a red liquid. "Sandy must have got a shot off before he took a bullet. Looks like Kozlov might have been hit."

A uniformed police officer walked up to them. "I just got off the radio with Lieutenant Childress. He asked me to tell you he's headed this way."

Kruger looked at the officers nametag. "Thank you, Officer Hampton."

Hampton continued, "We found a trail of blood that leads off toward the north. We've got cars headed that way and several men on foot following the trail."

"Make sure your men know this guy is extremely dangerous. He's already shot five individuals and killed four. Plus, he's a suspect in two murders in New York City. I'm not going to tell you what to do, but take this guy down if you can."

The officer nodded. "It's already a standing order, agent." He turned and walked back to a patrol car Kruger assumed was the command car.

One of the EMT technicians stood and walked to where Joseph was standing. "We're ready to transport, but he wants to talk to you."

Joseph hurried back to the medical gurney, and Kruger followed. Knoll's voice was weak as he said, "What about Mike?" Joseph shook his head. Knoll closed his eyes. "I got several shots off. I think I hit him, but I can't be sure."

Joseph put his hand on Sandy's arm. "You did. We'll find him. What was he wearing?"

"Looked like a homeless guy. Baggy pants and shirt, dark boonie hat, and sunglasses."

"Thanks, now let them take you to the hospital. I'll be there later."

Sandy nodded as the oxygen mask was placed back on his face and the gurney was wheeled to the waiting ambulance.

Kruger wandered over to the bushes next to the apartment after seeing something out of place. He bent down and moved the bushes a little. "I've got a gun here. Looks like a Ruger." He motioned for one of the uniformed officers, who came over and put a red flag next to the gun.

More police cars arrived and another ambulance. Kruger watched as the original chaos evolved into orchestrated effort to figure out what happened. He scrutinized the surrounding area. The buildings were old, clustered together, with lots of places to hide and lots of ways to move around without being detected. He said to Joseph, "If he's not found in the next few minutes, he'll be in the wind again."

Joseph nodded. "Most of the ones I dealt with in the eighties were well trained and knew how to evade capture. My guess is he's already in the wind."

Kruger stared off into the distance. "You're probably right."

***

The motel room smelled of insecticide and stale cigarette

smoke. The bored teenager at the front desk had taken his money and barely glanced at him when he registered. The room was on the ground floor as far away from the street as possible. The old tube television was on with a local channel frantically trying to report the mayhem.

One of the talking heads in the studio stared intently into the camera. "We have a live report from Penny Harrison in downtown Springfield. Penny."

"The apartment building behind me was the location of a gangland style shootout shortly after one this afternoon. One person was pronounced dead at the scene and another was taken to a local hospital. A third gunman is still on the loose and considered armed and dangerous. Police are not commenting about motive or who the suspected assailant might be. The FBI has been called in to help with the investigation. I spoke to an eyewitness a few minutes ago."

The view of the reporter was replaced with a video of a tall, lanky woman with stringy blond hair. Her name was displayed under the video as she said, "I seen this homeless guy hangin' around for several hours. He was a tall dude, at least six foot. He had a beard, he did. He just walked up to those two other fella's and started shootin'."

Kozlov laughed and turned off the television. With eyewitnesses like her, he would have no issues evading the manhunt. The bullet wound in his left arm throbbed. Checking it in the bathroom mirror, he noticed blood soaking through the gauze. While the bullet had not struck bone, it had passed through the bicep muscle. Using techniques his instructors had pounded into his head all those years ago, he'd been able to mostly stop the bleeding. But the wound would continue to ooze blood for a few more hours. He would survive without the help of a doctor. The clothes from the old man's closet had been placed in a plastic garbage bag and tossed into a dumpster a mile from Diminski's place.

Remembering the words of a long-dead instructor, he was hiding in plain sight. Before checking into the motel, he had driven the nurse's car to a crowded Walmart on the north side of Springfield. After purchasing a small electric screwdriver inside the store, he had swapped the license plates with one from another white Focus he'd found in the employee parking area. This plan would work as long as the owner didn't get stopped by the police. All Kozlov needed was a few days and he would be gone.

After changing the gauze on his wound, he put on a long-sleeved shirt to cover the bandage and left the motel room to find something to eat.

***

Mia had been upgraded from critical to stable, so JR sat next to her bed holding her hand as they listened to Kruger summarizing the search for Kozlov. "Weber will be extradited back to New York for the murder of Sharon. He faces other charges in both Greene and Stone County for your kidnapping and attempted murder, but I thought it best to get him out of the state."

She nodded but remained quiet for a moment. She looked at JR then back to Kruger. "Where's Kozlov?"

"He vanished. The police followed a blood trail for about a quarter of mile. They lost the trail after that."

JR stared at Kruger and was silent. Mia said, "Where's Joseph and his men. I wanted to thank them. I wouldn't be here if they hadn't found me."

"They're downstairs sitting in the waiting area. Sandy's still in surgery."

Having not said a word since Kruger's arrival, JR finally said, "All of this is my fault."

Kruger shook his head. "Not really. They started it, JR."

JR stood and walked to the window. The scenery was stark. The front lobby rooftop was two stories below, littered with air-conditioning units and piping. The wall across from the window was another wing of the hospital. He stared out the window and unconsciously watched a nurse pull shades together on a window in the other wing. Finally he walked back to Mia's bed and held her hand again. After kissing her on the forehead, he said, "I need to do something. I'll be back as soon as I can. Okay?"

She looked up at him and smiled. "Be careful."

He nodded and walked out of the room, followed by Kruger.

As they walked toward the elevators, Kruger said, "What do you have in mind?"

JR turned to look at him. "Something I have to do. Something you might not want to know about."

Kruger smiled as the elevator door opened. "I have a really bad memory. Tell me."

***

Five minutes after arriving at his apartment, he had hacked into the Verizon servers and found the phone number he needed. JR set up the call using various servers across the globe to hide his true location. When he was ready, he made the call using VoIP and waited for the call to be answered. The first call rang seven times before going to voice mail. The second call was answered on the fifth ring.

"Hello."

"Abel Plymel, this is the man you've been looking for."

There was silence on the other end of the call. Finally, "How do I know this?"

JR was somewhat surprised at the slight Russian accent he detected. "That's the trouble with guys like you; you never take responsibility for your actions."

"You have my money. I want it back." Kozlov's voice was low and menacing.

JR smiled. "I want you to leave me alone."

"The money first, then we will discuss leaving you alone."

"Plymel, I can find you anywhere. I found you today. I can find you tomorrow. Here's my offer. You get your money back, you disappear, and you never bother me again. In exchange, I won't tell the authorities where you are. You come after me again and I'll burn you."

Silence was JR's answer. He continued, "I have a little of the money in a safe deposit box and will give you the accounts and access codes to get the rest."

"That will do me no good, the US government has frozen all of my money."

"I'll release them."

"How can you do that?"

"Because I'm the one denying your access."

There was silence on the call. After what seemed like an hour, Kozlov said, "Your proposal has merit. How do I know you aren't setting a trap?"

"You don't, but then you could plan to kill me after I give you the money. So we both have a problem with trust, don't we?"

"Yes."

"Here is my proposal. I'll put the cash I have in a computer bag. In addition, the bag will contain a flash drive with the account numbers and access codes for your money. I will then place the bag in an open field in a remote location. Far enough from any structure the FBI might use to hide and wait for you. However, I won't tell you about this location until I have the money in place. You can then take your time making sure I haven't set a trap."

"This is interesting proposal. Let me think about it."

"Nope, that's not how this works. You accept it right now or I'll call the FBI and tell them where you are."

"You do not know where I am. You just have the number for this phone."

"False again, Plymel. I know you're in a No Tell Motel on the northeast side of town about a half a mile from I-44."

"Impressive. Okay, I agree to your terms. When will we make the exchange? I don't have a lot of time to wait."

"Everything is ready. I'll call you when the money's in place." He ended the call and smiled.

Kruger had been listening to the call in a chair next to

JR. "Remind me after this is over never to piss you off."

JR stared at the computer screen for a few minutes. "I have to do this myself Sean. I can't be responsible for any more deaths."

"I can't let you take the law into your own hands, JR."

"Yes you can. This guy is responsible for the deaths of your partner and three innocent people. That's not even counting Crigler and his driver. There are too many bodies associated with this man. If my idea fails, you can do what you need to do, but my plan is better."

Kruger stared at him and was silent for a long time. "Okay, we'll try it your way. I'll go to the hospital and check on Sandy. Call me if you need me."

JR nodded. "If things go sideways, tell Mia I love her."

Kruger stood and walked to the computer room door. As he was about to leave, he turned around. "Tell her yourself when you get back." He smiled and left the room.

Leaning back in his chair, JR took a deep breath and said to the empty room, "Yeah, when I get back."

CHAPTER 37

Greene County, MO

The land was in a remote part of northwestern Greene County Missouri, halfway between Bois D'Arc and Ash Grove off Missouri Route F. Access was by gravel road and there wasn't a tree or hill for half a mile in any direction. The only structure visible from where JR stood was an old dilapidated barn a little over eight hundred yards to the north. The Camry was parked and hidden in a grove of Black Walnut trees a mile and a half west. The hike to this spot had taken a little over thirty minutes.

The location had been discovered using Google Earth. Once he had decided to use this location, he was concerned about the age of the satellite photos, but now that he was here, the site was perfect. The long duffel bag he carried was from the cargo section of Sandy Knoll's SUV, which was still parked at his apartment building. He placed the duffel bag on the ground and slid his backpack off of his shoulders. From the backpack, he extracted a black leather computer bag, which contained twenty-thousand dollars in hundred-dollar bills and a flash drive. He placed the bag on the ground.

The next item he pulled from his backpack was a small

red flag, left over from the parking-lot crime scene. He stuck it in the ground next to the bag. Satisfied everything was in place, he started hiking toward the barn.

JR wasn't sure how long it had been abandoned, and he was a little concerned about its structural integrity. As he approached, his concern was justified. The building leaned slightly and the wood exposed to the sunlight felt brittle to the touch. Carefully, he opened a side door and entered. The barn smelled of rotting hay and mildew. Sunlight poured into the structure through gaps between the side planks. Looking up, he found what he needed: a loft ten feet off the barn floor. On the opposite side of the structure were wooden stair steps leading to the loft. He quickly walked across the barn and set the duffel on the floor. Carefully placing his weight on the bottom stair, he was rewarded with it snapping in two. Trying the next step, it also cracked and buckled downward.

Taking a deep breath, he frowned and looked around the interior of the barn.

On the opposite side, to the left of the door he had entered from, was a wooden ladder hanging on the wall. Returning to the other side of the barn, he slipped the backpack off. He took the ladder off the hooks and stood it up against the lip of the loft. It was at least fifteen feet long and extended beyond the edge of the loft. Placing his foot on the first rung, he gradually applied pressure. It held and felt solid. Smiling briefly, he carefully repeated the process on each of the remaining rungs. The ladder was strong and held his weight with no problems. Not wanting to test his luck, he retrieved the duffel bag and only carried it as he made the ascent to the loft.

Once in place in the barn's loft, he called Alexei Kozlov. It was answered on the second ring.

"Where is the bag?"

JR read off the directions, telling Kozlov which farm road to turn on and how far the bag was from the road. Then he said, "You can drive up to it. There will be a small red flag to mark the spot."

"No tricks, hacker. I'll be checking the area out before I retrieve the bag."

"Do what you want to do. The bag is there waiting for you."

JR ended the call and glanced at the time on his phone. Four hours of daylight left. Kozlov would not be able to find the bag in the dark, so he concluded everything would be over before nightfall. JR smiled and opened the duffel bag.

***

After the first call from Diminski, Kozlov left the motel room. He wasn't sure how he had been found, but he wasn't going to take any chances. Sitting in a Bob Evans diner three hours later, he received the information on the bag's location. He knew he was running out of time driving the nurse's white Ford, so once he had the bag he would drive to Kansas City. Once there, he would decide where to go.

The instructions Diminski gave were exact and led him to a remote piece of land. He drove around for another fifteen minutes until he was confident no one was staking out the site. Smiling, he turned the little Ford onto a gravel road that led to the field. The red flag was visible about a hundred feet from the entrance to the field, and he accelerated the Ford toward it.

Ten feet from the black bag, he parked the car. He carefully opened the car door and stood. The only sound he could hear was the ticking of the car's hot engine. He smiled again and walked toward the bag.

***

Diminski had not shot a rifle at this distance for more than ten years. But once he was behind the scope on the M110 SASS semiautomatic sniper rifle, all of his training flooded back. He watched from the barn's loft as the white

Ford pulled up to the red flag and stopped a few yards from the bag. Kozlov exited the car and surveyed the area before he walked toward the bag. At this distance, a headshot would be difficult, but the man's chest was possible.

Peering through the scope, he made slight adjustments to his aim based on the heat shimmers from the field and the slight breeze he could see from the red flag. As Kozlov walked, JR tried to relax, hoping his training would take over. As he prepared for the shot, he took a breath, released it slowly, and squeezed the trigger of the rifle. It broke and the rifle jumped back with the recoil. He sighted again and watched the bullet strike the ground two feet to Kozlov's left. Before the man could react, JR adjusted his aim and squeezed the trigger again. This bullet struck Kozlov just above the heart and the body slumped to the ground. It remained still as JR peered through the scope.

Diminski didn't take the time to admire his work; instead, he dissembled the rifle and placed it back inside the long duffel bag. He climbed down the rickety ladder, picked up his backpack, and slung it on to his shoulder. Exiting the barn, he jogged toward the white Ford.

When he arrived, Kozlov was lying on the ground, his hand over a spot on his chest that was bleeding profusely. He looked up at JR. "I continue to underestimate you, hacker."

"Your mistake."

Kozlov stared at JR for a few more moments, opened his mouth to say something, but only exhaled. His eyes remained open, but his chest did not rise.

Without emotion, JR looked down at the now dead man. This surprised him, all during the planning stage, he had worried about his emotions. He was afraid he would feel something, something to trip him up. A moment of regret or fear would make him hesitate. Now that it was over, he felt nothing. No remorse, no jubilation, no relief, nothing. In the back of his mind, he wondered what having no emotions about killing a person meant. He shook his head to clear the thought.

Walking back to the white Ford, he opened the back door and placed the duffel bag on the back seat. He took the backpack and placed it on the ground next to the rear wheel close to the car's bumper. After opening the trunk, he returned to the body. He then dragged Kozlov back to the car and with difficulty lifted him into the trunk. Before closing the lid, he searched the pockets of the jacket the man was wearing. He found a passport, driver's license, and a credit card in the name of Alexei Kozlov. These items were placed in the backpack. He removed a similar-looking passport from the backpack and placed it in the pocket of Kozlov's jacket. Satisfied, he closed the trunk lid and put the backpack on the back seat next to the duffel bag. The last thing to do was retrieve the red flag and computer bag, which he threw into the back seat as he got behind the steering wheel and started the car.

The trip to his gray Camry took five minutes. He transferred the duffel bag, backpack, computer bag, and red flag to the trunk of the Camry. Returning to the Focus, he activated the GPS function on his phone and entered a destination.

An hour later, he was in Bolivar, Missouri, purchasing two sixty-pound sandbag tubes at a farm supply store. His next stop was a Walmart a half-mile to the north. There, he purchased a set of black sheets, a boonie hat, a large plaid shirt, sunglasses, a cigarette lighter, and two bicycle locking chains. With his purchases in the back seat, he left the parking lot and drove to the north side of Bolivar. At the intersection with Highway Thirty-Two, he turned west.

Just past the town of Fair Play, a Polk County sheriff's car passed him heading east. The sun was just starting to set as he watched the sheriff's car do a K-turn in the rearview mirror. It accelerated to catch up, slowed, and followed the white Focus.

Diminski kept his speed steady at fifty-five miles an hour and took a deep breath. He had hoped to complete this part of his plan without incident, but if the deputy stopped him, it would be over. Resisting arrest or running was not an option at this point. Seconds ticked by as he continued to glance at the sheriff's car in the rearview mirror. He could see the deputy speaking into his microphone, calling in the license plate number. Soon the flashing lights and siren would be turned on. JR kept his speed at fifty-five, glancing at the rearview mirror every five seconds.

A minute later, he saw a turn-off up ahead. Switching on the right blinker, he touched the brakes to slow the car. As he made the turn, he watched in the rear-view mirror. The sheriff's car passed the turn-off and continue on west.

Not realizing he had been holding his breath, he blew it out and shook his head slowly. Apparently, Kozlov had switched the license plates at some point. The memory of doing the same thing at Lehigh Valley International eight months ago made him smile.

Returning to the highway, he continued west to the intersection of State Road 245 and turned left. A half-mile later, he turned left again onto a narrow asphalt road. Several miles later, he found the gravel lane he needed and turned right. Slowing, he navigated the loose gravel pathway that eventually degraded to a rutted dirt trail which meandered through the woods next to Stockton Lake. Once again, he had used Google Earth to find the location. Now he was here in person, it was suitable for his needs. There was a full moon and the trees still had leaves, but they were starting to turn toward the fiery reds, gold, and yellows of autumn. In a few weeks the leaves would have fallen, making this part of his task more dangerous. He slowly drove the last one hundred yards on the trail with the car's headlights off. If anyone was watching on the other side of the lake, they wouldn't remember seeing headlights where there shouldn't be any. The full moon provided plenty of light for his next action. As soon as the car exited the canopy of trees, he was only thirty feet from the bluff.

JR turned the engine off and sat in the quiet. The only sound were waves from the lake slapping at the side of the bluff. There were a few lights across the lake, but they were stationary. After several minutes of sitting there, he opened the car door. Taking one of the black sheets, he carefully spread it out flat next to the bluff's edge. He then placed the long tubes of sand adjacent to the sheet. JR struggled to lift the body of Kozlov out of the trunk. Once it was on the ground, he dragged the body over and placed it on top of the sheet. After the body was wrapped, he rolled the long sandbags next to it, one on each side. He then took one of the bike chains and wrapped it around the bundle, securing the bags to the legs of the body. He used the second chain to secure the bags to Kozlov's shoulders.

Satisfied with his labor, he pushed the bundle closer to the bluff where the water was fifteen feet below the edge. Through his research, JR had discovered the water depth in this part of the lake was over fifty feet. Deep enough for his needs. Without hesitation, he shoved the bundle farther until body and sandbags toppled over the edge into the water below. Breathing hard from his effort, he stood and listened. The splash was relatively inaudible, considering the quiet night on the lake.

JR stood at the edge and watched the bundle slowly submerge as moonlight reflected off the surface of the lake. Thirty seconds after Kozlov disappeared, JR turned back to the white Ford and drove it back through the woods to the highway.

He drove east toward Bolivar and stopped at a convenience store at the intersection of Highway 13 and 32. Using Kozlov's credit card, he filled the car with gas.

Two hours after the body had slipped below the surface of Stockton Lake, JR had the white Focus parked in a dry creek bed. After removing the license plates and placing them in the trunk of the Camry, he checked to make sure he had left nothing in the car and then closed the door. He ripped the remaining black sheet into strips and threw the unused parts into the trunk of the Focus and closed the lid. Opening the gas cap, he pushed the end of the long strip of fabric into the tank.

As soon as he felt the cloth outside grow moist with gas, he stopped pushing. The long wick soaked up more gas as JR stretched the cloth away from the car. He lit the end of the makeshift wick with the lighter and walked away.

As flame raced along the long strip of fabric toward the Focus, JR got into his Camry, started the engine, and drove away from the dry creek bed. He heard a loud *whomph* as the Focus's gas tank erupted in flame. As he drove the Camry onto the two-lane farm road running next to the dry creek bed, he saw flames engulf the Ford in his rearview mirror.

CHAPTER 38

Springfield, MO

The next thing JR knew, his cell phone was chirping. Checking the ID and time with one eye open, he laid the phone back down and let the call go to voicemail. He put his head back on the pillow and fell into a dreamless sleep until his consciousness was stirred by a pounding on his apartment door. He glanced at the digital clock on the nightstand: 10:42 a.m. He threw the covers back and shuffled to the front door and put his forehead against it. "Yeah, who is it?"

"Kruger."

JR unbolted the deadbolt and opened the door. Kruger stood there with his arms crossed, breathing heavily. He said in a loud tone, "Where the hell have you been?"

"Sleeping. Why?"

"You have a girlfriend recovering from a traumatic experience and she's worried sick about you."

As Kruger spoke, JR shuffled toward the kitchen in a zombielike state and started making coffee. "I got home late. Sue me."

Kruger leaned against the doorframe of the kitchen. "Did he pick up the package?"

JR stared at the Keurig as he watched it warm up. The blue light started flashing as he put a coffee pod in the receptacle, closed the lid, and pressed the large-cup button. He shook his head. "No."

"What do you mean he didn't pick up the package?"

JR turned toward Kruger. "Very simple. He did not pick up the package."

"He didn't show up?"

JR shrugged. "I didn't say that. I said, he didn't pick up the package."

"You didn't watch him?"

JR remained silent as he watched the mug fill with coffee.

"What kind of a cluster fuck have you gotten us into, JR? Did he show up or not?"

JR turned and stared at Kruger but remained silent.

It took Kruger several minutes to figure out what JR meant. "Oh, he didn't pick up the package."

JR nodded, turned back to the Keurig, took his cup and raised it in Kruger's direction. "Want some?"

"No thank you. Where is he?"

JR shrugged. "How should I know."

"You're not telling me everything, are you?"

JR shrugged again. "As I said before, you don't want to know. Now, if you don't mind, I'm going to take a shower and head over to the hospital."

***

The next day, Mia's condition was upgraded to good, and she was able to sit up in bed. JR held a cup of 7 Up and shaved ice to her lips as she sipped on the straw. "I think I want to buy the entire building where I live."

Her lips let go of the straw. "Are you sure? I thought you wanted to find a quiet neighborhood on the south side of town?"

"The building's for sale. The first-floor apartment was

empty and the other tenant moved out suddenly after the shooting."

She chuckled; it was the first time since the incident. "What would you do with it?"

"We could design the third floor as our home. The second floor would be the computer space, and the ground floor could be the reception area. Maybe a few offices, some cubicles, storage—you know, basic office space."

She smiled. "Whatever you want to do will be fine. But, I reserve the right to decorate the top floor."

He smiled. "That works for me."

The door to Mia's room opened, and Joseph and Kruger walked in. JR said, "How's Sandy?"

Joseph smiled. "He's going to be fine after some PT. He's already fussing about being restricted to bed."

Kruger had a scowl on his face, his demeanor dark, and he stood off to the side as JR and Joseph spoke. JR looked at him. "What's your problem?"

Kruger was leaning against the wall next to the restroom; he stared at JR. "I was just informed Kozlov's credit card was used to purchase gas at a convenience store on Highway 13 the night he disappeared. Security cameras show a man in a boonie hat, sunglasses, and a plaid shirt filling up a white Ford Focus. The bureau is scrambling several teams to Kansas City to cover the bus stations and airports. Also, a white Focus was found burned in a dry creek bed east of Ash Grove. Do you know anything about either of those events?"

JR shrugged. "Ford made more than one white Focus, Sean."

Kruger stared at him, started to say something, but stopped.

Joseph glared at both of them. "If you two need to talk, take it outside. Mia doesn't need the stress."

Kruger stood up and walked out of the room. JR followed and frowned at Joseph as he passed. He caught up to Kruger and they walked to the elevator in silence. The door opened and they took it to the ground floor. Once outside in the parking lot, Kruger turned abruptly and got into JR's face. "You'd better tell me what happened if you want me to support you."

JR stared back. "Are you sure you want to know?"

Kruger nodded.

JR hesitated for a few moments. "Very well, Kozlov showed up and left without the bag."

Kruger stared into JR's eyes, but remained quiet.

JR looked away, his gaze toward the sea of parked cars. "I can tell you he won't be bothering anyone again."

"How do you know that?" Kruger said, his face turning a new shade of red.

JR was tired of the conversation. He turned back to face Kruger. "Because he's dead—that's why."

Kruger backed away from JR and relaxed. "How?'

JR shook his head. "A body with his identification on it will be found in Mexico City tomorrow. Trust me, he will never be seen again."

Kruger frowned but was silent for a moment. "How?"

"There's a hacker in Mexico City. He's as good as I am, maybe better. I sent Kozlov's passport and twenty-thousand dollars to him via FedEx yesterday afternoon. He'll make sure it's found on a body that's unrecognizable."

Kruger said nothing, turned, walked about twenty yards away and then returned. "Is there a record of him entering Mexico?"

JR nodded. "His passport was stamped at Nuevo Laredo. He stayed at a hotel in San Luis Potosi before getting to Mexico City."

"How did you do that?"

"Really, Sean, do you want to know the technical details?"

Kruger shook his head. "Will you tell me where he really is?"

JR shook his head. "I told you, his passport will be found on a body in Mexico City. Let's face it, if I'd turned Kozlov over to you, the guys in black suits would have shown up and whisked him away. They weren't going to allow him to tell the world how the CIA turned him loose to rape and pillage the rich and stupid in New York City. "

Kruger smiled. "I was concerned about that too."

"I couldn't take a chance on them putting him in a witness protection program where in a few years he'd be back knocking on my door. We were lucky this time Mia wasn't killed. I won't take that chance again. My way was the best, Sean. We don't have to worry about Kozlov ever again."

Kruger crossed his arms in front of his chest and looked back at the hospital. He took a deep breath. "I have another problem."

"What is it?"

"I'm getting heat about finding you."

JR was silent; he turned his head and stared out into the parking lot again. "What are you going to tell them?"

Kruger sighed. "Nothing at the moment. I told you when we first met, I would help clear your name. But you'll have to go back to New York and testify."

JR shook his head. "I've been thinking. I'm not sure I want my old name cleared. I like my current situation."

"That's your decision. I'm still willing to help."

"I'm not sure if Kozlov's body will ever be found. It might be, but I doubt it. If someone does find it, there will be identification on it."

Kruger glared at JR, "What do you mean?"

"Before I disposed of the body," he paused, "I put my old passport in his jacket pocket."

CHAPTER 39

Kruger parked his Mustang in his assigned space just after four in the afternoon. He sat in the car for a few seconds, yawned, and then got out. After retrieving his overnight bag from the trunk, he noticed Stephanie's car was not in its assigned slot. Disappointed, he climbed the stairs to the second floor and opened the door to his apartment.

The place smelled musty and stale. Opening the sliding glass door to the balcony allowed a cool October breeze to flow into the apartment. Standing there, he smiled and tried to remember how long it had been since he had been home. The overnight bag and backpack were thrown onto his bed, to be unpacked later. Walking toward the bathroom, he stripped and got ready for a long shower.

Thirty minutes later, he was sitting on the balcony in a pair of Reebok wind pants and a sweatshirt sipping a cold beer. Stephanie had replied to an earlier text message. She would be home a little before six. Glancing at the time on his cell phone, he sighed and called his boss, Alan Seltzer. The call was answered on the third ring.

"It's about damn time you checked in. Talk to me."

"Alan, there really isn't anything new to tell you. You've read my reports and we've discussed them on a regular basis.

I sent one just before I drove back to Kansas City. You're as up to date as possible."

"Sean, we've known each other for a long time. You've never put everything in your official reports. This time, I need to know what's been left out."

"Not this time, Alan. Everything's there. We caught Adam Weber and extradited him to New York City. He will be charged with Sharon Crawford's murder and the DA told me they have ample evidence for a conviction. When I spoke to the sheriff of Stone County Missouri, he said their prosecutor was preparing to file numerous charges against Weber as well.

"Alexi Kozlov was an ex-Soviet-era sleeper agent the CIA ran as a double agent back in the eighties. He killed four people in Springfield and escaped the manhunt thrown down by the city and county. Somehow he made his way to Mexico City, where he met an unfortunate accident."

"Very convenient." Seltzer paused for a second. "You've never once explained why Weber and Kozlov were in Springfield."

Kruger closed his eyes and pinched the bridge of his nose. He took a deep breath. "Weber told me he'd traced the fugitive to the area. I can only speculate about Kozlov; I didn't get an opportunity to question him."

"Indulge me."

"He needed to eliminate Weber because Weber knew the truth about P&G Global."

"That makes sense. So, did Weber find the fugitive?

Hesitating for a few moments, Kruger said, "I think he's dead. Weber traded the fugitive's location to buy time for his escape. Kozlov might have found him, but I can't confirm he did or didn't." Kruger smiled slightly as he spoke. "If you want me to keep trying, I will. But, I think it's a dead end."

There was silence on the other end of the call. Finally Seltzer said, "No, we'll close the file. Besides, unraveling the conspiracy at P&G Global was a bigger coup; the assistant director was pleased. The media frenzy over Crigler's corruption and Weber's arrest has been an embarrassment for the director. He was called to the White House today concerning the matter. From what I heard, the president asked for his resignation. But as usual the director talked his way out of it and blamed others."

Kruger chuckled. "Yeah, he seems to have nine lives."

"What are your plans for next week? I've had a few requests for your services, but I wanted to talk to you first."

Kruger smiled. "I appreciate that, Alan. I was hoping to take a few days off."

"Fine, call me when you get back."

He ended the call just as Stephanie walked into the apartment with a bag of groceries in her arms. "I hope you're hungry. I've got a special meal planned for us."

Kruger smiled, walked into the living room, gave her a kiss, and helped carry the groceries to the kitchen.

Later that night, after making love, they lay in bed holding each other, enjoying being together. During dinner, Kruger had told her everything about the events of the past week. But now he was quiet.

Stephanie picked up on his mood. "Sean, don't be upset with JR. He was protecting Mia."

Kruger nodded. "I know, but the fact he's being vague about the details bothers me. I'm not sure he trusts me."

She laughed, broke from his embrace, rose up slightly, and leaned on one elbow. "How long have you known him? Less than a month. Of course he doesn't trust you yet. Look at what he's been through. Give him time. Someday he will."

He stared at the dark ceiling. "I know. Guess I'm being impatient."

"Of course you are. Now, consider this. How would you have handled the situation if you were in his shoes? Think about that."

He was silent for a long time, staring at the ceiling. "I would have handled it the exact same way."

***

Four weeks after Mia was released from the hospital, JR and Mia were at the closing company signing papers giving his company possession of the entire building. A cashier's check for the purchase amount was used, so he owned the building free and clear. After the signing, he and Mia met Joseph and Mary at a five-star restaurant in downtown Springfield. Mary was in town to join Joseph before they left on a long-planned vacation in New Zealand.

After the introductions and a lot of small talk over cocktails and wine, Mary said, "I'm not sure any of you know this, but Adam Weber struck a deal with the attorney general. He's spilling his guts about P&G Global." She took a sip of a dark-red Cabernet and continued, "It seems Crigler was siphoning off more money than Plymel. Some beltway pundits are calling for new legislation aimed at curtailing private equity companies." She chuckled. "Or at least regulating them."

JR was quiet as he stared into his wine glass. Finally he said, "Too many politicians are being paid too much money for that to ever happen."

Joseph nodded. "Our political system is being challenged by this influx of silent money."

JR continued, "The money isn't that silent, Joseph. When I hacked into P&G Global's computer, I found information about the amounts being paid to senators, congressmen, and even some of the president's advisors. The sums were obscene. Until we get the big money out of politics, we will continue to have men like Crigler and Plymel."

Mary nodded. "I agree, but the number of women getting into politics should help."

JR laughed but said nothing. Mia lightly hit him on the shoulder and said, "She's right. Women have higher moral standards than some of you men. The more women in politics, the better things will be."

Joseph sipped his glass of single-malt scotch and smiled. "You don't agree with our two female friends, JR?"

JR shook his head and stayed quiet.

Mia looked at him. "Why not?"

"Anything I say at this point will piss somebody off. I'll keep my opinions to myself. That way, we can continue enjoying the evening."

They all laughed and finished the evening without any further political discussions.

Later, when the two women excused themselves to visit the ladies room, Joseph leaned forward toward JR. "Okay, exactly what did you find on P&G Global's computer?"

JR looked at Joseph. "The corruption extends to all levels of the government—men, women, you name it. Becoming a member of Congress is a fast ticket to wealth. And for those that want it, media exposure."

"Help us fight it, JR. Use your abilities to chip away at the corruption."

JR stared at his friend, "How?"

"Expose the corruption like you did with P&G Global."

Chuckling, JR said, "You want me to hack into every computer on Wall Street?"

Joseph shook his head. "No, nothing like that—only when we have leads or suspicions."

JR's smile disappeared. He leaned forward and whispered, "Isn't that brushing aside everyone's constitutional rights?"

"Depends on what the money is being used for."

Both men stopped their conversation and smiled as Mia and Mary sat down in their seats. Mia's face was serious. "JR, is Sean Kruger going to clear your old name?"

JR shook his head but remained quiet.

"Why not? He said he would."

With a grim smile, JR said, "Because I asked him not to."

Mia's eyebrows rose and she looked shocked.

JR smiled. "I like my current life. The old one." He paused and stared into Mia's eyes. "Well, it kind of sucked.

You're in my life now and I'm making a difference to a bunch of companies that need technical help. Sean told me I'd have to return to New York and testify to clear my name." He slowly shook his head. "I'm not willing to do that, at least not right now."

Mia took his hand and touched it to her chest just below her neck. She then kissed it, smiling warmly at JR.

Joseph quickly said, "Mia, JR can do a lot—"

"Oh hush, Joseph." Mary frowned at him. "Mia's smarter than the rest of us combined. She figured out what you do, Joseph, and knows you've asked JR to work with you. So stop treating us like we're oblivious to the world around us."

Joseph laughed and JR stared at Mia. "You know?"

Mia smiled. "Mary confirmed my suspicions. I'll support you, whatever you do, JR. Joseph is doing good work, he needs you."

JR continued staring at Mia and slowly started to smile.

Joseph continued to chuckle. "That's why I love Mary. She cuts through the bullshit and says what's needed."

JR nodded.

ABOUT THE AUTHOR

J.C. Fields is a life-long resident of Missouri. He has a degree in Psychology and published a research paper before graduation. After college he joined a large computer corporation and has utilized skills learned there to introduce computer usage to numerous company's ever since.

His first short story was written while still in high school and he continued writing through-out his university days. Writing took a back seat during the family raising years. But in 2006 he opened his laptop and starting putting words on paper again.

Research for the Sean Kruger novels started while traveling extensively throughout the United States. He also has weapons training in both short and long guns.

Currently he resides in Southwest Missouri with his wife and their rescue cat, Asia.